The Best of Ring Lardner

Ringgold Wilmer Lardner was born in Niles, Michigan, in 1885. After briefly studying engineering at Armour Institute in Chicago, he worked as a freight agent and a book-keeper and then embarked on a career as a reporter with the *South Bend Times* in 1905. From 1910 he edited *Sporting News* at St Louis, and he was an increasingly popular columnist on the *Chicago Tribune* from 1913 to 1916. He became famous as a writer on sport, especially baseball, and started to write short stories, the first of which appeared in the *Saturday Evening Post* in 1914. Published collections of his stories include *You Know Me Al* (1916), *Own Your Own Home* (1919), and *How to Write Short Stories* (1924); his best stories were collected in *The Love Nest* (1926) and *Round Up* (1929).

After a brief, unproductive period as a First World War correspondent in France, Lardner settled at Great Neck, Long Island, where he became a neighbour and friend of Scott and Zelda Fitzgerald. (Abe North in Fitzgerald's *Tender is the Night* is partially based on Lardner.) During the 1920s he wrote songs, revue sketches and plays as well as stories. He worked for Ziegfeld, and he collaborated with George Kaufman on *June Moon*, a stage adaptation of Lardner's story 'Some Like Them Cold'. Tuberculosis was diagnosed in 1926, and thereafter Lardner was in and out of hospital until he died of a heart attack in 1933.

David Lodge, Professor of Modern English Literature at the University of Birmingham, is well known both as a critic and as a novelist. His most recent critical books are *Working with Structuralism* and *The Modes of Modern Writing*. Two of his novels, *Changing Places* (1975) and *How Far Can You Go?* (1980), have been awarded major literary prizes. His latest novel, published in 1984, is *Small World*.

EF.

THE BEST OF
RING LARDNER

Chosen and introduced by
DAVID LODGE

J. M. Dent & Sons Ltd
London Melbourne

This paperback edition first published by J. M. Dent & Sons Ltd 1984
Selection, Introduction and 'Some Notes on Baseball' © David Lodge 1984

This book is set in 10/11½ VIP Sabon by
Inforum Ltd, Portsmouth
Printed in Great Britain by
Guernsey Press Co. Ltd, Guernsey, C.I., for
J. M. Dent & Sons Ltd
Aldine House, 33 Welbeck Street, London W1M 8LX

British Library Cataloguing in Publication Data

Lardner, Ring
    The best of Ring Lardner.—(Everyman fiction)
    I. Title II. Lodge, David III. Series
    813'.4[F]   PS3523.A7

    ISBN 0–460–02270–9

Contents

Introduction

DAVID LODGE

There are at least two good reasons for re-issuing a selection of Ring Lardner's stories, which have been out of print in Britain for some time. The first is that he is a wonderfully entertaining writer. Anyone picking up this book who has not previously encountered his work—a category that must include a whole generation of young British readers—has a treat in store. The second reason is that Ring Lardner is a key figure in the development of modern American fiction, and no student of that literary tradition can afford to ignore him.

The most obvious recommendation of Ring Lardner is that he is a very funny writer. Humour is the most ephemeral of all literary qualities, but Lardner, at his very best, belongs to that select company of writers who can make posterity lift its head from the page and laugh aloud. But he is not just a humorist. His stories constitute a fascinating and illuminating record of a certain phase of American social history—the teens and twenties of the present century, when America was coming of age as a major modern power, with all the awkwardness, ebullience and occasional dissipation of a young man reaching his majority. It was a time of restless social mobility, of fortunes made and lost in a rapidly expanding capitalist economy, of conspicuous consumption and dismal poverty, of struggle between the traditional values of small towns and agrarian communities and the more sophisticated and cynical life-styles of big cities like New York and Chicago. It was a period that saw the advent of commercialised spectator sport, mass-circulation newspapers and magazines, jazz-based popular music, Prohibition and speak-easies. The Ring Lardner stories are vivid verbal snapshots of that America: baseball players and commercial travellers, Broadway impresarios and small town barbers, flappers and gold-diggers, are preserved in these pages, luminously lifelike but bathed in a sepia tint of yesteryear.

In spite of the United States' involvement in the Great War, and thus in world politics, Europe was still a week's voyage away, and for most Americans infinitely more distant in psychological and cultural terms. America remained in many ways a very provincial, inward-looking society—naïve, philistine and materialistic. Many American writers—T S Eliot, Ezra Pound, Gertrude Stein, Ernest Hemingway, for instance—found it inhospitable to literary art, and settled or travelled extensively in Europe. Ring Lardner made few trips to Europe and these left very little mark on his writing. In terms of Philip Rhav's celebrated division of American writers into Palefaces (those oriented to the European and specifically English literary tradition) and Redskins (those trying to create a distinctively American literature 'on native ground') Lardner is definitely a Redskin. But he was an urban, or suburban, Redskin. He did not yearn nostalgically for the frontier and the wilderness, from which Redskin writing derives its positive values and mythopoeic inspiration. He moved almost exclusively in those areas of his native land already thoroughly tamed and domesticated by the railroad and the motor car. Perhaps for that reason, his picture of his society is sardonic and far from flattering. His perspective may have been narrow, compared to that of his expatriate contemporaries, but it was clear-sighted and critical. Beneath the humour of these stories there is sometimes detectable an almost Swiftian misanthropy. This puzzled many who knew him personally. As Elizabeth Hardwick has succinctly put it: 'He came from a charming, talented family and married a woman he loved. He was kind, reserved, hardworking; his fictional world is loud, cruel, filled with desperate marriages, hideous old age, suburban wretchedness, fraud, drunkenness.' Ring Lardner himself, however, was given to sporadic bouts of self-destructive drinking, in which, if we need it, we can find some biographical clue to the dark side of his literary imagination.

Ringgold Wilmer Lardner—to unfurl in its full splendour a name he was glad to conceal behind the homely abbreviation 'Ring'—was born in 1885, in the small mid-western town of Niles, Michigan. His father owned a prosperous farming business, and Ring enjoyed a comfortable, almost idyllic upbringing, until, in his teens, the family fortunes suffered a reverse, which, among other consequences, prevented him from proceeding to college. After an abortive attempt to make a mechanical engineer out of him ('I can't think of no walk in life for which I had more of a natural bent,' he remarked later, 'unless it would be hostess at a roller rink') Ring became a sports journalist on a local paper, and showed such aptitude, especially as a baseball reporter, that he swiftly graduated to the big newspapers of Chicago and the East Coast. He wrote a daily baseball column for five years between 1908 and 1913, and continued to cover big games until the early '20s, though he became somewhat disillusioned with the sport after the so-called Black Sox scandal of 1919, when the Chicago White Sox conspired with a betting syndicate to 'throw' the World Series. The incident has been immortalised in a reference in *The Great Gatsby* by Scott Fitzgerald, who undoubtedly discussed it privately with Lardner. In 1922 Fitzgerald and Zelda moved to the fashionable community of Great Neck, Long Island (the original of East Egg and West Egg in *The Great Gatsby*), where Ring Lardner had a house, and the two men became friends.

By this time Lardner had more or less abandoned sports journalism, and was a successful freelance writer of humorous columns and short stories. This was a period when magazines such as the *Saturday Evening Post* occupied much the same position in popular culture as TV does today: they commanded huge national audiences and could pay immense sums to writers like Ring Lardner who enjoyed a strong personal following. In his heyday, Ring Lardner was among the highest-paid writers in America. In 1927 *Cosmopolitan* (not to be confused with the present-day bearer of that name) was paying him $4,500 for a single story (a sum equivalent to $25,000 in today's currency). Though he wrote for the same lucrative market, Scott Fitzgerald had his eyes fixed on literary immortality, and was continually badgering his friend to adopt a more serious attitude to the art of letters. Fitzgerald introduced Lardner to his editor, the famous Maxwell Perkins, at Scribner's, who then became the publishers of his short fiction, but together they never succeeded in persuading him to write a novel, or, for that matter, to put his stories before the public with the dignity appropriate to a modern literary master. His first collection for Scribner's was prefaced by a spoof introduction entitled 'How To Write Short Stories' (included in this collection), and each item was prefaced with a surrealistically misleading synopsis. For example, a baseball yarn is described as 'The love story, half earthly, half spiritual, of a beautiful snare drummer and a hospital interne, unique for its word pictures of the unpleasant after effects of anaesthesia. It explains what radio is and how it works.'

Something of Scott Fitzgerald's exasperation at Lardner's refusal to take his vocation with a high modern seriousness came out in his obituary on Lardner's death in 1933 (a premature one, brought on by TB and excessive drinking). 'Whatever Ring's achievement was it fell short of the achievement he was capable of, and this because of a cynical attitude towards his work.' Fitzgerald traced this back to Ring Lardner's youthful infatuation with baseball.

> During those years, when most men of promise achieve an adult education, if only in the school of war, Ring moved in the company of a few dozen illiterates playing a boy's game. A boy's game, with no more possibilities in it than a boy could master, a game bounded by walls which kept out novelty or danger, change or adventure.

There is perhaps some truth in this harsh judgment, but there is also the paradox that it was through baseball that Ring Lardner found his voice (or rather, voices) as a creative writer, and thus made his distinctive contribution to modern American fiction—the development of a vernacular literary style. The process has been well documented by his most recent biographer, Jonathan Yardley (*Ring: A Biography of Ring Lardner*, New York, 1977).

When Ring Lardner was travelling around the country with the Chicago Cubs in 1910–11 he began to use in his daily column (which had to be filled whether there was a game to report or not) the quoted comments of one of the players, Frank Schulte. Schulte had a sardonic wit that was akin to Lardner's own, and was often exercised at the expense of his teammates:

> 'They didn't trip us today because they played better ball. Oh no . . . You saw Jack Murray hit that one out of the ball yard? Well, that's no credit to Murray. He had his eyes shut or was talking to someone back in the grandstand when he let that one loose. He didn't meet the ball square. Oh no. The ball hit his little finger nail and bounded off it over the fence.'

How much of this is quotation, and how much Lardner's invention, we shall never know; but, as Yardley observes, we can see here the first burgeoning of the style of mature baseball stories like 'Alibi Ike'*, in which a richly resourceful vernacular rhetoric expresses and exposes human vanity, folly and pretence in a way that is both specific to the small, self-obsessed world of baseball and yet universally recognisable. The actual transition from sports journalism to prose fiction was made in 1916, with 'A Bushman's Letters Home', a series of letters ostensibly written by a brash and barely literate rookie, trying to make it in big-league baseball, to his friend back home in Bedford, Indiana. These pieces were collected and published, with considerable success, under the title *You Know Me Al*.

That title illustrates and encapsulates Ring Lardner's mastery of the vernacular style. The absence of the comma that would be conventional in written English after 'Me' compels the reader to punctuate the phrase himself in order to interpret it—thus compels him to pronounce it silently to himself, hearing its rhythm and intonation, recognising and relishing its rhetorical function, at once phatic and self-congratulatory. Virginia Woolf paid a surprising but characteristically acute tribute to the achievement:

> With extraordinary ease and aptitude, with the quickest strokes, the surest touch, the sharpest insight, he lets Jack Keefe the baseball player cut out his own outline, fill in his own depths, until the figure of the foolish, boastful, innocent athlete lives before us.

She also provided (in advance, for she was writing in *The Dial* in 1925) a riposte to Scott Fitzgerald's obituary criticism:

> It is no coincidence that the best of Mr Lardner's stories are about games, for one may guess that Mr Lardner's interest in games has solved one of the most difficult problems of the American writer; it has given him a clue, a centre, a meeting place for the divers activities of people whom a vast continent isolates, whom no tradition controls. Games give him what society gives his English brother.

* See 'Some Notes on Baseball', p. 211.

In fact not all Ring Lardner's best stories are about games, and some of them are about social manners (for example, 'Ex Parte' and 'Mr and Mrs Fixit'), but most of them are cast in the form of monologues, letters or journals, uttered or written in the American vernacular by invented characters, and this was a mode of writing that Ring Lardner discovered through baseball. In order to explain the importance of this discovery, it is necessary to indulge in a little literary history, and even literary theory—doing our best to ignore the derisive shade of Ring Lardner hovering over the exercise.

A distinctive feature of the novel as a genre (some would say, its most important distinguishing feature) is that it assimilated and combined a whole range of discourses suppressed and excluded by the decorums of classical epic and traditional romance—not only by the vivid imitation of different kinds of speech in dialogue, but by letting characters tell their own stories in their own language. The pseudo-autobiographies of Defoe, the epistolary novels of Samuel Richardson, in the eighteenth century, revolutionised narrative literature and prepared the way for more subtle and self-conscious experiments by modern novelists with unreliable narrators, streams of consciousness and interior monologues. The effect of letting the characters' distinctive voices be heard in, and on occasion take over, the narrative discourse, is not only to gain realism and immediacy, but also to 'defamiliarise' the world we inhabit (thus making it more perceptible) by refusing the familiar, conventional ways of representing it in literature.

This was always a particularly urgent need for American writers, struggling to articulate the experience of a new and emergent nation in a literary language suffocated under the weight of European tradition. The great breakthrough was made by Mark Twain who, in *Huckleberry Finn* (1884), made the informal speech of an uneducated country boy a wonderfully eloquent medium through which to express profound insights into the nature of America and American society. Ernest Hemingway paid famous homage to the achievement, and acknowledged his own debt to Twain, when he declared, 'All modern American literature comes from one book by Mark Twain called *Huckleberry Finn*.' But, arguably, it was Ring Lardner's early stories and journalism that showed the young Hemingway how the stylistic lessons of *Huckleberry Finn* might be applied and adapted to more modern subject-matter. Charles A Fenton records in *The Apprenticeship of Ernest Hemingway* that a teacher at his high school 'was always having to fight criticism by the superintendent that Ernie was writing like Ring Lardner' in the school newspaper; and in 1932 Hemingway inscribed a copy of *Death in the Afternoon*, 'To Ring Lardner, from his early imitator and always admirer.' Other writers directly influenced by Lardner include Sherwood Anderson, James T Farrell, Nathanael West, John O'Hara, James Thurber and Damon Runyon. There are scores of others indirectly influenced by his experiments with vernacular narrative.

In terms of literary history, Ring Lardner's example was as important as his actual achievement, and one must be careful not to exaggerate the latter. He left comparatively few stories that are indisputably first class, and these are invariably ones in which the form of vernacular narration disguises or displaces those aspects of the art of fiction in which he was weak. He was, for instance, as he readily admitted, a poor hand at constructing a plot, and tended to rely on stock formulae and melodramatic stereotypes. 'Haircut', with its poetic justice for the town bully who teased the idiot boy and persecuted the innocent heroine, is an example; but we are hardly aware of the artificiality of the story because of the fascinating indirection of its telling. The town barber is regaling a customer with an admiring and nostalgic account of the bully's brutal and humourless practical jokes, and everything he says has to be interpreted in a sense opposite to what he intends. The barber's shop is a perfect setting for a dramatic monologue of which Browning himself might have been proud, for the reader is compelled to place himself, as it were, in the position of the silent listener, trapped in the chair, inwardly disgusted yet unable to stem the flow of mean-minded, bigoted, complacent, sexist garrulity.

'Champion' is another story about a bully which undoubtedly has its moments, but is less successful as a whole than 'Haircut'. It is no coincidence, I think, that this story is more conventional in form, narrated by an authorial voice that often sounds stilted and uneasy in contrast to the colloquial speech of the characters:

> Midge, on the contrary, gave his new manager's wife the many times over, *and seemed loath to end the feast of his eyes*.

'Some doll,' he said to Grace when they were alone.

'Doll is right,' the lady replied, 'and sawdust where her brains ought to be.'

'I'm li'ble to steal that baby,' said Midge, and he smiled as *he noted the effect of his words on his audience's face.* [Italics mine]

Edmund Wilson recorded a revealing conversation with Ring Lardner that took place in the Fitzgeralds' house at Great Neck.

When we were talking about his own work, Lardner said that the trouble was he couldn't write straight English. I asked him what he meant and he said: 'I can't write a sentence like, "We were sitting in the Fitzgeralds' house and the fire was burning brightly." '

What he *could* write were sentences like:

This is our first separation since we have been engaged, nearly 17 days. It will be 17 days tomorrow. And the hotel orchestra at dinner this evening played that old thing 'Oh how I miss you tonight' and it seemed as if they must be playing it for my benefit though of course the person in that song is talking about how they miss their mother though of course I miss mother too, but a person gets used to missing their mother and it isn't like Walter or the person you are engaged to. ('I Can't Breathe')

Or:

You must write and tell me how you are getting along in the 'battle of Broadway' (I laughed when I read that) and whether the publishers like your songs though I know they will. Am crazy to hear them and hear you play the piano as I love good jazz music even better than classical, though I suppose it is terrible to say such a thing. But I usually say just what I think though sometimes I wish afterwards I had not of. But I still believe it is better for a girl to be her own self and natural instead of always acting. But am afraid I will never have a chance to hear you play unless you come back to Chi and pay us a visit as my 'threat' was just a 'threat' and I don't see any hope of ever getting there unless some rich New Yorker should fall in love with me and take me there to live. Fine chance for poor little me, eh, Mr Lewis? ('Some Like Them Cold')

Or:

After dinner we made them come up to our house and we all set in the parlor, which the young woman had give us the use of to entertain company. We begun talking over old times and Mother said she was a-scared Mrs Hartsell would find it tiresome listening to we three talk over old times, but as it turned out they wasn't much chance for nobody else to talk with Mrs Hartsell in the company. I have heard lots of women that could go it, but Hartsell's wife takes the cake of all the women I ever seen. She told us the family history of everybody in the State of Michigan and bragged for a half hour about her son, who she said is in the drug business in Grand Rapids, and a Rotarian. ('The Golden Honeymoon')

Ring Lardner is at his best when he allows his men and women to speak for themselves, without authorial intervention or interpretation. These characters reveal themselves—their hopes and fears and vanities and flaws—to hilarious or pitiful effect in language that is, by conventional literary standards, impoverished and imperfect, but, when subtly manipulated by the invisible Lardner, wonderfully expressive. That apparently redundant distinction in the first passage between 'Walter or the person you are engaged to', for instance, is a kind of Freudian slip since, as we soon discover, the young lady in question is rather promiscuous in her engagements. Behind the arch quotation marks, the tortuous qualifications, the unsubtle flattery and self-justification of the second passage, we sense the desperate anxiety of a woman trying to attract a potential husband without violating the code of gentility to which she pretends. Through speech, or speech transcribed into writing, a character and a whole way of life are revealed to us, and the plot line is essentially a pretext for this exposure.

Perhaps the most daring, technically speaking, of the three stories cited above is 'The Golden Honeymoon', which is virtually plotless. An elderly couple from New Jersey take a winter vacation in Florida in a resort filled with other old people. The husband records the trivial minutiae of the journey, the accommodation, and the banal diversions of the resort. They meet another couple, the male half of whom was an old flame of the narrator's wife, keep irritable company with them for a while, compete at various games, quarrel and fall out. The narrator and his wife are reconciled. Then they go home. Nothing is said or done that is not of the utmost banality, yet it would be hard to say whether the story redeems or exposes that banality. It is positively Chekhovian in the flawless realism of its surface and the ambiguity of its import. One may read it as either a horrifying indictment of the vacancy of old age in modern western society, or as a tender celebration of marriage as companionship. Significantly, the *Saturday Evening Post*, to whom it was first offered, turned it down because they thought it would surprise and unsettle Ring Lardner's regular readers. It is in some ways his most 'modern', most experimental story.

Ring Lardner himself, as Fitzgerald discovered, had no pretensions to Parnassus. He liked to regard himself as an entertainer who wrote by instinct and from experience. 'I don't worry about plots', he said once. 'I just start writing about someone I think I know something about. I try to get him down cold. The other characters seem to walk into the story naturally enough. I seldom write a story of more than 5000 words—my mind seems geared to that length. I write about 3000 words about nothing; that is a terrible struggle. Then I come to, and say to myself, "I must get a punch in this." I stop and figure out the punch, then sail through to the finish.' Though the tone is characteristically throwaway and self-deprecating, this is probably a reliable account of Ring Lardner's working method. And the phrase 'terrible struggle', in spite of its ironical placing, gives us a glimpse of the hard work and creative concentration that must have gone into the composition of the best of his stories. Writing of that quality was never easy.

THE BEST OF RING LARDNER

Haircut

I got another barber that comes over from Carterville and helps me out Saturdays, but the rest of the time I can get along all right alone. You can see for yourself that this ain't no New York City and besides that, the most of the boys works all day and don't have no leisure to drop in here and get themselves prettied up.

You're a newcomer, ain't you? I thought I hadn't seen you round before. I hope you like it good enough to stay. As I say, we ain't no New York City or Chicago, but we have pretty good times. Not as good, though, since Jim Kendall got killed. When he was alive, him and Hod Meyers used to keep this town in an uproar. I bet they was more laughin' done here than any town its size in America.

Jim was comical, and Hod was pretty near a match for him. Since Jim's gone, Hod tried to hold his end up just the same as ever, but it's tough goin' when you ain't got nobody to kind of work with.

They used to be plenty fun in here Saturdays. This place is jam-packed Saturdays, from four o'clock on. Jim and Hod would show up right after their supper, round six o'clock. Jim would set himself down in that big chair, nearest the blue spittoon. Whoever had been settin' in that chair, why they'd get up when Jim come in and give it to him.

You'd of thought it was a reserved seat like they have sometimes in a theayter. Hod would generally always stand or walk up and down, or some Saturdays, of course, he'd be settin' in this chair part of the time, gettin' a haircut.

Well, Jim would set there a wile without openin' his mouth only to spit, and then finally he'd say to me, 'Whitey,'—my right name, that is, my right first name, is Dick, but everybody round here calls me Whitey—Jim would say, 'Whitey, your nose looks like a rosebud tonight. You must of been drinkin' some of your aw de cologne.'

So I'd say, 'No, Jim, but you look like you'd been drinkin' somethin' of that kind or somethin' worse.'

Jim would have to laugh at that, but then he'd speak up and say, 'No, I ain't had nothin' to drink, but that ain't sayin' I wouldn't like somethin'. I wouldn't even mind if it was wood alcohol.'

Then Hod Meyers would say, 'Neither would your wife.' That would set everybody to laughin' because Jim and his wife wasn't on very good terms. She'd of divorced him only they wasn't no chance to get alimony and she didn't have no way to take care of herself and the kids. She couldn't never understand Jim. He *was* kind of rough, but a good fella at heart.

Him and Hod had all kinds of sport with Milt Sheppard. I don't suppose you've seen Milt. Well, he's got an Adam's apple that looks more like a mushmelon. So I'd be shavin' Milt and when I'd start to shave down here on his neck, Hod would holler, 'Hey, Whitey, wait a minute! Before you cut into it, let's make up a pool and see who can guess closest to the number of seeds.'

And Jim would say, 'If Milt hadn't of been so hoggish, he'd of ordered a half a cantaloupe instead of a whole one and it might not of stuck in this throat.'

All the boys would roar at this and Milt himself would force a smile, though the joke was on him. Jim certainly was a card!

There's his shavin' mug, settin' on the shelf, right next to Charley Vail's. 'Charles M. Vail.' That's the druggist. He comes in regular for his shave, three times a week. And Jim's is the cup next to Charley's. 'James H. Kendall.' Jim won't need no shavin' mug no more, but I'll leave it there just the same for old time's sake. Jim certainly was a character!

Years ago, Jim used to travel for a canned goods concern over in Carterville. They sold canned goods. Jim had the whole northern half of the State and was on the road five days out of every week. He'd drop in here Saturdays and tell his experiences for that week. It was rich.

I guess he paid more attention to playin' jokes than makin' sales. Finally the concern let him out and he come right home here and told everybody he'd been fired instead of sayin' he'd resigned like most fellas would of.

It was a Saturday and the shop was full and Jim got up out of

4

that chair and says, 'Gentlemen, I got an important announcement to make. I been fired from my job.'

Well, they asked him if he was in earnest and he said he was and nobody could think of nothin' to say till Jim finally broke the ice himself. He says, 'I been sellin' canned goods and now I'm canned goods myself.'

You see, the concern he'd been workin' for was a factory that made canned goods. Over in Carterville. And now Jim said he was canned himself. He was certainly a card!

Jim had a great trick that he used to play wile he was travelin'. For instance, he'd be ridin' on a train and they'd come to some little town like, well, like, we'll say, like Benton. Jim would look out the train window and read the signs on the stores.

For instance, they'd be a sign, 'Henry Smith, Dry Goods.' Well, Jim would write down the name and the name of the town and when he got to wherever he was goin' he'd mail back a postal card to Henry Smith at Benton and not sign no name to it, but he'd write on the card, well, somethin' like 'Ask your wife about that book agent that spent the afternoon last week,' or 'Ask your Missus who kept her from gettin' lonesome the last time you was in Carterville.' And he'd sign the card, 'A Friend.'

Of course, he never knew what really come of none of these jokes, but he could picture what *probably* happened and that was enough.

Jim didn't work very steady after he lost his position with the Carterville people. What he did earn, doin' odd jobs round town, why he spent pretty near all of it on gin and his family might of starved if the stores hadn't of carried them along. Jim's wife tried her hand at dressmakin', but they ain't nobody goin' to get rich makin' dresses in this town.

As I say, she'd of divorced Jim, only she seen that she couldn't support herself and the kids and she was always hopin' that some day Jim would cut out his habits and give her more than two or three dollars a week.

They was a time when she would go to whoever he was workin' for and ask them to give her his wages, but after she done this once or twice, he beat her to it by borrowin' most of his pay in advance. He told it all round town, how he had outfoxed his Missus. He certainly was a caution!

But he wasn't satisfied with just outwittin' her. He was sore the

5

way she had acted, tryin' to grab off his pay. And he made up his mind he'd get even. Well, he waited till Evans's Circus was advertised to come to town. Then he told his wife and two kiddies that he was goin' to take them to the circus. The day of the circus, he told them he would get the tickets and meet them outside the entrance to the tent.

Well, he didn't have no intentions of bein' there or buyin' tickets or nothin'. He got full of gin and laid round Wright's poolroom all day. His wife and the kids waited and waited and of course he didn't show up. His wife didn't have a dime with her, or nowhere else, I guess. So she finally had to tell the kids it was all off and they cried like they wasn't never goin' to stop.

Well, it seems, wile they was cryin', Doc Stair came along and he asked what was the matter, but Mrs. Kendall was stubborn and wouldn't tell him, but the kids told him and he insisted on takin' them and their mother in the show. Jim found this out afterwards and it was one reason why he had it in for Doc Stair.

Doc Stair come here about a year and a half ago. He's a mighty handsome young fella and his clothes always look like he has them made to order. He goes to Detroit two or three times a year and wile he's there he must have a tailor take his measure and then make him a suit to order. They cost pretty near twice as much, but they fit a whole lot better than if you just bought them in a store.

For a wile everybody was wonderin' why a young doctor like Doc Stair should come to a town like this where we already got old Doc Gamble and Doc Foote that's both been here for years and all the practice in town was always divided between the two of them.

Then they was a story got round that Doc Stair's gal had throwed him over, a gal up in the Northern Peninsula somewheres, and the reason he come here was to hide himself away and forget it. He said himself that he thought they wasn't nothin' like general practice in a place like ours to fit a man to be a good all round doctor. And that's why he'd came.

Anyways, it wasn't long before he was makin' enough to live on, though they tell me that he never dunned nobody for what they owed him, and the folks here certainly has got the owin' habit, even in my business. If I had all that was comin' to me for just shaves alone, I could go to Carterville and put up at the

Mercer for a week and see a different picture every night. For instance, they's old George Purdy—but I guess I shouldn't ought to be gossipin'.

Well, last year, our coroner died, died of the flu. Ken Beatty, that was his name. He was the coroner. So they had to choose another man to be coroner in his place and they picked Doc Stair. He laughed at first and said he didn't want it, but they made him take it. It ain't no job that anybody would fight for and what a man makes out of it in a year would just about buy seeds for their garden. Doc's the kind, though, that can't say no to nothin' if you keep at him long enough.

But I was goin' to tell you about a poor boy we got here in town—Paul Dickson. He fell out of a tree when he was about ten years old. Lit on his head and it done somethin' to him and he ain't never been right. No harm in him, but just silly. Jim Kendall used to call him cuckoo; that's a name Jim had for anybody that was off their head, only he called people's head their bean. That was another of his gags, callin' head bean and callin' crazy people cuckoo. Only poor Paul ain't crazy, but just silly.

You can imagine that Jim used to have all kinds of fun with Paul. He'd send him to the White Front Garage for a left-handed monkey wrench. Of course they ain't no such a thing as a left-handed monkey wrench.

And once we had a kind of a fair here and they was a baseball game between the fats and the leans and before the game started Jim called Paul over and sent him way down to Schrader's hardware store to get a key for the pitcher's box.

They wasn't nothin' in the way of gags that Jim couldn't think up, when he put his mind to it.

Poor Paul was always kind of suspicious of people, maybe on account of how Jim had kept foolin' him. Paul wouldn't have much to do with anybody only his own mother and Doc Stair and a girl here in town named Julie Gregg. That is, she ain't a girl no more, but pretty near thirty or over.

When Doc first come to town, Paul seemed to feel like here was a real friend and he hung around Doc's office most of the wile; the only time he wasn't there was whcn hc'd go home to eat or sleep or when he seen Julie Gregg doin' her shoppin'.

When he looked out Doc's window and seen her, he'd run downstairs and join her and tag along with her to the different

7

stores. The poor boy was crazy about Julie and she always treated him mighty nice and made him feel like he was welcome, though of course it wasn't nothin' but pity on her side.

Doc done all he could to improve Paul's mind and he told me once that he really thought the boy was gettin' better, that they was times when he was as bright and sensible as anybody else.

But I was goin' to tell you about Julie Gregg. Old Man Gregg was in the lumber business, but got to drinkin' and lost the most of his money and when he died, he didn't leave nothin' but the house and just enough insurance for the girl to skimp along on.

Her mother was a kind of a half invalid and didn't hardly ever leave the house. Julie wanted to sell the place and move somewheres else after the old man died, but the mother said she was born here and would die here. It was tough on Julie, as the young people round this town—well she's too good for them.

She's been away to school and Chicago and New York and different places and they ain't no subject she can't talk on, where you take the rest of the young folks here and you mention anything to them outside of Gloria Swanson or Tommy Meighan and they think you're delirious. Did you see Gloria in Wages of Virtue? You missed somethin'!

Well, Doc Stair hadn't been here more than a week when he come in one day to get shaved and I recognized who he was as he had been pointed out to me, so I told him about my old lady. She's been ailin' for a couple of years and either Doc Gamble or Doc Foote, neither one, seemed to be helpin' her. So he said he would come out and see her, but if she was able to get out herself, it would be better to bring her to his office where he could make a completer examination.

So I took her to his office and wile I was waitin' for her in the reception room, in come Julie Gregg. When somebody comes in Doc Stair's office, they's a bell that rings in his inside office so as he can tell they's somebody to see him.

So he left my old lady inside and come out to the front office and that's the first time him and Julie met and I guess it was what they call love at first sight. But it wasn't fifty-fifty. This young fella was the slickest lookin' fella she'd ever seen in this town and she went wild over him. To him she was just a young lady that wanted to see the doctor.

She'd came on about the same business I had. Her mother had

been doctorin' for years with Doc Gamble and Doc Foote and without no results. So she'd heard they was a new doc in town and decided to give him a try. He promised to call and see her mother that same day.

I said a minute ago that it was love at first sight on her part. I'm not only judgin' by how she acted afterwards but how she looked at him that first day in his office. I ain't no mind reader, but it was wrote all over her face that she was gone.

Now Jim Kendall, besides bein' a jokesmith and a pretty good drinker, well, Jim was quite a lady-killer. I guess he run pretty wild durin' the time he was on the road for them Carterville people, and besides that, he'd had a couple little affairs of the heart right here in town. As I say, his wife could of divorced him, only she couldn't.

But Jim was like the majority of men, and women, too, I guess. He wanted what he couldn't get. He wanted Julie Gregg and worked his head off tryin' to land her. Only he'd of said bean instead of head.

Well, Jim's habits and his jokes didn't appeal to Julie and of course he was a married man, so he didn't have no more chance than, well, than a rabbit. That's an expression of Jim's himself. When somebody didn't have no chance to get elected or somethin', Jim would always say they didn't have no more chance than a rabbit.

He didn't make no bones about how he felt. Right in here, more than once, in front of the whole crowd, he said he was stuck on Julie and anybody that could get her for him was welcome to his house and his wife and kids included. But she wouldn't have nothin' to do with him; wouldn't even speak to him on the street. He finally seen he wasn't gettin' nowheres with his usual line so he decided to try the rough stuff. He went right up to her house one evenin' and when she opened the door he forced his way in and grabbed her. But she broke loose and before he could stop her, she run in the next room and locked the door and phoned to Joe Barnes. Joe's the marshal. Jim could hear who she was phonin' to and he beat it before Joe got there.

Joe was an old friend of Julie's pa. Joe went to Jim the next day and told him what would happen if he ever done it again.

I don't know how the news of this little affair leaked out. Chances is that Joe Barnes told his wife and she told somebody else's wife and they told their husband. Anyways, it did leak out and Hod Meyers had the nerve to kid Jim about it, right here in this shop. Jim didn't deny nothin' and kind of laughed it off and said for us all to wait; that lots of people had tried to make a monkey out of him, but he always got even.

Meanwile everybody in town was wise to Julie's bein' wild mad over the Doc. I don't suppose she had any idear how her face changed when him and her was together; of course she couldn't of, or she'd of kept away from him. And she didn't know that we was all noticin' how many times she made excuses to go up to his office or pass it on the other side of the street and look up in his window to see if he was there. I felt sorry for her and so did most other people.

Hod Meyers kept rubbin' it into Jim about how the Doc had cut him out. Jim didn't pay no attention to the kiddin' and you could see he was plannin' one of his jokes.

One trick Jim had was the knack of changin' his voice. He could make you think he was a girl talkin' and he could mimic any man's voice. To show you how good he was along this line, I'll tell you the joke he played on me once.

You know, in most towns of any size, when a man is dead and needs a shave, why the barber that shaves him soaks him five dollars for the job; that is, he don't soak *him*, but whoever ordered the shave. I just charge three dollars because personally I don't mind much shavin' a dead person. They lay a whole lot stiller than live customers. The only thing is that you don't feel like talkin' to them and you get kind of lonesome.

Well, about the coldest day we ever had here, two years ago last winter, the phone rung at the house wile I was home to dinner and I answered the phone and it was a woman's voice and she said she was Mrs. John Scott and her husband was dead and would I come out and shave him.

Old John had always been a good customer of mine. But they live seven miles out in the country, on the Streeter road. Still I didn't see how I could say no.

So I said I would be there, but would have to come in a jitney and it might cost three or four dollars besides the price of the shave. So she, or the voice, it said that was all right, so I got Frank Abbott to drive me out to the place and when I got there, who should open the door but old John himself! He wasn't no more dead than, well, than a rabbit.

It didn't take no private detective to figure out who had played me this little joke. Nobody could of thought it up but Jim Kendall. He certainly was a card!

I tell you this incident just to show you how he could disguise his voice and make you believe it was somebody else talkin'. I'd of swore it was Mrs. Scott had called me. Anyways, some woman.

Well, Jim waited till he had Doc Stair's voice down pat; then he went after revenge.

He called Julie up on a night when he knew Doc was over in Carterville. She never questioned but what it was Doc's voice. Jim said he must see her that night; he couldn't wait no longer to tell her somethin'. She was all excited and told him to come to the house. But he said he was expectin' an important long distance call and wouldn't she please forget her manners for once and come to his office. He said they couldn't nothin' hurt her and nobody would see her and he just *must* talk to her a little wile. Well, poor Julie fell for it.

Doc always keeps a night light in his office, so it looked to Julie like they was somebody there.

Meanwile Jim Kendall had went to Wright's poolroom, where they was a whole gang amusin' themselves. The most of them had drank plenty of gin, and they was a rough bunch even when sober. They was always strong for Jim's jokes and when he told them to come with him and see some fun they give up their card games and pool games and followed along.

Doc's office is on the second floor. Right outside his door they's a flight of stairs leadin' to the floor above. Jim and his gang hid in the dark behind these stairs.

Well, Julie come up to Doc's door and rung the bell and they was nothin' doin'. She rung it again and rung it seven or eight times. Then she tried the door and found it locked. Then Jim made some kind of a noise and she heard it and waited a minute, and then she says, 'Is that you, Ralph?' Ralph is Doc's first name.

They was no answer and it must of come to her all of a sudden that she'd been bunked. She pretty near fell downstairs and the whole gang after her. They chased her all the way home, hollerin', 'Is that you, Ralph?' and 'Oh, Ralphie, dear, is that you?' Jim says he couldn't holler it himself, as he was laughin' too hard.

Poor Julie! She didn't show up here on Main Street for a long, long time afterward.

And of course Jim and his gang told everybody in town, everybody but Doc Stair. They was scared to tell him, and he might of never knowed only for Paul Dickson. The poor cuckoo, as Jim called him, he was here in the shop one night when Jim was still gloatin' yet over what he'd done to Julie. And Paul took in as much of it as he could understand and he run to Doc with the story.

It's a cinch Doc went up in the air and swore he'd make Jim suffer. But it was a kind of a delicate thing, because if it got out that he had beat Jim up, Julie was bound to hear of it and then she'd know that Doc knew and of course knowin' that he knew would make it worse for her than ever. He was goin' to do something', but it took a lot of figurin'.

Well, it was a couple days later when Jim was here in the shop again, and so was the cuckoo. Jim was goin' duck-shootin' the next day and had came in lookin' for Hod Meyers to go with him. I happened to know that Hod had went over to Carterville and wouldn't be home till the end of the week. So Jim said he hated to go alone and he guessed he would call it off. Then poor Paul spoke up and said if Jim would take him he would go along. Jim thought a wile and then he said, well, he guessed a half-wit was better than nothin'.

I suppose he was plottin' to get Paul out in the boat and play some joke on him, like pushin' him in the water. Anyways, he said Paul could go. He asked him had he ever shot a duck and Paul said no, he'd never even had a gun in his hands. So Jim said he could set in the boat and watch him and if he behaved himself, he might lend him his gun for a couple of shots. They made a date to meet in the mornin' and that's the last I seen of Jim alive.

Next mornin', I hadn't been open more than ten minutes when Doc Stair come in. He looked kind of nervous. He asked me had I seen Paul Dickson. I said no, but I knew where he was, out duck-shootin' with Jim Kendall. So Doc says that's what he had heard, and he couldn't understand it because Paul had told him he wouldn't never have no more to do with Jim as long as he lived.

He said Paul had told him about the joke Jim had played on Julie. He said Paul had asked him what he thought of the joke and the Doc had told him that anybody that would do a thing like that ought not to be let live.

12

I said it had been a kind of a raw thing, but Jim just couldn't resist no kind of a joke, no matter how raw. I said I thought he was all right at heart, but just bubblin' over with mischief. Doc turned and walked out.

At noon he got a phone call from old John Scott. The lake where Jim and Paul had went shootin' is on John's place. Paul had come runnin' up to the house a few minutes before and said they'd been an accident. Jim had shot a few ducks and then give the gun to Paul and told him to try his luck. Paul hadn't never handled a gun and he was nervous. He was shakin' so hard that he couldn't control the gun. He let fire and Jim sunk back in the boat, dead.

Doc Stair, bein' the coroner, jumped in Frank Abbott's flivver and rushed out to Scott's farm. Paul and old John was down on the shore of the lake. Paul had rowed the boat to shore, but they'd left the body in it, waitin' for Doc to come.

Doc examined the body and said they might as well fetch it back to town. They was no use leavin' it there or callin' a jury, as it was a plain case of accidental shootin'.

Personally I wouldn't never leave a person shoot a gun in the same boat I was in unless I was sure they knew somethin' about guns. Jim was a sucker to leave a new beginner have his gun, let alone a half-wit. It probably served Jim right, what he got. But still we miss him round here. He certainly was a card!

Comb it wet or dry?

I Can't Breathe

I am staying here at the Inn for two weeks with my Uncle Nat and Aunt Jule and I think I will keep a kind of a diary while I am here to help pass the time and so I can have a record of things that happen though goodness knows there isn't lightly to anything happen, that is anything exciting with Uncle Nat and Aunt Jule making the plans as they are both at least 35 years old and maybe older.

Dad and mother are abroad to be gone a month and me coming here is supposed to be a recompence for them not taking me with them. A fine recompence to be left with old people that come to a place like this to rest. Still it would be a heavenly place under different conditions, for instance if Walter were here, too. It would be heavenly if he were here, the very thought of it makes my heart stop.

I can't stand it. I won't think about it.

This is our first separation since we have been engaged, nearly 17 days. It will be 17 days tomorrow. And the hotel orchestra at dinner this evening played that old thing 'Oh how I miss you tonight' and it seemed as if they must be playing it for my benefit though of course the person in that song is talking about how they miss their mother though of course I miss mother too, but a person gets used to missing their mother and it isn't like Walter or the person you are engaged to.

But there won't be any more separations much longer, we are going to be married in December even if mother does laugh when I talk to her about it because she says I am crazy to even think of getting married at 18.

She got married herself when she was 18, but of course that was 'different,' she wasn't crazy like I am, she knew whom she was

14

marrying. As if Walter were a policeman or a foreigner or something. And she says she was only engaged once while I have been engaged at least five times a year since I was 14, of course it really isn't as bad as that and I have really only been really what I call engaged six times altogether, but is getting engaged my fault when they keep insisting and hammering at you and if you didn't say yes they would never go home.

But it is different with Walter. I honestly believe if he had not asked me I would have asked him. Of course I wouldn't have, but I would have died. And this is the first time I have ever been engaged to be really married. The other times when they talked about when should we get married I just laughed at them, but I hadn't been engaged to Walter ten minutes when he brought up the subject of marriage and I didn't laugh. I wouldn't be engaged to him unless it was to be married. I couldn't stand it.

Anyway mother may as well get used to the idea because it is 'No Foolin' ' this time and we have got our plans all made and I am going to be married at home and go out to California and Hollywood on our honeymoon. December, five months away. I can't stand it. I can't wait.

There were a couple of awfully nice looking boys sitting together alone in the dining-room tonight. One of them wasn't so much, but the other was cute. And he——

There's the dance orchestra playing 'Always,' what they played at the Biltmore the day I met Walter. 'Not for just an hour not for just a day.' I can't live. I can't breathe.

July 13

This has been a much more exciting day than I expected under the circumstances. In the first place I got two long night letters, one from Walter and one from Gordon Flint. I don't see how Walter ever had the nerve to send his, there was everything in it and it must have been horribly embarrassing for him while the telegraph operator was reading it over and counting the words to say nothing of embarrassing for the operator.

But the one from Gordon was a kind of a shock. He just got back from a trip around the world, left last December to go on it and got back yesterday and called up our house and Helga gave him my address, and his telegram, well it was nearly as bad as

15

Walter's. The trouble is that Gordon and I were engaged when he went away, or at least he thought so and he wrote to me right along all the time he was away and sent cables and things and for a while I answered his letters, but then I lost track of his itinery and couldn't write to him any more and when I got really engaged to Walter I couldn't let Gordon know because I had no idea where he was besides not wanting to spoil his trip.

And now he still thinks we are engaged and he is going to call me up tomorrow from Chicago and how in the world can I explain things and get him to understand because he is really serious and I like him ever and ever so much and in lots of ways he is nicer than Walter, not really nicer but better looking and there is no comparison between their dancing. Walter simply can't learn to dance, that is really dance. He says it is because he is flat footed, he says that as a joke, but it is true and I wish to heavens it wasn't.

All forenoon I thought and thought and thought about what to say to Gordon when he calls up and finally I couldn't stand thinking about it any more and just made up my mind I wouldn't think about it any more. But I will tell the truth though it will kill me to hurt him.

I went down to lunch with Uncle Nat and Aunt Jule and they were going out to play golf this afternoon and were insisting that I go with them, but I told them I had a headache and then I had a terrible time getting them to go without me. I didn't have a headache at all and just wanted to be alone to think about Walter and besides when you play with Uncle Nat he is always correcting your stance or your swing or something and always puts his hands on my arms or shoulders to show me the right way and I can't stand it to have old men touch me, even if they are your uncle.

I finally got rid of them and I was sitting watching the tennis when that boy that I saw last night, the cute one, came and sat right next to me and of course I didn't look at him and I was going to smoke a cigarette and found I had left my lighter upstairs and I started to get up and go after it when all of a sudden he was offering me his lighter and I couldn't very well refuse it without being rude. So we got to talking and he is even cuter than he looks, the most original and wittiest person I believe I ever met and I haven't laughed so much in I don't know how long.

For one thing he asked me if I had heard Rockefeller's song and

I said no and he began singing 'Oil alone.' Then he asked me if I knew the orange juice song and I told him no again and he said it was 'Orange juice sorry you made me cry.' I was in hysterics before we had been together ten minutes.

His name is Frank Caswell and he has been out of Dartmouth a year and is 24 years old. That isn't so terribly old, only two years older than Walter and three years older than Gordon. I hate the name Frank, but Caswell is all right and he is so cute.

He was out in California last winter and visited Hollywood and met everybody in the world and it is fascinating to listen to him. He met Norma Shearer and he said he thought she was the prettiest thing he had ever seen. What he said was 'I did think she was the prettiest girl in the world, till today.' I was going to pretend I didn't get it, but I finally told him to be sensible or I would never be able to believe anything he said.

Well, he wanted me to dance with him tonight after dinner and the next question was how to explain how we had met each other to Uncle Nat and Aunt Jule. Frank said he would fix that all right and sure enough he got himself introduced to Uncle Nat when Uncle Nat came in from golf and after dinner Uncle Nat introduced him to me and Aunt Jule too and we danced together all evening, that is not Aunt Jule. They went to bed, thank heavens.

He is a heavenly dancer, as good as Gordon. One dance we were dancing and for one of the encores the orchestra played 'In a cottage small by a waterfall' and I simply couldn't dance to it. I just stopped still and said 'Listen, I can't bear it, I can't breathe' and poor Frank thought I was sick or something and I had to explain that that was the tune the orchestra played the night I sat at the next table to Jack Barrymore at Barney Gallant's.

I made him sit out that encore and wouldn't let him talk till they got through playing it. Then they played something else and I was all right again and Frank told me about meeting Jack Barrymore. Imagine meeting him. I couldn't live.

I promised Aunt Jule I would go to bed at eleven and it is way past that now, but I am all ready for bed and have just been writing this. Tomorrow Gordon is going to call up and what will I say to him? I just won't think about it.

*

17

Gordon called up this morning from Chicago and it was wonderful to hear his voice again though the connection was terrible. He asked me if I still loved him and I tried to tell him no, but I knew that would mean an explanation and the connection was so bad that I never could make him understand so I said yes, but I almost whispered it purposely, thinking he wouldn't hear me, but he heard me all right and he said that made everything all right with the world. He said he thought I had stopped loving him because I had stopped writing.

I wish the connection had been decent and I could have told him how things were, but now it is terrible because he is planning to get to New York the day I get there and heaven knows what I will do because Walter will be there, too. I just won't think about it.

Aunt Jule came in my room just after I was through talking to Gordon, thank heavens. The room was full of flowers. Walter had sent me some and so had Frank. I got another long night letter from Walter, just as silly as the first one. I wish he would say those things in letters instead of night letters so everybody in the world wouldn't see them. Aunt Jule wanted me to read it aloud to her. I would have died.

While she was still in the room, Frank called up and asked me to play golf with him and I said all right and Aunt Jule said she was glad my headache was gone. She was trying to be funny.

I played golf with Frank this afternoon. He is a beautiful golfer and it is thrilling to watch him drive, his swing is so much more graceful than Walter's. I asked him to watch me swing and tell me what was the matter with me, but he said he couldn't look at anything but my face and there wasn't anything the matter with that.

He told me the boy who was here with him had been called home and he was glad of it because I might have liked him, the other boy, better than himself. I told him that couldn't be possible and he asked me if I really meant that and I said of course, but I smiled when I said it so he wouldn't take it too seriously.

We danced again tonight and Uncle Nat and Aunt Jule sat with us a while and danced a couple of dances themselves, but they were really there to get better acquainted with Frank and see if he was all right for me to be with. I know they certainly couldn't have enjoyed their own dancing, no old people really can enjoy it because they can't really *do* anything.

They were favorably impressed with Frank I think, at least Aunt Jule didn't say I must be in bed at eleven, but just not to stay up too late. I guess it is a big surprise to a girl's parents and aunts and uncles to find out that the boys you go around with are all right, they always seem to think that if I seem to like somebody and the person pays a little attention to me, why he must be a convict or a policeman or a drunkard or something queer.

Frank had some more songs for me tonight. He asked me if I knew the asthma song and I said I didn't and he said 'Oh, you must know that. It goes yes, sir, asthma baby.' Then he told me about the underwear song, 'I underwear my baby is tonight.' He keeps you in hysterics and yet he has his serious side, in fact he was awfully serious when he said good night to me and his eyes simply shown. I wish Walter were more like him in some ways, but I mustn't think about that.

July 15

I simply can't live and I know I'll never sleep tonight. I am in a terrible predicament or rather I won't know whether I really am or not till tomorrow and that is what makes it so terrible.

After we had danced two or three dances, Frank asked me to go for a ride with him and we went for a ride in his car and he had had some cocktails and during the ride he had some drinks out of a flask and finally he told me he loved me and I said not to be silly, but he said he was perfectly serious and he certainly acted that way. He asked me if I loved anybody else and I said yes and he asked if I didn't love him more than anybody else and I said yes, but only because I thought he had probably had too much to drink and wouldn't remember it anyway and the best thing to do was humor him under the circumstances.

Then all of a sudden he asked me when I could marry him and I said, just as a joke, that I couldn't possibly marry him before December. He said that was a long time to wait, but I was certainly worth waiting for and he said a lot of other things and maybe I humored him a little too much, but that is just the trouble, I don't know.

I was absolutely sure he was tight and would forget the whole

19

thing, but that was early in the evening, and when we said good night he was a whole lot more sober than he had been and now I am not sure how it stands. If he doesn't remember anything about it, of course I am all right. But if he does remember and if he took me seriously, I will simply have to tell him about Walter and maybe about Gordon, too. And it isn't going to be easy. The suspense is what is maddening and I know I'll never live through this night.

July 16

I can't stand it, I can't breathe, life is impossible. Frank remembered everything about last night and firmly believes we are engaged and going to be married in December. His people live in New York and he says he is going back when I do and have them meet me.

Of course it can't go on and tomorrow I will tell him about Walter or Gordon or both of them. I know it is going to hurt him terribly, perhaps spoil his life and I would give anything in the world not to have had it happen. I hate so to hurt him because he is so nice besides being so cute and attractive.

He sent me the loveliest flowers this morning and called up at ten and wanted to know how soon he could see me and I hope the girl wasn't listening in because the things he said were, well, like Walter's night letters.

And that is another terrible thing, today I didn't get a night letter from Walter, but there was a regular letter instead and I carried it around in my purse all this afternoon and evening and never remembered to read it till ten minutes ago when I came up in the room. Walter is worried because I have only sent him two telegrams and written him one letter since I have been here, he would be a lot more worried if he knew what has happened now, though of course it can't make any difference because he is the one I am really engaged to be married to and the one I told mother I was going to marry in December and I wouldn't dare tell her it was somebody else.

I met Frank for lunch and we went for a ride this afternoon and he was so much in love and so lovely to me that I simply did not have the heart to tell him the truth, I am surely going to tell him tomorrow and telling him today would have just meant one more day of unhappiness for both of us.

He said his people had plenty of money and his father had offered to take him into partnership and he might accept, but he thinks his true vocation is journalism with a view to eventually writing novels and if I was willing to undergo a few hardships just at first we would probably both be happier later on if he was doing something he really liked. I didn't know what to say, but finally I said I wanted him to suit himself and money wasn't everything.

He asked me where I would like to go on my honeymoon and I suppose I ought to have told him my honeymoon was all planned, that I was going to California, with Walter, but all I said was that I had always wanted to go to California and he was enthusiastic and said that is where we would surely go and he would take me to Hollywood and introduce me to all those wonderful people he met there last winter. It nearly takes my breath away to think of it, going there with someone who really knows people and has the entrée.

We danced again tonight, just two or three dances, and then went out and sat in the tennis-court, but I came upstairs early because Aunt Jule had acted kind of funny at dinner. And I wanted to be alone, too, and think, but the more I think the worse it gets.

Sometimes I wish I were dead, maybe that is the only solution and it would be best for everyone concerned. I *will* die if things keep on the way they have been. But of course tomorrow it will be all over, with Frank I mean, for I must tell him the truth no matter how much it hurts us both. Though I don't care how much it hurts me. The thought of hurting him is what is driving me mad. I can't bear it.

July 18

I have skipped a day. I was busy every minute of yesterday and so exhausted when I came upstairs that I was tempted to fall into bed with all my clothes on. First Gordon called me up from Chicago to remind me that he would be in New York the day I got there and that when he comes he wants me all to himself all the time and we can make plans for our wedding. The connection was bad again and I just couldn't explain to him about Walter.

21

I had an engagement with Frank for lunch and just as we were going in another long distance call came, from Walter this time. He wanted to know why I haven't written more letters and sent him more telegrams and asked me if I still loved him and of course I told him yes because I really do. Then he asked if I had met any men here and I told him I had met one, a friend of Uncle Nat's. After all it was Uncle Nat who introduced me to Frank. He reminded me that he would be in New York on the 25th which is the day I expect to get home, and said he would have theater tickets for that night and we would go somewhere afterwards and dance.

Frank insisted on knowing who had kept me talking so long and I told him it was a boy I had known a long while, a very dear friend of mine and a friend of my family's. Frank was jealous and kept asking questions till I thought I would go mad. He was so serious and kind of cross and gruff that I gave up the plan of telling him the truth till some time when he is in better spirits.

I played golf with Frank in the afternoon and we took a ride last night and I wanted to get in early because I had promised both Walter and Gordon that I would write them long letters, but Frank wouldn't bring me back to the Inn till I had named a definite date in December. I finally told him the 10th and he said all right if I was sure that wasn't a Sunday. I said I would have to look it up, but as a matter of fact I know the 10th falls on a Friday because the date Walter and I have agreed on for our wedding is Saturday the 11th.

Today has just been the same thing over again, two more night letters, a long distance call from Chicago, golf and a ride with Frank, and the room full of flowers. But tomorrow I am going to tell Frank and I am going to write Gordon a long letter and tell him, too, because this simply can't go on any longer. I can't breathe. I can't live.

July 21

I wrote to Gordon yesterday, but I didn't say anything about Walter because I don't think it is a thing a person ought to do by letter. I can tell him when he gets to New York and then I will be sure that he doesn't take it too hard and I can promise him that I will be friends with him always and make him promise not to do anything silly, while if I told it to him in a letter there is no telling

22

what he would do, there all alone.

And I haven't told Frank because he hasn't been feeling well, he is terribly sunburned and it hurts him terribly so he can hardly play golf or dance, and I want him to be feeling his best when I do tell him, but whether he is all right or not I simply must tell him tomorrow because he is actually planning to leave here on the same train with us Saturday night and I can't let him do that.

Life is so hopeless and it could be so wonderful. For instance how heavenly it would be if I could marry Frank first and stay married to him five years and he would be the one who would take me to Hollywood and maybe we could go on parties with Norman Kerry and Jack Barrymore and Buster Collier and Marion Davies and Lois Moran.

And at the end of five years Frank could go into journalism and write novels and I would only be 23 and I could marry Gordon and he would be ready for another trip around the world and he could show me things better than someone who had never seen them before.

Gordon and I would separate at the end of five years and I would be 28 and I know of lots of women that never even got married the first time till they were 28 though I don't suppose that was their fault, but I would marry Walter then, for after all he is the one I really love and want to spend most of my life with and I wouldn't care whether he could dance or not when I was that old. Before long we would be as old as Uncle Nat and Aunt Jule and I certainly wouldn't want to dance at their age when all you can do is just hobble around the floor. But Walter is so wonderful as a companion and we would enjoy the same things and be pals and maybe we would begin to have children.

But that is all impossible though it wouldn't be if older people just had sense and would look at things the right way.

It is only half past ten, the earliest I have gone to bed in weeks, but I am worn out, and Frank went to bed early so he could put cold cream on his sunburn.

Listen, diary, the orchestra is playing 'Limehouse Blues.' The first tune I danced to with Merle Oliver, two years ago. I can't stand it. And how funny that they should play that old tune tonight of all nights, when I have been thinking of Merle off and on all day, and I hadn't thought of him before in weeks and weeks. I wonder where he is, I wonder if it is just an accident or if it means

I am going to see him again. I simply mustn't think about it or I'll die.

I knew it wasn't an accident. I knew it must mean something, and it did.

Merle is coming here today, here to this Inn, and just to see me. And there can only be one reason. And only one answer. I knew that when I heard his voice calling from Boston. How could I ever had thought I loved anyone else? How could he ever have thought I meant it when I told him I was engaged to George Morse?

A whole year and he still cares and I still care. That shows we were always intended for each other and for no one else. I won't make *him* wait till December. I doubt if we even wait till dad and mother get home. And as for a honeymoon I will go with him to Long Beach or the Bronx Zoo, wherever he wants to take me.

After all this is the best way out of it, the only way. I won't have to say anything to Frank, he will guess when he sees me with Merle. And when I get home Sunday and Walter and Gordon call me up, I will invite them both to dinner and Merle can tell them himself, with two of them there it will only hurt each one half as much as if they were alone.

The train is due at 2:40, almost three hours from now. I can't wait. And what if it should be late? I can't stand it.

Alibi Ike

His right name was Frank X. Farrell, and I guess the X stood for 'Excuse me.' Because he never pulled a play, good or bad, on or off the field, without apologizin' for it.

'Alibi Ike' was the name Carey wished on him the first day he reported down South. O' course we all cut out the 'Alibi' part of it right away for the fear he would overhear it and bust somebody. But we called him 'Ike' right to his face and the rest of it was understood by everybody on the club except Ike himself.

He ast me one time, he says:

'What do you all call me Ike for? I ain't no Yid.'

'Carey give you the name,' I says. 'It's his nickname for everybody he takes a likin' to.'

'He mustn't have only a few friends then,' says Ike. 'I never heard him say "Ike" to nobody else.'

But I was goin' to tell you about Carey namin' him. We'd been workin' out two weeks and the pitchers was showin' somethin' when this bird joined us. His first day out he stood up there so good and took such a reef at the old pill that he had everyone lookin'. Then him and Carey was together in left field, catchin' fungoes, and it was after we was through for the day that Carey told me about him.

'What do you think of Alibi Ike?' ast Carey.

'Who's that?' I says.

'This here Farrell in the outfield,' says Carey.

'He looks like he could hit,' I says.

'Yes,' says Carey, 'but he can't hit near as good as he can apologize.'

Then Carey went on to tell me what Ike had been pullin' out

there. He'd dropped the first fly ball that was hit to him and told Carey his glove wasn't broke in good yet, and Carey says the glove could easy of been Kid Gleason's gran'father. He made a whale of a catch out o' the next one and Carey says 'Nice work!' or somethin' like that, but Ike says he could of caught the ball with his back turned only he slipped when he started after it and, besides that, the air currents fooled him.

'I thought you done well to get to the ball,' says Carey.

'I ought to been settin' under it,' says Ike.

'What did you hit last year?' Carey ast him.

'I had malaria most o' the season,' says Ike. 'I wound up with .356.'

'Where would I have to go to get malaria?' says Carey, but Ike didn't wise up.

I and Carey and him set at the same table together for supper. It took him half an hour longer'n us to eat because he had to excuse himself every time he lifted his fork.

'Doctor told me I needed starch,' he'd say, and then toss a shoveful o' potatoes into him. Or, 'They ain't much meat on one o' these chops,' he'd tell us, and grab another one. Or he'd say: 'Nothin' like onions for a cold,' and then he'd dip into the perfumery.

'Better try that apple sauce,' says Carey. 'It'll help your malaria.'

'Whose malaria?' says Ike. He'd forgot already why he didn't only hit .356 last year.

I and Carey begin to lead him on.

'Whereabouts did you say your home was?' I ast him.

'I live with my folks,' he says. 'We live in Kansas City—not right down in the business part—outside a ways.'

'How's that come?' says Carey. 'I should think you'd get rooms in the post office.'

But Ike was too busy curin' his cold to get that one.

'Are you married?' I ast him.

'No,' he says. 'I never run round much with girls, except to shows onct in a wile and parties and dances and roller skatin'.'

'Never take 'em to the prize fights, eh?' says Carey.

'We don't have no real good bouts,' says Ike. 'Just bush stuff. And I never figured a boxin' match was a place for the ladies.'

Well, after supper he pulled a cigar out and lit it. I was just goin'

26

to ask him what he done it for, but he beat me to it.

'Kind o' rests a man to smoke after a good work-out,' he says. 'Kind o' settles a man's supper, too.'

'Looks like a pretty good cigar,' says Carey.

'Yes,' says Ike. 'A friend o' mine give it to me—a fella in Kansas City that runs a billiard room.'

'Do you play billiards?' I ast him.

'I used to play a fair game,' he says. 'I'm all out o' practice now—can't hardly make a shot.'

We coaxed him into a four-handed battle, him and Carey against Jack Mack and I. Say, he couldn't play billiards as good as Willie Hoppe; not quite. But to hear him tell it, he didn't make a good shot all evenin'. I'd leave him an awful-lookin' layout and he'd gather 'em up in one try and then run a couple o' hundred, and between every carom he'd say he'd put too much stuff on the ball, or the English didn't take, or the table wasn't true, or his stick was crooked, or somethin'. And all the time he had the balls actin' like they was Dutch soldiers and him Kaiser William. We started out to play fifty points, but we had to make it a thousand so as I and Jack and Carey could try the table.

The four of us set round the lobby a wile after we was through playin', and when it got along toward bedtime Carey whispered to me and says:

'Ike'd like to go to bed, but he can't think up no excuse.'

Carey hadn't hardly finished whisperin' when Ike got up and pulled it:

'Well, good night, boys,' he says. 'I ain't sleepy, but I got some gravel in my shoes and it's killin' my feet.'

We knowed he hadn't never left the hotel since we'd came in from the grounds and changed our clo'es. So Carey says:

'I should think they'd take them gravel pits out o' the billiard room.'

But Ike was already on his way to the elevator, limpin'.

'He's got the world beat,' says Carey to Jack and I. 'I've knew lots o' guys that had an alibi for every mistake they made; I've heard pitchers say that the ball slipped when somebody cracked one off'n 'em; I've heard infielders complain of a sore arm after heavin' one into the stand, and I've saw outfielders tooken sick with a dizzy spell when they've misjudged a fly ball. But this baby can't even go to bed without apologizin', and I bet he excuses himself to the razor when he gets ready to shave.'

'And at that,' says Jack, 'he's goin' to make us a good man.'

'Yes,' says Carey, 'unless rheumatism keeps his battin' average down to .400.'

Well, sir, Ike kept whalin' away at the ball all through the trip till everybody knowed he'd won a job. Cap had him in there regular the last few exhibition games and told the newspaper boys a week before the season opened that he was goin' to start him in Kane's place.

'You're there, kid,' says Carey to Ike, the night Cap made the 'nnouncement. 'They ain't many boys that wins a big league berth their third year out.'

'I'd of been up here a year ago,' says Ike, 'only I was bent over all season with lumbago.'

II

It rained down in Cincinnati one day and somebody organized a little game o' cards. They was shy two men to make six and ast I and Carey to play.

'I'm with you if you get Ike and make it seven-handed,' says Carey.

So they got a hold of Ike and we went up to Smitty's room.

'I pretty near forgot how many you deal,' says Ike. 'It's been a long wile since I played.'

I and Carey give each other the wink, and sure enough, he was just as ig'orant about poker as billiards. About the second hand, the pot was opened two or three ahead of him, and they was three in when it comes his turn. It cost a buck, and he throwed in two.

'It's raised, boys,' somebody says.

'Gosh, that's right, I did raise it,' says Ike.

'Take out a buck if you didn't mean to tilt her,' says Carey.

'No,' says Ike, 'I'll leave it go.'

Well, it was raised back at him and then he made another mistake and raised again. They was only three left in when the draw come. Smitty'd opened with a pair o' kings and he didn't help 'em. Ike stood pat. The guy that'd raised him back was flushin' and he didn't fill. So Smitty checked and Ike bet and didn't get no call. He tossed his hand away, but I grabbed it and give it a

28

look. He had king, queen, jack and two tens. Alibi Ike he must have seen me peekin', for he leaned over and whispered to me.

'I overlooked my hand,' he says. 'I thought all the wile it was a straight.'

'Yes,' I says, 'that's why you raised twice by mistake.'

They was another pot that he come into with tens and fours. It was tilted a couple o' times and two o' the strong fellas drawed ahead of Ike. They each drawed one. So Ike throwed away his little pair and come out with four tens. And they was four treys against him. Carey'd looked at Ike's discards and then he says:

'This lucky bum busted two pair.'

'No, no, I didn't,' says Ike.

'Yes, yes, you did,' says Carey, and showed us the two fours.

'What do you know about that?' says Ike. 'I'd of swore one was a five spot.'

Well, we hadn't had no pay day yet, and after a wile everybody except Ike was goin' shy. I could see him gettin' restless and I was wonderin' how he'd make the get-away. He tried two or three times. 'I got to buy some collars before supper,' he says.

'No hurry,' says Smitty. 'The stores here keeps open all night in April.'

After a minute he opened up again.

'My uncle out in Nebraska ain't expected to live,' he says. 'I ought to send a telegram.'

'Would that save him?' says Carey.

'No, it sure wouldn't,' says Ike, 'but I ought to leave my old man know where I'm at.'

'When did you hear about your uncle?' says Carey.

'Just this mornin',' says Ike.

'Who told you?' ast Carey.

'I got a wire from my old man,' says Ike.

'Well,' says Carey, 'your old man knows you're still here yet this afternoon if you was here this mornin'. Trains leavin' Cincinnati in the middle o' the day don't carry no ball clubs.'

'Yes,' says Ike, 'that's true. But he don't know where I'm goin' to be next week.'

'Ain't he got no schedule?' ast Carey.

'I sent him one openin' day,' says Ike, 'but it takes mail a long time to get to Idaho.'

'I thought your old man lived in Kansas City,' says Carey.

'He does when he's home,' says Ike.

'But now,' says Carey, 'I s'pose he's went to Idaho so as he can be near your sick uncle in Nebraska.'

'He's visitin' my other uncle in Idaho.'

'Then how does he keep posted about your sick uncle?' ast Carey.

'He don't,' says Ike. 'He don't even know my other uncle's sick. That's why I ought to wire and tell him.'

'Good night!' says Carey.

'What town in Idaho is your old man at?' I says.

Ike thought it over.

'No town at all,' he says. 'But he's near a town.'

'Near what town?' I says.

'Yuma,' says Ike.

Well, by this time he'd lost two or three pots and he was desperate. We was playin' just as fast as we could, because we seen we couldn't hold him much longer. But he was tryin' so hard to frame an escape that he couldn't pay no attention to the cards, and it looked like we'd get his whole pile away from him if we could make him stick.

The telephone saved him. The minute it begun to ring, five of us jumped for it. But Ike was there first.

'Yes,' he says, answerin' it. 'This is him. I'll come right down.'

And he slammed up the receiver and beat it out o' the door without even sayin' good-by.

'Smitty'd ought to locked the door,' says Carey.

'What did he win?' ast Carey.

We figured it up—sixty-odd bucks.

'And the next time we ask him to play,' says Carey, 'his fingers will be so stiff he can't hold the cards.'

Well, we set round a wile talkin' it over, and pretty soon the telephone rung again. Smitty answered it. It was a friend of his'n from Hamilton and he wanted to know why Smitty didn't hurry down. He was the one that had called before and Ike had told him he was Smitty.

'Ike'd ought to split with Smitty's friend,' says Carey.

'No,' I says, 'he'll need all he won. It costs money to buy collars and to send telegrams from Cincinnati to your old man in Texas and keep him posted on the health o' your uncle in Cedar Rapids, D.C.'

30

III

And you ought to heard him out there on that field! They wasn't a day when he didn't pull six or seven, and it didn't make no difference whether he was goin' good or bad. If he popped up in the pinch he should of made a base hit and the reason he didn't was so-and-so. And if he cracked one for three bases he ought to had a home run, only the ball wasn't lively, or the wind brought it back, or he tripped on a lump o' dirt, roundin' first base.

They was one afternoon in New York when he beat all records. Big Marquard was workin' against us and he was good.

In the first innin' Ike hit one clear over that right field stand, but it was a few feet foul. Then he got another foul and then the count come to two and two. Then Rube slipped one acrost on him and he was called out.

'What do you know about that!' he says afterward on the bench. 'I lost count. I thought it was three and one, and I took a strike.'

'You took a strike all right,' says Carey. 'Even the umps knowed it was a strike.'

'Yes,' says Ike, 'but you can bet I wouldn't of took it if I'd knew it was the third one. The score board had it wrong.'

'That score board ain't for you to look at,' says Cap. 'It's for you to hit that old pill against.'

'Well,' says Ike, 'I could of hit that one over the score board if I'd knew it was the third.'

'Was it a good ball?' I says.

'Well, no, it wasn't,' says Ike. 'It was inside.'

'How far inside?' says Carey.

'Oh, two or three inches or half a foot,' says Ike.

'I guess you wouldn't of threatened the score board with it then,' says Cap.

'I'd of pulled it down the right foul line if I hadn't thought he'd call it a ball,' says Ike.

Well, in New York's part o' the innin' Doyle cracked one and Ike run back a mile and a half and caught it with one hand. We was all sayin' what a whale of a play it was, but he had to apologize just the same as for gettin' struck out.

'That stand's so high,' he says, 'that a man don't never see a ball till it's right on top o' you.'

31

'Didn't you see that one?' ast Cap.

'Not at first,' says Ike; 'not till it raised up above the roof o' the stand.'

'Then why did you start back as soon as the ball was hit?' says Cap.

'I knowed by the sound that he'd got a good hold of it,' says Ike.

'Yes,' says Cap, 'but how'd you know what direction to run in?'

'Doyle usually hits 'em that way, the way I run,' says Ike.

'Why don't you play blindfolded?' says Carey.

'Might as well, with that big high stand to bother a man,' says Ike. 'If I could of saw the ball all the time I'd of got it in my hip pocket.'

Along in the fifth we was one run to the bad and Ike got on with one out. On the first ball throwed to Smitty, Ike went down. The ball was outside and Meyers throwed Ike out by ten feet.

You could see Ike's lips movin' all the way to the bench and when he got there he had his piece learned.

'Why didn't he swing?' he says.

'Why didn't you wait for his sign?' says Cap.

'He give me his sign,' says Ike.

'What is his sign with you?' says Cap.

'Pickin' up some dirt with his right hand,' says Ike.

'Well, I didn't see him do it,' Cap says.

'He done it all right,' says Ike.

Well, Smitty went out and they wasn't no more argument till they come in for the next innin'. Then Cap opened it up.

'You fellas better get your signs straight,' he says.

'Do you mean me?' says Smitty.

'Yes,' Cap says. 'What's your sign with Ike?'

'Slidin' my left hand up to the end o' the bat and back,' says Smitty.

'Do you hear that, Ike?' ast Cap.

'What of it?' says Ike.

'You says his sign was pickin' up dirt and he says it's slidin' his hand. Which is right?'

'I'm right,' says Smitty. 'But if you're arguin' about him goin' last innin', I didn't give him no sign.'

'You pulled your cap down with your right hand, didn't you?' ast Ike.

'Well, s'pose I did,' says Smitty. 'That don't mean nothin'. I never told you to take that for a sign, did I?'

'I thought maybe you meant to tell me and forgot,' says Ike.

They couldn't none of us answer that and they wouldn't of been no more said if Ike had of shut up. But wile we was settin' there Carey got on with two out and stole second clean.

'There!' says Ike. 'That's what I was tryin' to do and I'd of got away with it if Smitty'd swang and bothered the Indian.'

'Oh!' says Smitty. 'You was tryin' to steal then, was you? I thought you claimed I give you the hit and run.'

'I didn't claim no such a thing,' says Ike. 'I thought maybe you might of gave me a sign, but I was goin' anyway because I thought I had a good start.'

Cap prob'ly would of hit him with a bat, only just about that time Doyle booted one on Hayes and Carey come acrost with the run that tied.

Well, we go into the ninth finally, one and one, and Marquard walks McDonald with nobody out.

'Lay it down,' says Cap to Ike.

And Ike goes up there with orders to bunt and cracks the first ball into that right-field stand! It was fair this time, and we're two ahead, but I didn't think about that at the time. I was too busy watchin' Cap's face. First he turned pale and then he got red as fire and then he got blue and purple, and finally he just laid back and busted out laughin'. So we wasn't afraid to laugh ourselfs when we seen him doin' it, and when Ike come in everybody on the bench was in hysterics.

But instead o' takin' advantage, Ike had to try and excuse himself. His play was to shut up and he didn't know how to make it.

'Well,' he says, 'if I hadn't hit quite so quick at that one I bet it'd of cleared the center-field fence.'

Cap stopped laughin'.

'It'll cost you plain fifty,' he says.

'What for?' says Ike.

'When I say "bunt" I mean "bunt," ' says Cap.

'You didn't say "bunt," ' says Ike.

'I says "Lay it down," ' says Cap. 'If that don't mean "bunt," what does it mean?'

' "Lay it down" means "bunt" all right,' says Ike, 'but I understood you to say "Lay on it." '

33

'All right,' says Cap, 'and the little misunderstandin' will cost you fifty.'

Ike didn't say nothin' for a few minutes. Then he had another bright idear.

'I was just kiddin' about misunderstandin' you,' he says. 'I knowed you wanted me to bunt.'

'Well, then, why didn't you bunt?' ast Cap.

'I was goin' to on the next ball,' says Ike. 'But I thought if I took a good wallop I'd have 'em all fooled. So I walloped at the first one to fool 'em, and I didn't have no intention o' hittin' it.'

'You tried to miss it, did you?' says Cap.

'Yes,' says Ike.

'How'd you happen to hit it?' ast Cap.

'Well,' Ike says, 'I was lookin' for him to throw me a fast one and I was goin' to swing under it. But he come with a hook and I met it right square where I was swingin' to go under the fast one.'

'Great!' says Cap. 'Boys,' he says, 'Ike's learned how to hit Marquard's curve. Pretend a fast one's comin' and then try to miss it. It's a good thing to know and Ike'd ought to be willin' to pay for the lesson. So I'm goin' to make it a hundred instead o' fifty.'

The game wound up 3 to 1. The fine didn't go, because Ike hit like a wild man all through that trip and we made pretty near a clean-up. The night we went to Philly I got him cornered in the car and I says to him:

'Forget them alibis for a wile and tell me somethin'. What'd you do that for, swing that time against Marquard when you was told to bunt?'

'I'll tell you,' he says. 'That ball he throwed me looked just like the one I struck out on in the first innin' and I wanted to show Cap what I could of done to that other one if I'd knew it was the third strike.'

'But,' I says, 'the one you struck out on in the first innin' was a fast ball.'

'So was the one I cracked in the ninth,' says Ike.

IV

You've saw Cap's wife, o' course. Well, her sister's about twict as good-lookin' as her, and that's goin' some.

Cap took his missus down to St. Louis the second trip and the

34

other one come down from St. Joe to visit her. Her name is Dolly, and some doll is right.

Well, Cap was goin' to take the two sisters to a show and he wanted a beau for Dolly. He left it to her and she picked Ike. He'd hit three on the nose that afternoon—off'n Sallee, too.

They fell for each other that first evenin'. Cap told us how it come off. She begin flatterin' Ike for the star game he'd played and o' course he begin excusin' himself for not doin' better. So she thought he was modest and it went strong with her. And she believed everything he said and that made her solid with him—that and her make-up. They was together every mornin' and evenin' for the five days we was there. In the afternoons Ike played the grandest ball you ever see, hittin' and runnin' the bases like a fool and catchin' everything that stayed in the park.

I told Cap, I says: 'You'd ought to keep the doll with us and he'd make Cobb's figures look sick.'

But Dolly had to go back to St. Joe and we come home for a long serious.

Well, for the next three weeks Ike had a letter to read every day and he'd set in the clubhouse readin' it till mornin' practice was half over. Cap didn't say nothin' to him, because he was goin' so good. But I and Carey wasted a lot of our time tryin' to get him to own up who the letters was from. Fine chanct!

'What are you readin'?' Carey'd say. 'A bill?'

'No,' Ike'd say, 'not exactly a bill. It's a letter from a fella I used to go to school with.'

'High school or college?' I'd ask him.

'College,' he'd say.

'What college?' I'd say.

Then he'd stall a wile and then he'd say:

'I didn't go to the college myself, but my friend went there.'

'How did it happen you didn't go?' Carey'd ask him.

'Well,' he'd say, 'they wasn't no colleges near where I lived.'

'Didn't you live in Kansas City?' I'd say to him.

One time he'd say he did and another time he didn't. One time he says he lived in Michigan.

'Where at?' says Carey.

'Near Detroit,' he says.

'Well,' I says, 'Detroit's near Ann Arbor and that's where they got the university.'

35

'Yes,' says Ike, 'they got it there now, but they didn't have it there then.'

'I come pretty near goin' to Syracuse,' I says, 'only they wasn't no railroads runnin' through there in them days.'

'Where'd this friend o' yours go to college?' says Carey.

'I forget now,' says Ike.

'Was it Carlisle?' ast Carey.

'No,' says Ike, 'his folks wasn't very well off.'

'That's what barred me from Smith,' I says.

'I was goin' to tackle Cornell's,' says Carey, 'but the doctor told me I'd have hay fever if I didn't stay up North.'

'Your friend writes long letters,' I says.

'Yes,' says Ike; 'he's tellin' me about a ball player.'

'Where does he play?' ast Carey.

'Down in the Texas League—Fort Wayne,' says Ike.

'It looks like a girl's writin',' Carey says.

'A girl wrote it,' says Ike. 'That's my friend's sister, writin' for him.'

'Didn't they teach writin' at this here college where he went?' says Carey.

'Sure,' Ike says, 'they taught writin', but he got his hand cut off in a railroad wreck.'

'How long ago?' I says.

'Right after he got out o' college,' says Ike.

'Well,' I says, 'I should think he'd of learned to write with his left hand by this time.'

'It's his left hand that was cut off,' says Ike; 'and he was left-handed.'

'You get a letter every day,' says Carey. 'They're all the same writin'. Is he tellin' you about a different ball player every time he writes?'

'No,' Ike says. 'It's the same ball player. He just tells me what he does every day.'

'From the size o' the letters, they don't play nothin' but double-headers down there,' says Carey.

We figured that Ike spent most of his evenin's answerin' the letters from his 'friend's sister,' so we kept tryin' to date him up for shows and parties to see how he'd duck out of 'em. He was bugs over spaghetti, so we told him one day that they was goin' to be a big feed of it over to Joe's that night and he was invited.

36

'How long'll it last?' he says.

'Well,' we says, 'we goin' right over there after the game and stay till they close up.'

'I can't go,' he says, 'unless they leave me come home at eight bells.'

'Nothin' doin',' says Carey. 'Joe'd get sore.'

'I can't go then,' says Ike.

'Why not?' I ast him.

'Well,' he says, 'my landlady locks up the house at eight and I left my key home.'

'You can come and stay with me,' says Carey.

'No,' he says, 'I can't sleep in a strange bed.'

'How do you get along when we're on the road?' says I.

'I don't never sleep the first night anywheres,' he says. 'After that I'm all right.'

'You'll have time to chase home and get your key right after the game,' I told him.

'The key ain't home,' says Ike. 'I lent it to one o' the other fellas and he's went out o' town and took it with him.'

'Couldn't you borry another key off'n the landlady?' Carey ast him.

'No,' he says, 'that's the only one they is.'

Well, the day before we started East again, Ike come into the clubhouse all smiles.

'Your birthday?' I ast him.

'No,' he says.

'What do you feel so good about?' I says.

'Got a letter from my old man,' he says. 'My uncle's goin' to get well.'

'Is that the one in Nebraska?' says I.

'Not right in Nebraska,' says Ike. 'Near there.'

But afterwards we got the right dope from Cap. Dolly'd blew in from Missouri and was goin' to make the trip with her sister.

V

Well, I want to alibi Carey and I for what come off in Boston. If we'd of had any idear what we was doin', we'd never did it. They wasn't nobody outside o' maybe Ike and the dame that felt worse over it than I and Carey.

37

The first two days we didn't see nothin' of Ike and her except out to the park. The rest o' the time they was sight-seein' over to Cambridge and down to Revere and out to Brook-a-line and all the other places where the rubes go.

But when we come into the beanery after the third game Cap's wife called us over.

'If you want to see somethin' pretty,' she says, 'look at the third finger on Sis's left hand.'

Well, o' course we knowed before we looked that it wasn't goin' to be no hangnail. Nobody was su'prised when Dolly blew into the din' room with it—a rock that Ike'd bought off'n Diamond Joe the first trip to New York. Only o' course it'd been set into a lady's-size ring instead o' the automobile tire he'd been wearin'.

Cap and his missus and Ike and Dolly ett supper together, only Ike didn't eat nothin', but just set there blushin' and spillin' things on the table-cloth. I heard him excusin' himself for not havin' no appetite. He says he couldn't never eat when he was clost to the ocean. He'd forgot about them sixty-five oysters he destroyed the first night o' the trip before.

He was goin' to take her to a show, so after supper he went upstairs to change his collar. She had to doll up, too, and o' course Ike was through long before her.

If you remember the hotel in Boston, they's a little parlor where the piano's at and then they's another little parlor openin' off o' that. Well, when Ike come down Smitty was playin' a few chords and I and Carey was harmonizin'. We seen Ike go up to the desk to leave his key and we called him in. He tried to duck away, but we wouldn't stand for it.

We ast him what he was all duded up for and he says he was goin' to the theayter.

'Goin' alone?' says Carey.

'No,' he says, 'a friend o' mine's goin' with me.'

'What do you say if we go along?' says Carey.

'I ain't only got two tickets,' he says.

'Well,' says Carey, 'we can go down there with you and buy our own seats; maybe we can all get together.'

'No,' says Ike. 'They ain't no more seats. They're all sold out.'

'We can buy some off'n the scalpers,' says Carey.

'I wouldn't if I was you,' says Ike. 'They say the show's rotten.'

38

'What are you goin' for, then?' I ast.

'I didn't hear about it bein' rotten till I got the tickets,' he says.

'Well,' I says, 'if you don't want to go I'll buy the tickets from you.'

'No,' says Ike, 'I wouldn't want to cheat you. I'm stung and I'll just have to stand for it.'

'What are you goin' to do with the girl, leave her here at the hotel?' I says.

'What girl?' says Ike.

'The girl you ett supper with,' I says.

'Oh,' he says, 'we just happened to go into the dinin' room together, that's all. Cap wanted I should set down with 'em.'

'I noticed,' says Carey, 'that she happened to be wearin' that rock you bought off'n Diamond Joe.'

'Yes,' says Ike. 'I lent it to her for a wile.'

'Did you lend her the new ring that goes with it?' I says.

'She had that already,' says Ike. 'She lost the set out of it.'

'I wouldn't trust no strange girl with a rock o' mine,' says Carey.

'Oh, I guess she's all right,' Ike says. 'Besides, I was tired o' the stone. When a girl asks you for somethin', what are you goin' to do?'

He started out toward the desk, but we flagged him.

'Wait a minute!' Carey says. 'I got a bet with Sam here, and it's up to you to settle it.'

'Well,' says Ike, 'make it snappy. My friend'll be here any minute.'

'I bet,' says Carey, 'that you and that girl was engaged to be married.'

'Nothin' to it,' says Ike.

'Now look here,' says Carey, 'this is goin' to cost me real money if I lose. Cut out the alibi stuff and give it to us straight. Cap's wife just as good as told us you was roped.'

Ike blushed like a kid.

'Well, boys,' he says, 'I may as well own up. You win, Carey.'

'Yatta boy!' says Carey. 'Congratulations!'

'You got a swell girl, Ike,' I says.

'She's a peach,' says Smitty.

'Well, I guess she's O.K.,' says Ike. 'I don't know much about girls.'

'Didn't you never run round with 'em?' I says.

'Oh, yes, plenty of 'em,' says Ike. 'But I never seen none I'd fall for.'

'That is, till you seen this one,' says Carey.

'Well,' says Ike, 'this one's O.K., but I wasn't thinkin' about gettin' married yet a wile.'

'Who done the askin'—her?' says Carey.

'Oh, no,' says Ike, 'but sometimes a man don't know what he's gettin' into. Take a good-lookin' girl, and a man gen'ally almost always does about what she wants him to.'

'They couldn't no girl lasso me unless I wanted to be lassoed,' says Smitty.

'Oh, I don't know,' says Ike. 'When a fella gets to feelin' sorry for one of 'em it's all off.'

Well, we left him go after shakin' hands all round. But he didn't take Dolly to no show that night. Some time wile we was talkin' she'd came into that other parlor and she'd stood there and heard us. I don't know how much she heard. But it was enough. Dolly and Cap's missus took the midnight train for New York. And from there Cap's wife sent her on her way back to Missouri.

She'd left the ring and a note for Ike with the clerk. But we didn't ask Ike if the note was from his friend in Fort Wayne, Texas.

VI

When we'd came to Boston Ike was hittin' plain .397. When we got back home he'd fell off to pretty near nothin'. He hadn't drove one out o' the infield in any o' them other Eastern parks, and he didn't even give no excuse for it.

To show you how bad he was, he struck out three times in Brooklyn one day and never opened his trap when Cap ast him what was the matter. Before, if he'd whiffed oncet in a game he'd of wrote a book tellin' why.

Well, we dropped from first place to fifth in four weeks and we was still goin' down. I and Carey was about the only ones in the club that spoke to each other, and all as we did was remind ourself o' what a boner we'd pulled.

'It's goin' to beat us out o' the big money,' says Carey.

'Yes,' I says. 'I don't want to knock my own ball club, but it

40

looks like a one-man team, and when that one man's dauber's down we couldn't trim our whiskers.'

'We ought to knew better,' says Carey.

'Yes,' I says, 'but why should a man pull an alibi for bein' engaged to such a bearcat as she was?'

'He shouldn't,' says Carey. 'But I and you knowed he would or we'd never start talkin' to him about it. He wasn't no more ashamed o' the girl than I am of a regular base hit. But he just can't come clean on no subjec'.'

Cap had the whole story, and I and Carey was as pop'lar with him as an umpire.

'What do you want me to do, Cap?' Carey'd say to him before goin' up to hit.

'Use your own judgment,' Cap'd tell him. 'We want to lose another game.'

But finally, one night in Pittsburgh, Cap had a letter from his missus and he come to us with it.

'You fellas,' he says, 'is the ones that put us on the bum, and if you're sorry I think they's a chancet for you to make good. The old lady's out to St Joe and she's been tryin' her hardest to fix things up. She's explained that Ike don't mean nothin' with his talk; I've wrote and explained that to Dolly, too. But the old lady says that Dolly says that she can't believe it. But Dolly's still stuck on this baby, and she's pinin' away just the same as Ike. And the old lady says she thinks if you two fellas would write to the girl and explain how you was always kiddin' with Ike and leadin' him on, and how the ball club was all shot to pieces since Ike quit hittin', and how he acted like he was goin' to kill himself, and this and that, she'd fall for it and maybe soften down. Dolly, the old lady says, would believe you before she'd believe I and the old lady, because she thinks it's her we're sorry for, and not him.'

Well, I and Carey was only too glad to try and see what we could do. But it wasn't no snap. We wrote about eight letters before we got one that looked good. Then we give it to the stenographer and had it wrote out on a typewriter and both of us signed it.

It was Carey's idear that made the letter good. He stuck in somethin' about the world's serious money that our wives wasn't goin' to spend unless she took pity on a 'boy who was so shy and modest that he was afraid to come right out and say that he had asked such a beautiful and handsome girl to become his bride.'

That's prob'ly what got her, or maybe she couldn't of held out much longer anyway. It was four days after we sent the letter that Cap heard from his Missus again. We was in Cincinnati.

'We've won,' he says to us. 'The old lady says that Dolly says she'll give him another chance. But the old lady says it won't do no good for Ike to write a letter. He'll have to go out there.'

'Send him to-night,' says Carey.

'I'll pay half his fare,' I says.

'I'll pay the other half,' says Carey.

'No,' says Cap, 'the club'll pay his expenses. I'll send him scoutin'.'

'Are you goin' to send him to-night?'

'Sure,' says Cap. 'But I'm goin' to break the news to him right now. It's time we win a ball game.'

So in the clubhouse, just before the game, Cap told him. And I certainly felt sorry for Rube Benton and Red Ames that afternoon! I and Carey was standin' in front o' the hotel that night when Ike come out with his suitcase.

'Sent home?' I says to him.

'No,' he says, 'I'm goin' scoutin'.'

'Where to?' I says. 'Fort Wayne?'

'No, not exactly,' he says.

'Well,' says Carey, 'have a good time.'

'I ain't lookin' for no good time,' says Ike. 'I says I was goin' scoutin'.'

'Well, then,' says Carey, 'I hope you see somebody you like.'

'And you better have a drink before you go,' I says.

'Well,' says Ike, 'they claim it helps a cold.'

Zone of Quiet

'Well,' said the Doctor briskly, 'how do you feel?'

'Oh, I guess I'm all right,' replied the man in bed. 'I'm still kind of drowsy, that's all.'

'You were under the anesthetic an hour and a half. It's no wonder you aren't wide awake yet. But you'll be better after a good night's rest, and I've left something with Miss Lyons that'll make you sleep. I'm going along now. Miss Lyons will take good care of you.'

'I'm off at seven o'clock,' said Miss Lyons. 'I'm going to a show with my G.F. But Miss Halsey's all right. She's the night floor nurse. Anything you want, she'll get it for you. What can I give him to eat, Doctor?'

'Nothing at all; not till after I've been here tomorrow. He'll be better off without anything. Just see that he's kept quiet. Don't let him talk, and don't talk to him; that is, if you can help it.'

'Help it!' said Miss Lyons. 'Say, I can be old lady Sphinx herself when I want to! Sometimes I sit for hours—not alone, neither— and never say a word. Just think and think. And dream.

'I had a G.F. in Baltimore, where I took my training; she used to call me Dummy. Not because I'm dumb like some people—you know—but because I'd sit there and not say nothing. She'd say, "A penny for your thoughts, Eleanor." That's my first name— Eleanor.'

'Well, I must run along. I'll see you in the morning.'

'Good-by, Doctor,' said the man in bed, as he went out.

'Good-by, Doctor Cox,' said Miss Lyons as the door closed.

'He seems like an awful nice fella,' said Miss Lyons. 'And a good doctor, too. This is the first time I've been on a case with him. He gives a girl credit for having some sense. Most of these doctors treat us like they thought we were Mormons or something. Like Doctor Holland. I was on a case with him last week.

43

He treated me like I was a Mormon or something. Finally, I told him, I said, "I'm not as dumb as I look." She died Friday night.'

'Who?' asked the man in bed.

'The woman; the case I was on,' said Miss Lyons.

'And what did the doctor say when you told him you weren't as dumb as you look?'

'I don't remember,' said Miss Lyons. 'He said, "I hope not," or something. What *could* he say? Gee! It's quarter to seven. I hadn't no idear it was so late. I must get busy and fix you up for the night. And I'll tell Miss Halsey to take good care of you. We're going to see "What Price Glory?" I'm going with my G.F. Her B.F. gave her the tickets and he's going to meet us after the show and take us to supper.

'Marian—that's my G.F.—she's crazy wild about him. And he's crazy about her, to hear her tell it. But I said to her this noon—she called me up on the phone—I said to her, "If he's so crazy about you, why don't he propose? He's got plenty of money and no strings tied to him, and as far as I can see there's no reason why he shouldn't marry you if he wants you as bad as you say he does." So she said maybe he was going to ask her tonight. I told her, "Don't be silly! Would he drag me along if he was going to ask you?"

'That about him having plenty money, though, that's a joke. He told her he had and she believes him. I haven't met him yet, but he looks in his picture like he's lucky if he's getting twenty-five dollars a week. She thinks he must be rich because he's in Wall Street. I told her, I said, "That being in Wall Street don't mean nothing. What does he do there? is the question. You know they have to have janitors in those buildings just the same like anywhere else." But she think's he's God or somebody.

'She keeps asking me if I don't think he's the best looking thing I ever saw. I tell her yes, sure, but between you and I, I don't believe anybody'd ever mistake him for Richard Barthelmess.

'Oh, say! I saw him the other day, coming out of the Algonquin! He's the best looking thing! Even better looking than on the screen. Roy Stewart.'

'What about Roy Stewart?' asked the man in bed.

'Oh, he's the fella I was telling you about,' said Miss Lyons. 'He's my G.F.'s B.F.'

44

'Maybe I'm a D.F. not to know, but would you tell me what a B.F. and G.F. are?'

'Well, you *are* dumb, aren't you!' said Miss Lyons. 'A G.F., that's a girl friend, and a B.F. is a boy friend. I thought everybody knew that.

'I'm going out now and find Miss Halsey and tell her to be nice to you. But maybe I better not.'

'Why not?' asked the man in bed.

'Oh, nothing. I was just thinking of something funny that happened last time I was on a case in this hospital. It was the day the man had been operated on and he was the best looking somebody you ever saw. So when I went off duty I told Miss Halsey to be nice to him, like I was going to tell her about you. And when I came back in the morning he was dead. Isn't that funny?'

'Very!'

'Well,' said Miss Lyons, 'did you have a good night? You look a lot better anyway. How'd you like Miss Halsey? Did you notice her ankles? She's got pretty near the smallest ankles I ever saw. Cute. I remember one day Tyler—that's one of the internes—he said if he could just see our ankles, mine and Miss Halsey's, he wouldn't know which was which. Of course we don't look anything alike other ways. She's pretty close to thirty and—well, nobody'd ever take her for Julia Hoyt. Helen.'

'Who's Helen?' asked the man in bed.

'Helen Halsey. Helen; that's her first name. She was engaged to a man in Boston. He was going to Tufts College. He was going to be a doctor. But he died. She still carries his picture with her. I tell her she's silly to mope about a man that's been dead four years. And besides a girl's a fool to marry a doctor. They've got too many alibis.

'When I marry somebody, he's got to be somebody that has regular office hours like he's in Wall Street or somewhere. Then when he don't come home, he'll have to think up something better than being "on a case." I used to use that on my sister when we were living together. When I happened to be out late, I'd tell her I was on a case. She never knew the difference. Poor sis! She married a terrible oil can! But she didn't have the looks to get a real somebody. I'm making this for her. It's a bridge table cover

45

for her birthday. She'll be twenty-nine. Don't that seem old?'

'Maybe to you; not to me,' said the man in bed.

'You're about forty, aren't you?' said Miss Lyons.

'Just about.'

'And how old would you say I am?'

'Twenty-three.'

'I'm twenty-five,' said Miss Lyons. 'Twenty-five and forty. That's fifteen years' difference. But I know a married couple that the husband is forty-five and she's only twenty-four, and they get along fine.'

'I'm married myself,' said the man in bed.

'You would be!' said Miss Lyons. 'The last four cases I've been on was all married men. But at that, I'd rather have any kind of a man than a woman. I hate women! I mean sick ones. They treat a nurse like a dog, especially a pretty nurse. What's that you're reading?'

' "Vanity Fair," ' replied the man in bed.

' "Vanity Fair." I thought that was a magazine.'

'Well, there's a magazine *and* a book. This is the book.'

'Is it about a girl?'

'Yes.'

'I haven't read it yet. I've been busy making this thing for my sister's birthday. She'll be twenty-nine. It's a bridge table cover. When you get that old, about all there is left is bridge or cross-word puzzles. Are you a puzzle fan? I did them religiously for a while, but I got sick of them. They put in such crazy words. Like one day they had a word with only three letters and it said "A e-longated fish" and the first letter had to be an *e*. And only three letters. That *couldn't* be right. So I said if they put things wrong like that, what's the use? Life's too short. And we only live once. When you're dead, you stay a long time dead.

'That's what a B.F. of mine used to say. He was a caution! But he was crazy about me. I might of married him only for a G.F. telling him lies about me. And called herself my friend! Charley Pierce.'

'Who's Charley Pierce?'

'That was my B.F. that the other girl lied to him about me. I told him, I said, "Well, if you believe all them stories about me, maybe we better part once and for all. I don't want to be tied up to a somebody that believes all the dirt they hear about me." So he said he didn't really believe it and if I would take him back he wouldn't quarrel with me no more. But I said I thought it was best for us to part. I got their announcement two years ago, while I was still in training in Baltimore.'

'Did he marry the girl that lied to him about you?'

'Yes, the poor fish! And I bet he's satisfied! They're a match for each other! He was all right, though, at that, till he fell for her. He used to be so thoughtful of me, like I was his sister or something.

'I like a man to respect me. Most fellas wants to kiss you before they know your name.

'Golly! I'm sleepy this morning! And got a right to be, too. Do you know what time I got home last night, or this morning rather? Well, it was half past three. What would mama say if she could see her little girl now! But we did have a good time. First we went to the show—"What Price Glory?"—I and my G.F.—and afterwards her B.F. met us and took us in a taxi down to Barney Gallant's. Peewee Byers has got the orchestra there now. Used to be with Whiteman's. Gee! How can he dance! I mean Roy.'

'Your G.F.'s B.F.?'

'Yes, but I don't believe he's as crazy about her as she thinks he is. Anyway—but this is a secret—he took down the phone number of the hospital while Marian was out powdering her nose, and he said he'd give me a ring about noon. Gee! I'm sleepy! Roy Stewart!'

'Well,' said Miss Lyons, 'how's my patient? I'm twenty minutes late, but honest, it's a wonder I got up at all! Two nights in succession is too much for this child!'

'Barney Gallant's again?' asked the man in bed.

'No, but it was dancing, and pretty near as late. It'll be different tonight. I'm going to bed just the minute I get home. But I did have a dandy time. And I'm crazy about a certain somebody.'

'Roy Stewart?'

'How'd you guess it? But honest, he's wonderful! And so different than most of the fellas I've met. He says the craziest things, just keeps you in hysterics. We were talking about books and reading, and he asked me if I liked poetry—only he called it "poultry"—and I said I was wild about it and Edgar M. Guest was just about my favorite, and then I asked him if he liked Kipling and what do you think he said? He said he didn't know; he'd never kipled.

47

'He's a scream! We just sat there in the house till half past eleven and didn't do nothing but just talk and the time went like we was at a show. He's better than a show. But finally I noticed how late it was and I asked him didn't he think he better be going and he said he'd go if I'd go with him, so I asked him where could we go at that hour of the night, and he said he knew a roadhouse just a little ways away, and I didn't want to go, but he said we wouldn't stay for only just one dance, so I went with him. To the Jericho Inn.

'I don't know what the woman thought of me where I stay, going out that time of night. But he *is* such a wonderful dancer and such a perfect gentleman! Of course we had more than one dance and it was after two o'clock before I knew it. We had some gin, too, but he just kissed me once and that was when we said good night.'

'What about your G.F., Marian? Does she know?'

'About Roy and I? No. I always say that what a person don't know don't hurt them. Besides, there's nothing *for* her to know— yet. But listen: If there was a chance in the world for her, if I thought he cared anything about her, I'd be the last one in the world to accept his intentions. I hope I'm not that kind! But as far as anything serious between them is concerned, well, it's cold. I happen to *know* that. She's not the girl for him.

'In the first place, while she's pretty in a way, her complexion's bad and her hair's scraggy and her figure, well, it's like some woman in the funny pictures. And she's not peppy enough for Roy. She'd rather stay home than do anything. Stay home! It'll be time enough for that when you can't get somebody to take you out.

'She'd never make a wife for him. He'll be a rich man in another year; that is, if things go right for him in Wall Street like he expects. And a man as rich as he'll be wants a wife that can live up to it and entertain and step out once in a while. He don't want a wife that's a drag on him. And he's too good-looking for Marian. A fella as good-looking as him needs a pretty wife or the first thing you know some girl that is pretty will steal him off of you. But it's silly to talk about them marrying each other. He'd have to ask her first, and he's not going to. I know! So I don't feel at all like I'm trespassing.

'Anyway, you know the old saying, everything goes in love. And I—— But I'm keeping you from reading your book. Oh, yes; I almost forgot a T.L. that Miss Halsey said about you. Do you know what a T.L. is?'

'Yes.'

'Well, then, you give me one and I'll give you this one.'

'But I haven't talked to anybody but the Doctor. I can give you one from myself. He asked me how I liked you and I said all right.'

'Well, that's better than nothing. Here's what Miss Halsey said: She said if you were shaved and fixed up, you wouldn't be bad. And now I'm going out and see if there's any mail for me. Most of my mail goes to where I live, but some of it comes here sometimes. What I'm looking for is a letter from the state board telling me if I passed my state examination. They ask you the craziest questions. Like "Is ice a disinfectant?" Who cares! Nobody's going to waste ice to kill germs when there's so much of it needed in high-balls. Do you like high-balls? Roy says it spoils whisky to mix it with water. He takes it straight. He's a terror! But maybe you want to read.'

'Good morning,' said Miss Lyons. 'Did you sleep good?'

'Not so good,' said the man in bed. 'I——'

'I bet you got more sleep than I did,' said Miss Lyons. 'He's the most persistent somebody I ever knew! I asked him last night, I said, "Don't you never get tired of dancing?" So he said, well, he did get tired of dancing with some people, but there was others who he never got tired of dancing with them. So I said, "Yes, Mr. Jollier, but I wasn't born yesterday and I know apple sauce when I hear it and I bet you've told that to fifty girls." I guess he really did mean it, though.

'Of course most anybody'd rather dance with slender girls than stout girls. I remember a B.F. I had one time in Washington. He said dancing with me was just like dancing with nothing. That sounds like he was insulting me, but it was really a compliment. He meant it wasn't any effort to dance with me like with some girls. You take Marian, for instance, and while I'm crazy about her, still that don't make her a good dancer and dancing with her must be a good deal like moving the piano or something.

'I'd die if I was fat! People are always making jokes about fat people. And there's the old saying, "Nobody loves a fat man." And it's even worse with a girl. Besides people making jokes about them and don't want to dance with them and so forth, besides that they're always trying to reduce and can't eat what they want to. I bet, though, if I was fat, I'd eat everything in sight. Though I guess not, either. Because I hardly eat anything as it is. But they do make jokes about them.

'I'll never forget one day last winter, I was on a case in Great Neck and the man's wife was the fattest thing! So they had a radio in the house and one day she saw in the paper where Bugs Baer was going to talk on the radio and it would probably be awfully funny because he writes so crazy. Do you ever read his articles? But this woman, she was awfully sensitive about being fat and I nearly died sitting there with her listening to Bugs Baer, because his whole talk was all about some fat woman and he said the craziest things, but I couldn't laugh on account of she being there in the room with me. One thing he said was that the woman, this woman he was talking about, he said she was so fat that she wore a wrist watch on her thumb. Henry J. Belden.'

'Who is Henry J. Belden? Is that the name of Bugs Baer's fat lady?'

'No, you crazy!' said Miss Lyons. 'Mr. Belden was the case I was on in Great Neck. He died.'

'It seems to me a good many of your cases die.'

'Isn't it a scream!' said Miss Lyons. 'But it's true; that is, it's been true lately. The last five cases I've been on has all died. Of course it's just luck, but the girls have been kidding me about it and calling me a jinx, and when Miss Halsey saw me here the evening of the day you was operated, she said, "God help him!" That's the night floor nurse's name. But you're going to be mean and live through it and spoil my record, aren't you? I'm just kidding. Of course I want you to get all right.

'But it *is* queer, the way things have happened, and it's made me feel kind of creepy. And besides, I'm not like some of the girls and don't care. I get awfully fond of some of my cases and I hate to see them die, especially if they're men and not very sick and treat you half-way decent and don't yell for you the minute you go out of the room. There's only one case I was ever on where I didn't mind her dying and that was a woman. She had nephritis. Mrs. Judson.

'Do you want some gum? I chew it just when I'm nervous. And I always get nervous when I don't have enough sleep. You can bet I'll stay home tonight, B.F. or no B.F. But anyway he's got an engagement tonight, some directors' meeting or something. He's the busiest somebody in the world. And I told him last night, I said, "I should think you'd need sleep, too, even more than I do because you have to have all your wits about you in your business or those big bankers would take advantage and rob you. You can't afford to be sleepy," I told him.

'So he said, "No, but of course it's all right for you, because if you go to sleep on your job, there's no danger of you doing any damage except maybe give one of your patients a bichloride of mercury tablet instead of an alcohol rub." He's terrible! But you can't help from laughing.

'There was four of us in the party last night. He brought along his B.F. and another girl. She was just blah, but the B.F. wasn't so bad, only he insisted on me helping him drink a half a bottle of Scotch, and on top of gin, too. I guess I was the life of the party; that is, at first. Afterwards I got sick and it wasn't so good.

'But at first I was certainly going strong. And I guess I made quite a hit with Roy's B.F. He knows Marian, too, but he won't say anything, and if he does, I don't care. If she don't want to lose her beaus, she ought to know better than to introduce them to all the pretty girls in the world. I don't mean that I'm any Norma Talmadge, but at least—well—but I sure was sick when I *was* sick!

'I must give Marian a ring this noon. I haven't talked to her since the night she introduced me to him. I've been kind of scared. But I've got to find out what she knows. Or if she's sore at me. Though I don't see how she can be, do you? But maybe you want to read.'

'I called Marian up, but I didn't get her. She's out of town but she'll be back tonight. She's been out on a case. Hudson, New York. That's where she went. The message was waiting for her when she got home the other night, the night she introduced me to Roy.'

'Good morning,' said Miss Lyons.

'Good morning,' said the man in bed. 'Did you sleep enough?'

'Yes,' said Miss Lyons. 'I mean no, not enough.'

'Your eyes look bad. They almost look as if you'd been crying.'

'Who? Me? It'd take more than—I mean, I'm not a baby! But go on and read your book.'

51

'Well, good morning,' said Miss Lyons. 'And how's my patient? And this is the last morning I can call you that, isn't it? I think you're mean to get well so quick and leave me out of a job. I'm just kidding. I'm glad you're all right again, and I can use a little rest myself.'

'Another big night?' asked the man in bed.

'Pretty big,' said Miss Lyons. 'And another one coming. But tomorrow I won't ever get up. Honest, I danced so much last night that I thought my feet would drop off. But he certainly is a dancing fool! And the nicest somebody to talk to that I've met since I came to this town. Not a smart Alex and not always trying to be funny like some people, but just nice. He understands. He seems to know just what you're thinking. George Morse.'

'George Morse!' exclaimed the man in bed.

'Why yes,' said Miss Lyons. 'Do you know him?'

'No. But I thought you were talking about this Stewart, this Roy.'

'Oh, him!' said Miss Lyons. 'I should say not! He's private property; other people's property, not mine. He's engaged to my G.F. Marian. It happened day before yesterday, after she got home from Hudson. She was on a case up there. She told me about it night before last. I told her congratulations. Because I wouldn't hurt her feelings for the world! But heavens! what a mess she's going to be in, married to that dumb-bell. But of course some people can't be choosey. And I doubt if they ever get married unless some friend loans him the price of a license.

'He's got her believing he's in Wall Street, but I bet if he ever goes there at all, it's to sweep it. He's one of these kind of fellas that's got a great line for a little while, but you don't want to live with a clown. And I'd hate to marry a man that all he thinks about is to step out every night and dance and drink.

'I had a notion to tell her what I really thought. But that'd only of made her sore, or she'd of thought I was jealous or something. As if I couldn't of had him myself! Though even if he wasn't so awful, if I'd liked him instead of loathed him, I wouldn't of taken him from her on account of she being my G.F. And especially while she was out of town.

'He's the kind of a fella that'd marry a nurse in the hopes that some day he'd be an invalid. You know, that kind.

'But say—did you ever hear of J.P. Morgan and Company?

52

That's where my B.F. works, and he don't claim to own it neither. George Morse.

'Haven't you finished that book yet?'

Champion

Midge Kelly scored his first knockout when he was seventeen. The knockee was his brother Connie, three years his junior and a cripple. The purse was a half dollar given to the younger Kelly by a lady whose electric had just missed bumping his soul from his frail little body.

Connie did not know Midge was in the house, else he never would have risked laying the prize on the arm of the least comfortable chair in the room, the better to observe its shining beauty. As Midge entered from the kitchen, the crippled boy covered the coin with his hand, but the movement lacked the speed requisite to escape his brother's quick eye.

'Watcha got there?' demanded Midge.

'Nothin',' said Connie.

'You're a one legged liar!' said Midge.

He strode over to his brother's chair and grasped the hand that concealed the coin.

'Let loose!' he ordered.

Connie began to cry.

'Let loose and shut up your noise,' said the elder, and jerked his brother's hand from the chair arm.

The coin fell onto the bare floor. Midge pounced on it. His weak mouth widened in a triumphant smile.

'Nothin', huh?' he said. 'All right, if it's nothin' you don't want it.'

'Give that back,' sobbed the younger.

'I'll give you a red nose, you little sneak! Where'd you steal it?'

'I didn't steal it. It's mine. A lady give it to me after she pretty near hit me with a car.'

'It's a crime she missed you,' said Midge.

Midge started for the front door. The cripple picked up his crutch, rose from his chair with difficulty, and, still sobbing, came toward Midge. The latter heard him and stopped.

'You better stay where you're at,' he said.

'I want my money,' cried the boy.

'I know what you want,' said Midge.

Doubling up the fist that held the half dollar, he landed with all his strength on his brother's mouth. Connie fell to the floor with a thud, the crutch tumbling on top of him. Midge stood beside the prostrate form.

'Is that enough?' he said. 'Or do you want this, too?'

And he kicked him in the crippled leg.

'I guess that'll hold you,' he said.

There was no response from the boy on the floor. Midge looked at him a moment, then at the coin in his hand, and then went out into the street, whistling.

An hour later, when Mrs Kelly came home from her day's work at Faulkner's Steam Laundry, she found Connie on the floor, moaning. Dropping on her knees beside him, she called him by name a score of times. Then she got up and, pale as a ghost, dashed from the house. Dr Ryan left the Kelly abode about dusk and walked toward Halsted Street. Mrs Dorgan spied him as he passed her gate.

'Who's sick, Doctor?' she called.

'Poor little Connie,' he replied. 'He had a bad fall.'

'How did it happen?'

'I can't say for sure, Margaret, but I'd almost bet he was knocked down.'

'Knocked down!' exclaimed Mrs Dorgan.

'Why, who——?'

'Have you seen the other one lately?'

'Michael? No, not since mornin'. You can't be thinkin'——'

'I wouldn't put it past him, Margaret,' said the doctor gravely. 'The lad's mouth is swollen and cut, and his poor, skinny little leg is bruised. He surely didn't do it to himself and I think Helen suspects the other one.'

'Lord save us!' said Mrs Dorgan. 'I'll run over and see if I can help.'

'That's a good woman,' said Dr Ryan, and went on down the street.

Near midnight, when Midge came home, his mother was sitting at Connie's bedside. She did not look up.

'Well,' said Midge, 'what's the matter?'

She remained silent. Midge repeated his question.

'Michael, you know what's the matter,' she said at length.

'I don't know nothin',' said Midge.

'Don't lie to me, Michael. What did you do to your brother?'

'Nothin'.'

'You hit him.'

'Well, then, I hit him. What of it? It ain't the first time.'

Her lips pressed tightly together, her face like chalk, Ellen Kelly rose from her chair and made straight for him. Midge backed against the door.

'Lay off'n me, Ma. I don't want to fight no woman.'

Still she came on breathing heavily.

'Stop where you're at, Ma,' he warned.

There was a brief struggle and Midge's mother lay on the floor before him.

'You ain't hurt, Ma. You're lucky I didn't land good. And I told you to lay off'n me.'

'God forgive you, Michael!'

Midge found Hap Collins in the showdown game at the Royal.

'Come on out a minute,' he said.

Hap followed him out on the walk.

'I'm leavin' town for a wile,' said Midge.

'What for?'

'Well, we had a little run-in up to the house. The kid stole a half buck off'n me, and when I went after it he cracked me with his crutch. So I nailed him. And the old lady came at me with a chair and I took it off'n her and she fell down.'

'How is Connie hurt?'

'Not bad.'

'What are you runnin' away for?'

'Who the hell said I was runnin' away? I'm sick and tired o' gettin' picked on; that's all. So I'm leavin' for a wile and I want a piece o' money.'

'I ain't only got six bits,' said Happy.

'You're in bad shape, ain't you? Well, come through with it.'

Happy came through.

'You oughtn't to hit the kid,' he said.

'I ain't astin' you who can I hit,' snarled Midge. 'You try to put somethin' over on me and you'll get the same dose. I'm goin' now.'

56

'Go as far as you like,' said Happy, but not until he was sure that Kelly was out of hearing.

Early the following morning, Midge boarded a train for Milwaukee. He had no ticket, but no one knew the difference. The conductor remained in the caboose.

On a night six months later, Midge hurried out of the 'stage door' of the Star Boxing Club and made for Duane's saloon, two blocks away. In his pocket were twelve dollars, his reward for having battered up one Demon Dempsey through the six rounds of the first preliminary.

It was Midge's first professional engagement in the manly art. Also it was the first time in weeks that he had earned twelve dollars.

On the way to Duane's he had to pass Niemann's. He pulled his cap over his eyes and increased his pace until he had gone by. Inside Niemann's stood a trusting bartender, who for ten days had staked Midge to drinks and allowed him to ravage the lunch on a promise to come in and settle the moment he was paid for the 'prelim.'

Midge strode into Duane's and aroused the napping bartender by slapping a silver dollar on the festive board.

'Gimme a shot,' said Midge.

The shooting continued until the wind-up at the Star was over and part of the fight crowd joined Midge in front of Duane's bar. A youth in the early twenties, standing next to young Kelly, finally summoned sufficient courage to address him.

'Wasn't you in the first bout?' he ventured.

'Yeh,' Midge replied.

'My name's Hersch,' said the other.

Midge received the startling information in silence.

'I don't want to butt in,' continued Mr. Hersch, 'but I'd like to buy you a drink.'

'All right,' said Midge, 'but don't overstrain yourself.'

Mr Hersch laughed uproariously and beckoned to the bartender.

'You certainly gave that wop a trimmin' tonight,' said the buyer of the drink, when they had been served. 'I thought you'd kill him.'

'I would if I hadn't let up,' Midge replied. 'I'll kill 'em all.'

'You got the wallop all right,' the other said admiringly.

57

'Have I got the wallop?' said Midge. 'Say, I can kick like a mule. Did you notice them muscles in my shoulders?'

'Notice 'em? I couldn't help from noticin' 'em,' said Hersch. 'I says to the fella settin' alongside o' me, I says: "Look at them shoulders! No wonder he can hit," I says to him.'

'Just let me land and it's good-by, baby,' said Midge. 'I'll kill 'em all.'

The oral manslaughter continued until Duane's closed for the night. At parting, Midge and his new friend shook hands and arranged for a meeting the following evening.

For nearly a week the two were together almost constantly. It was Hersch's pleasant rôle to listen to Midge's modest revelations concerning himself, and to buy every time Midge's glass was empty. But there came an evening when Hersch regretfully announced that he must go home to supper.

'I got a date for eight bells,' he confided. 'I could stick till then, only I must clean up and put on the Sunday clo'es, 'cause she's the prettiest little thing in Milwaukee.'

'Can't you fix it for two?' asked Midge.

'I don't know who to get,' Hersch replied. 'Wait, though. I got a sister and if she ain't busy, it'll be O.K. She's no bum for looks herself.'

So it came about that Midge and Emma Hersch and Emma's brother and the prettiest little thing in Milwaukee foregathered at Wall's and danced half the night away. And Midge and Emma danced every dance together, for though every little onestep seemed to induce a new thirst of its own, Lou Hersch stayed too sober to dance with his own sister.

The next day, penniless at last in spite of his phenomenal ability to make someone else settle, Midge Kelly sought out Doc Hammond, matchmaker for the Star, and asked to be booked for the next show.

'I could put you on with Tracy for the next bout,' said Doc.

'What's they in it?' asked Midge.

'Twenty if you cop,' Doc told him.

'Have a heart,' protested Midge. 'Didn't I look good the other night?'

'You looked all right. But you aren't Freddie Welsh yet by a consid'able margin.'

'I ain't scared of Freddie Welsh or none of 'em,' said Midge.

58

'Well, we don't pay our boxers by the size of their chests,' Doc said. 'I'm offerin' you this Tracy bout. Take it or leave it.'

'All right; I'm on,' said Midge, and he passed a pleasant afternoon at Duane's on the strength of his booking.

Young Tracy's manager came to Midge the night before the show.

'How do you feel about this go?' he asked.

'Me?' said Midge, 'I feel all right. What do you mean, how do I feel?'

'I mean,' said Tracy's manager, 'that we're mighty anxious to win, 'cause the boy's got a chanct in Philly if he cops this one.'

'What's your proposition?' asked Midge.

'Fifty bucks,' said Tracy's manager.

'What do you think I am, a crook? Me lay down for fifty bucks. Not me!'

'Seventy-five, then,' said Tracy's manager.

The market closed on eighty and the details were agreed on in short order. And the next night Midge was stopped in the second round by a terrific slap on the forearm.

This time Midge passed up both Niemann's and Duane's, having a sizeable account at each place, and sought his refreshment at Stein's farther down the street.

When the profits of his deal with Tracy were gone, he learned, by first-hand information from Doc Hammond and the matchmakers at other 'clubs,' that he was no longer desired for even the cheapest of preliminaries. There was no danger of his starving or dying of thirst while Emma and Lou Hersch lived. But he made up his mind, four months after his defeat by Young Tracy, that Milwaukee was not the ideal place for him to live.

'I can lick the best of 'em,' he reasoned, 'but there ain't no more chanct for me here. I can maybe go east and get on somewheres. And besides——'

But just after Midge had purchased a ticket to Chicago with the money he had 'borrowed' from Emma Hersch 'to buy shoes,' a heavy hand was laid on his shoulders and he turned to face two strangers.

'Where are you goin', Kelly?' inquired the owner of the heavy hand.

'Nowheres,' said Midge. 'What the hell do you care?'

The other stranger spoke:

'Kelly, I'm employed by Emma Hersch's mother to see that you do right by her. And we want you to say here till you've done it.'

'You won't get nothin' but the worst of it, monkeying with me,' said Midge.

Nevertheless he did not depart for Chicago that night. Two days later, Emma Hersch became Mrs Kelly, and the gift of the groom, when once they were alone, was a crushing blow on the bride's pale cheek.

Next morning, Midge left Milwaukee as he had entered it—by fast freight.

'They's no use kiddin' ourself any more,' said Tommy Haley. 'He might get down to thirty-seven in a pinch, but if he done below that a mouse could stop him. He's a welter; that's what he is and he knows it as well as I do. He's growed like a weed in the last six mont's. I told him, I says, "If you don't quit growin' they won't be nobody for you to box, only Willard and them." He says, "Well, I wouldn't run away from Willard if I weighed twenty pounds more."'

'He must hate himself,' said Tommy's brother.

'I never seen a good one that didn't,' said Tommy. 'And Midge is a good one; don't make no mistake about that. I wisht we could of got Welsh before the kid growed so big. But it's too late now. I won't make no holler, though, if we can match him up with the Dutchman.'

'Who do you mean?'

'Young Goetz, the welter champ. We mightn't not get so much dough for the bout itself, but it'd roll in afterward. What a drawin' card we'd be, 'cause the people pays their money to see the fella with the wallop, and that's Midge. And we'd keep the title just as long as Midge could make the weight.'

'Can't you land no match with Goetz?'

'Sure, 'cause he needs the money. But I've went careful with the kid so far and look at the results I got! So what's the use of takin' a chanct? The kid's comin' every minute and Goetz is goin' back faster'n big Johnson did. I think we could lick him now; I'd bet my life on it. But six mont's from now they won't be no risk. He'll of licked hisself before that time. Then all as we'll have to do is sign up with him and wait for the referee to stop it. But Midge is so crazy to get at him now that I can't hardly hold him back.'

60

The brothers Haley were lunching in a Boston hotel. Dan had come down from Holyoke to visit with Tommy and to watch the latter's protégé go twelve rounds, or less, with Bud Cross. The bout promised little in the way of a contest, for Midge had twice stopped the Baltimore youth and Bud's reputation for gameness was all that had earned him the date. The fans were willing to pay the price to see Midge's hay-making left, but they wanted to see it used on an opponent who would not jump out of the ring the first time he felt its crushing force. But Cross was such an opponent, and his willingness to stop boxing-gloves with his eyes, ears, nose and throat had long enabled him to escape the horrors of honest labor. A game boy was Bud, and he showed it in his battered, swollen, discolored face.

'I should think,' said Dan Haley, 'that the kid'd do whatever you tell him after all you done for him.'

'Well,' said Tommy, 'he's took my dope pretty straight so far, but he's so sure of hisself that he can't see no reason for waitin'. He'll do what I say, though; he'd be a sucker not to.'

'You got a contrac' with him?'

'No, I don't need no contrac'. He knows it was me that drug him out o' the gutter and he ain't goin' to turn me down now, when he's got the dough and bound to get more. Where'd he of been at if I hadn't listened to him when he first come to me? That's pretty near two years ago now, but it seems like last week. I was settin' in the s'loon acrost from the Pleasant Club in Philly, waitin' for McCann to count the dough and come over, when this little bum blowed in and tried to stand the house off for a drink. They told him nothin' doin' and to beat it out o' there, and then he seen me and come over to where I was settin' and ast me wasn't I a boxin' man and I told him who I was. Then he ast me for money to buy a shot and I told him to set down and I'd buy it for him.

'Then we got talkin' things over and he told me his name and told me about fightin' a couple o' prelims out to Milwaukee. So I says, "Well, boy, I don't know how good or how rotten you are, but you won't never get nowheres trainin' on that stuff." So he says he'd cut it out if he could get on in a bout and I says I would give him a chanct if he played square with me and didn't touch no more to drink. So we shook hands and I took him up to the hotel with me and give him a bath and the next day I bought him some clo'es. And I staked him to eats and sleeps for over six weeks. He

61

had a hard time breakin' away from the polish, but finally I thought he was fit and I give him his chanct. He went on with Smiley Sayer and stopped him so quick that Smiley thought sure he was poisoned.

'Well, you know what he's did since. The only beatin' in his record was by Tracy in Milwaukee before I got hold of him, and he's licked Tracy three times in the last year.

'I've gave him all the best of it in a money way and he's got seven thousand bucks in cold storage. How's that for a kid that was in the gutter two years ago? And he'd have still more yet if he wasn't so nuts over clo'es and got to stop at the good hotels and so forth.'

'Where's his home at?'

'Well, he ain't really got no home. He came from Chicago and his mother canned him out o' the house for bein' no good. She give him a raw deal, I guess, and he says he won't have nothin' to do with her unlest she comes to him first. She's got a pile o' money, he says, so he ain't worryin' about her.'

The gentleman under discussion entered the café and swaggered to Tommy's table, while the whole room turned to look.

Midge was the picture of health despite a slightly colored eye and an ear that seemed to have no opening. But perhaps it was not his healthiness that drew all eyes. His diamond horse-shoe tie pin, his purple cross-striped shirt, his orange shoes and his light blue suit fairly screamed for attention.

'Where you been?' he asked Tommy. 'I been lookin' all over for you.'

'Set down,' said his manager.

'No time,' said Midge. 'I'm goin' down to the w'arf and see 'em unload the fish.'

'Shake hands with my brother Dan,' said Tommy.

Midge shook hands with the Holyoke Haley.

'If you're Tommy's brother, you're O.K. with me,' said Midge, and the brothers beamed with pleasure.

Dan moistened his lips and murmured an embarrassed reply, but it was lost on the young gladiator.

'Leave me take twenty,' Midge was saying. 'I prob'ly won't need it, but I don't like to be caught short.'

Tommy parted with a twenty dollar bill and recorded the transaction in a small black book the insurance company had given him for Christmas.

'But,' he said, 'it won't cost you no twenty to look at them fish. Want me to go along?'

'No,' said Midge hastily. 'You and your brother here prob'ly got a lot to say to each other.'

'Well,' said Tommy, 'don't take no bad money and don't get lost. And you better be back at four o'clock and lay down a wile.'

'I don't need no rest to beat this guy,' said Midge. 'He'll do enough layin' down for the both of us.'

And laughing even more than the jest called for, he strode out through the fire of admiring and startled glances.

The corner of Boylston and Tremont was the nearest Midge got to the wharf, but the lady awaiting him was doubtless a more dazzling sight than the catch of the luckiest Massachusetts fisherman. She could talk, too—probably better than the fish.

'O you Kid!' she said, flashing a few silver teeth among the gold. 'O you fighting man!'

Midge smiled up at her.

'We'll go somewheres and get a drink,' he said. 'One won't hurt.'

In New Orleans, five months after he had rearranged the map of Bud Cross for the third time, Midge finished training for his championship bout with the Dutchman.

Back in his hotel after the final workout, Midge stopped to chat with some of the boys from up north, who had made the long trip to see a champion dethroned, for the result of this bout was so nearly a foregone conclusion that even the experts had guessed it.

Tommy Haley secured the key and the mail and ascended to the Kelly suite. He was bathing when Midge came in, half an hour later.

'Any mail?' asked Midge.

'There on the bed,' replied Tommy from the tub.

Midge picked up the stack of letters and postcards and glanced them over. From the pile he sorted out three letters and laid them on the table. The rest he tossed into the waste-basket. Then he picked up the three and sat for a few moments holding them, while his eyes gazed off into space. At length he looked again at the three unopened letters in his hand; then he put one in his pocket and tossed the other two at the basket. They missed their target and fell on the floor.

'Hell!' said Midge, and stooping over picked them up.
He opened one postmarked Milwaukee and read:

DEAR HUSBAND:

I have wrote to you so manny times and got no anser and I dont
know if you ever got them, so I am writeing again in the hopes you
will get this letter and anser. I dont like to bother you with my
trubles and I would not only for the baby and I am not asking you
should write to me but only send a little money and I am not asking
for myself but the baby has not been well a day sence last Aug. and
the dr. told me she cant live much longer unless I give her better
food and thats impossible the ways things are. Lou has not been
working for a year and what I make dont hardley pay for the rent. I
am not asking for you to give me any money, but only you should
send what I loaned when convenient and I think it amts. to about
$36.00. Please try and send that amt. and it will help me, but if you
cant send the whole amt. try and send me something.

Your wife,
EMMA

Midge tore the letter into a hundred pieces and scattered them
over the floor.

'Money, money, money!' he said. 'They must think I'm made o'
money. I s'pose the old woman's after it too.'

He opened his mother's letter:

dear Michael Connie wonted me to rite and say you must beet
the dutchman and he is sur you will and wonted me to say we wont
you to rite and tell us about it, but I gess you havent no time to rite
or we herd from you long beffore this but I wish you would rite jest
a line or 2 boy becaus it wuld be better for Connie then a barl of
medisin. It wuld help me to keep things going if you send me money
now and then when you can spair it but if you cant send no money
try and fine time to rite a letter onley a few lines and it will please
Connie, jest think boy he hasent got out of bed in over 3 yrs. Connie
says good luck.

Your Mother,
ELLEN F. KELLY

'I thought so,' said Midge. 'They're all alike.'
The third letter was from New York. It read:

64

Hon:—This is the last letter you will get from me before your champ, but I will send you a telegram Saturday, but I can't say as much in a telegram as in a letter and I am writeing this to let you know I am thinking of you and praying for good luck.

Lick him good hon and don't wait no longer than you have to and don't forget to wire me as soon as its over. Give him that little old left of yours on the nose hon and don't be afraid of spoiling his good looks because he couldn't be no homlier than he is. But don't let him spoil my baby's pretty face. You won't will you hon.

Well hon I would give anything to be there and see it, but I guess you love Haley better than me or you wouldn't let him keep me away. But when your champ hon we can do as we please and tell Haley to go to the devil.

Well hon I will send you a telegram Saturday and I almost forgot to tell you I will need some more money, a couple hundred say and you will have to wire it to me as soon as you get this. You will won't you hon.

I will send you a telegram Saturday and remember hon I am pulling for you.

Well good-by sweetheart and good luck.

GRACE

'They're all alike,' said Midge. 'Money, money, money.'

Tommy Haley, shining from his ablutions, came in from the adjoining room.

'Thought you'd be layin' down,' he said.

'I'm goin' to,' said Midge, unbuttoning his orange shoes.

'I'll call you at six and you can eat up here without no bugs to pester you. I got to go down and give them birds their tickets.'

'Did you hear from Goldberg?' asked Midge.

'Didn't I tell you? Sure; fifteen weeks at five hundred, if we win. And we can get a guarantee o' twelve thousand, with privileges either in New York or Milwaukee.'

'Who with?'

'Anybody that'll stand up in front of you. You don't care who it is, do you?'

'Not me. I'll make 'em all look like a monkey.'

'Well you better lay down aw'ile.'

'Oh, say, wire two hundred to Grace for me, will you? Right away; the New York address.'

'Two hundred! You just sent her three hundred last Sunday.'

'Well, what the hell do you care?'

65

'All right, all right. Don't get sore about it. Anything else?'

'That's all,' said Midge, and dropped onto the bed.

'And I want the deed done before I come back,' said Grace as she rose from the table. 'You won't fall down on me, will you, hon?'

'Leave it to me,' said Midge. 'And don't spend no more than you have to.'

Grace smiled a farewell and left the café. Midge continued to sip his coffee and read his paper.

They were in Chicago and they were in the middle of Midge's first week in vaudeville. He had come straight north to reap the rewards of his glorious victory over the broken down Dutchman. A fortnight had been spent in learning his act, which consisted of a gymnastic exhibition and a ten minutes' monologue on the various excellences of Midge Kelly. And now he was twice daily turning 'em away from the Madison Theater.

His breakfast over and his paper read, Midge sauntered into the lobby and asked for his key. He then beckoned to a bell-boy, who had been hoping for that very honor.

'Find Haley, Tommy Haley,' said Midge. 'Tell him to come up to my room.'

'Yes, sir, Mr Kelly,' said the boy, and proceeded to break all his former records for diligence.

Midge was looking out of his seventh-story window when Tommy answered the summons.

'What'll it be?' inquired his manager.

There was a pause before Midge replied.

'Haley,' he said, 'twenty-five per cent's a whole lot o' money.'

'I guess I got it comin', ain't I?' said Tommy.

'I don't see how you figger it. I don't see where you're worth it to me.'

'Well,' said Tommy, 'I didn't expect nothin' like this. I thought you was satisfied with the bargain. I don't want to beat nobody out o' nothin', but I don't see where you could have got anybody else that would of did all I done for you.'

'Sure, that's all right,' said the champion. 'You done a lot for me in Philly. And you got good money for it, didn't you?'

'I ain't makin' no holler. Still and all, the big money's still ahead of us yet. And if it hadn't of been for me, you wouldn't of never got within grabbin' distance.'

'Oh, I guess I could of went along all right,' said Midge. 'Who was it that hung that left on the Dutchman's jaw, me or you?'

'Yes, but you wouldn't been in the ring with the Dutchman if it wasn't for how I handled you.'

'Well, this won't get us nowheres. The idear is that you ain't worth no twenty-five per cent now and it don't make no difference what come off a year or two ago.'

'Don't it?' said Tommy. 'I'd say it made a whole lot of difference.'

'Well, I say it don't and I guess that settles it.'

'Look here, Midge,' Tommy said, 'I thought I was fair with you, but if you don't think so, I'm willin' to hear what you think is fair. I don't want nobody callin' me a Sherlock. Let's go down to business and sign up a contrac'. What's your figger?'

'I ain't namin' no figger,' Midge replied. 'I'm sayin' that twenty-five's too much. Now what are you willin' to take?'

'How about twenty?'

'Twenty's too much,' said Kelly.

'What ain't too much?' asked Tommy.

'Well, Haley, I might as well give it to you straight. They ain't nothin' that ain't too much.'

'You mean you don't want me at no figger?'

'That's the idear.'

There was a minute's silence. Then Tommy Haley walked toward the door.

'Midge,' he said, in a choking voice, 'you're makin' a big mistake, boy. You can't throw down your best friends and get away with it. That damn woman will ruin you.'

Midge sprang from his seat.

'You shut your mouth!' he stormed. 'Get out o' here before they have to carry you out. You been spongin' off o' me long enough. Say one more word about the girl or about anything else and you'll get what the Dutchman got. Now get out!'

And Tommy Haley, having a very vivid memory of the Dutchman's face as he fell, got out.

Grace came in later, dropped her numerous bundles on the lounge and perched herself on the arm of Midge's chair.

'Well?' she said.

'Well,' said Midge, 'I got rid of him.'

'Good boy!' said Grace. 'And now I think you might give me that twenty-five per cent.'

'Besides the seventy-five you're already gettin'?' said Midge.

'Don't be no grouch, hon. You don't look pretty when you're grouchy.'

'It ain't my business to look pretty,' Midge replied.

'Wait till you see how I look with the stuff I bought this mornin'!'

Midge glanced at the bundles on the lounge.

'There's Haley's twenty-five per cent,' he said, 'and then some.'

The champion did not remain long without a manager. Haley's successor was none other than Jerome Harris, who saw in Midge a better meal ticket than his popular-priced musical show had been.

The contract, giving Mr Harris twenty-five per cent of Midge's earnings, was signed in Detroit the week after Tommy Haley had heard his dismissal read. It had taken Midge just six days to learn that a popular actor cannot get on without the ministrations of a man who thinks, talks and means business. At first Grace objected to the new member of the firm, but when Mr. Harris had demanded and secured from the vaudeville people a one-hundred dollar increase in Midge's weekly stipend, she was convinced that the champion had acted for the best.

'You and my missus will have some great old times,' Harris told Grace. 'I'd of wired her to join us here, only I seen the Kid's bookin' takes us to Milwaukee next week, and that's where she is.'

But when they were introduced in the Milwaukee hotel, Grace admitted to herself that her feeling for Mrs Harris could hardly be called love at first sight. Midge, on the contrary, gave his new manager's wife the many times over and seemed loath to end the feast of his eyes.

'Some doll,' he said to Grace when they were alone.

'Doll is right,' the lady replied, 'and sawdust where her brains ought to be.'

'I'm li'ble to steal that baby,' said Midge, and he smiled as he noted the effect of his words on his audience's face.

On Tuesday of the Milwaukee week the champion successfully

defended his title in a bout that the newspapers never reported. Midge was alone in his room that morning when a visitor entered without knocking. The visitor was Lou Hersch.

Midge turned white at sight of him.

'What do you want?' he demanded.

'I guess you know,' said Lou Hersch. 'Your wife's starvin' to death and your baby's starvin' to death and I'm starvin' to death. And you're dirty with money.'

'Listen,' said Midge, 'if it wasn't for you, I wouldn't never saw your sister. And, if you ain't man enough to hold a job, what's that to me? The best thing you can do is keep away from me.'

'You give me a piece o' money and I'll go.'

Midge's reply to the ultimatum was a straight right to his brother-in-law's narrow chest.

'Take that home to your sister.'

And after Lou Hersch picked himself up and slunk away, Midge thought: 'It's lucky I didn't give him my left or I'd of croaked him. And if I'd hit him in the stomach, I'd of broke his spine.'

There was a party after each evening performance during the Milwaukee engagement. The wine flowed freely and Midge had more of it than Tommy Haley ever would have permitted him. Mr Harris offered no objection, which was possibly just as well for his own physical comfort.

In the dancing between drinks, Midge had his new manager's wife for a partner as often as Grace. The latter's face as she floundered round in the arms of the portly Harris, belied her frequent protestations that she was having the time of her life.

Several times that week, Midge thought Grace was on the point of starting the quarrel he hoped to have. But it was not until Friday night that she accommodated. He and Mrs Harris had disappeared after the matinee and when Grace saw him again at the close of the night show, she came to the point at once.

'What are you tryin' to pull off?' she demanded.

'It's none o' your business, is it?' said Midge.

'You bet it's my business; mine and Harris's. You cut it short or you'll find out.'

'Listen,' said Midge, 'have you got a mortgage on me or somethin'? You talk like we was married.'

'We're goin' to be, too. And to-morrow's as good a time as any.'

'Just about,' Midge said. 'You got as much chanct o' marryin' me to-morrow as the next day or next year and that ain't no chanct at all.'

'We'll find out,' said Grace.

'You're the one that's got somethin' to find out.'

'What do you mean?'

'I mean I'm married already.'

'You lie!'

'You think so, do you? Well, s'pose you go to this here address and get acquainted with my missus.'

Midge scrawled a number on a piece of paper and handed it to her. She stared at it unseeingly.

'Well,' said Midge, 'I ain't kiddin' you. You go there and ask for Mrs Michael Kelly, and if you don't find her, I'll marry you to-morrow before breakfast.'

Still Grace stared at the scrap of paper. To Midge it seemed an age before she spoke again.

'You lied to me all this wile.'

'You never ast me was I married. What's more, what the hell diff'rence did it make to you? You got a split, didn't you? Better'n fifty-fifty.'

He started away.

'Where you goin'?'

'I'm goin' to meet Harris and his wife.'

'I'm goin' with you. You're not goin' to shake me now.'

'Yes, I am, too,' said Midge quietly. 'When I leave town tomorrow night, you're going to stay here. And if I see where you're goin' to make a fuss, I'll put you in a hospital where they'll keep you quiet. You can get your stuff to-morrow mornin' and I'll slip you a hundred bucks. And then I don't want to see no more o' you. And don't try and tag along now or I'll have to add another K.O. to the old record.'

When Grace returned to the hotel that night, she discovered that Midge and the Harrises had moved to another. And when Midge left town the following night, he was again without a manager, and Mr Harris was without a wife.

Three days prior to Midge Kelly's ten-round bout with Young Milton in New York City, the sporting editor of *The News* assigned Joe Morgan to write two or three thousand words about the champion to run with a picture lay-out for Sunday.

Joe Morgan dropped in at Midge's training quarters Friday afternoon. Midge, he learned, was doing road work, but Midge's manager, Wallie Adams, stood ready and willing to supply reams of dope about the greatest fighter of the age.

'Let's hear what you've got,' said Joe, 'and then I'll try to fix up something.'

So Wallie stepped on the accelerator of his imagination and shot away.

'Just a kid; that's all he is; a regular boy. Get what I mean? Don't know the meanin' o' bad habits. Never tasted liquor in his life and would prob'bly get sick if he smelled it. Clean livin' put him up where he's at. Get what I mean? And modest and unassumin' as a school girl. He's so quiet you wouldn't never know he was round. And he'd go to jail before he'd talk about himself.

'No job at all to get him in shape, 'cause he's always that way. The only trouble we have with him is gettin' him to light into these poor bums they match him up with. He's scared he'll hurt somebody. Get what I mean? He's tickled to death over this match with Milton, 'cause everybody says Milton can stand the gaff. Midge'll maybe be able to cut loose a little this time. But the last two bouts he had, the guys hadn't no business in the ring with him, and he was holdin' back all the wile for the fear he'd kill somebody. Get what I mean?'

'Is he married?' inquired Joe.

'Say, you'd think he was married to hear him rave about them kiddies he's got. His fam'ly's up in Canada to their summer home and Midge is wild to get up there with 'em. He thinks more o' that wife and them kiddies than all the money in the world. Get what I mean?'

'How many children has he?'

'I don't know, four or five, I guess. All boys and every one of 'em a dead ringer for their dad.'

'Is his father living?'

'No, the old man died when he was a kid. But he's got a grand old mother and a kid brother out in Chi. They're the first ones he thinks about after a match, them and his wife and kiddies. And he don't forget to send the old woman a thousand bucks after every bout. He's goin' to buy her a new home as soon as they pay him off for this match.'

71

'How about his brother? Is he going to tackle the game?'

'Sure, and Midge says he'll be a champion before he's twenty years old. They're a fightin' fam'ly and all of 'em honest and straight as a die. Get what I mean? A fella that I can't tell you his name come to Midge in Milwaukee onct and wanted him to throw a fight and Midge give him such a trimmin' in the street that he couldn't go on that night. That's the kind he is. Get what I mean?'

Joe Morgan hung around the camp until Midge and his trainers returned.

'One o' the boys from *The News*' said Wallie by way of introduction. 'I been givin' him your fam'ly hist'ry.'

'Did he give you good dope?' he inquired.

'He's some historian,' said Joe.

'Don't call me no names,' said Wallie smiling. 'Call us up if they's anything more you want. And keep your eyes on us Monday night. Get what I mean?'

The story in Sunday's *News* was read by thousands of lovers of the manly art. It was well written and full of human interest. Its slight inaccuracies went unchallenged, though three readers, besides Wallie Adams and Midge Kelly, saw and recognized them. The three were Grace, Tommy Haley and Jerome Harris and the comments they made were not for publication.

Neither the Mrs Kelly in Chicago nor the Mrs Kelly in Milwaukee knew that there was such a paper as the New York *News*. And even if they had known of it and that it contained two columns of reading matter about Midge, neither mother nor wife could have bought it. For *The News* on Sunday is a nickel a copy.

Joe Morgan could have written more accurately, no doubt, if instead of Wallie Adams, he had interviewed Ellen Kelly and Connie Kelly and Emma Kelly and Lou Hersch and Grace and Jerome Harris and Tommy Haley and Hap Collins and two or three Milwaukee bartenders.

But a story built on their evidence would never have passed the sporting editor.

'Suppose you can prove it,' that gentleman would have said. 'It wouldn't get us anything but abuse to print it. The people don't want to see him knocked. He's champion.'

72

Some Like Them Cold

DEAR MISS GILLESPIE:

How about our bet now as you bet me I would forget all about you the minute I hit the big town and would never write you a letter. Well girlie it looks like you lose so pay me. Seriously we will call all bets off as I am not the kind that bet on a sure thing and it sure was a sure thing that I would not forget a girlie like you and all that is worrying me is whether it may not be the other way round and you are wondering who this fresh guy is that is writeing you this letter. I bet you are so will try and refreshen your memory.

Well girlie I am the handsome young man that was wondering round the Lasalle st station Monday and 'happened' to sit down beside of a mighty pretty girlie who was waiting to meet her sister from Toledo and the train was late and I am glad of it because if it had not of been that little girlie and I would never of met. So for once I was a lucky guy but still I guess it was time I had some luck as it was certainly tough luck for you and I to both be liveing in Chi all that time and never get together till a half hour before I was leaveing town for good.

Still 'better late than never' you know and maybe we can make up for lost time though it looks like we would have to do our makeing up at long distants unless you make good on your threat and come to N.Y. I wish you would do that little thing girlie as it looks like that was the only way we would get a chance to play round together as it looks like they was little or no chance of me comeing back to Chi as my whole future is in the big town. N.Y. is the only spot and specially for a man that expects to make my liveing in the song writeing game as here is the Mecca for that line of work and no matter how good a man may be they don't get no recognition unless they live in N.Y.

Well girlie you asked me to tell you all about my trip. Well I remember you saying that you would give anything to be makeing it yourself but as far as the trip itself was conserned you ought to be thankfull you did not have to make it as you would of sweat your head off. I know I did specially wile going through Ind. Monday p.m. but Monday night was the worst of all trying to sleep and finely I give it up and just layed there with the prespiration rolling off of me though I was laying on top of the covers and nothing on but my underwear.

Yesterday was not so bad as it rained most of the a.m. comeing through N.Y. state and in the p.m. we road along side of the Hudson all p.m. Some river girlie and just looking at it makes a man forget all about the heat and everything else except a certain girlie who I seen for the first time Monday and then only for a half hour but she is the kind of a girlie that a man don't need to see her only once and they would be no danger of forgetting her. There I guess I better lay off that subject or you will think I am a 'fresh guy.'

Well that is about all to tell you about the trip only they was one amuseing incidence that come off yesterday which I will tell you. Well they was a dame got on the train at Toledo Monday and had the birth opp. mine but I did not see nothing of her that night as I was out smokeing till late and she hit the hay early but yesterday a.m. she come in the dinner and sit at the same table with me and tried to make me and it was so raw that the dinge waiter seen it and give me the wink and of course I paid no tension and I waited till she got through so as they would be no danger of her folling me out but she stopped on the way out to get a tooth pick and when I come out she was out on the platform with it so I tried to brush right by but she spoke up and asked me what time it was and I told her and she said she guessed her watch was slow so I said maybe it just seemed slow on acct. of the company it was in.

I don't know if she got what I was driveing at or not but any way she give up trying to make me and got off at Albany. She was a good looker but I have no time for gals that tries to make strangers on a train.

Well if I don't quit you will think I am writing a book but will expect a long letter in answer to this letter and we will see if you can keep your promise like I have kept mine. Don't dissapoint me girlie as I am all alone in a large city and hearing from you will keep me from getting home sick for old Chi though I never thought so much of the old town till I found out you lived there. Don't think that is kidding girlie as I mean it.

You can address me at this hotel as it looks like I will be here right along as it is on 47th st right off of old Broadway and handy to everything and am only paying $21 per wk. for my rm. and could of got one for $16 but without bath but am glad to pay the difference as am lost without my bath in the a.m. and sometimes at night too.

Tomorrow I expect to commence fighting the 'battle of Broadway' and will let you know how I come out that is if you answer this letter. In the mean wile girlie au reservoir and don't do nothing I would not do.

Your new friend (?)
CHAS. F. LEWIS

Chicago, Ill., Aug. 6

MY DEAR MR LEWIS:

Well, that certainly was a 'surprise party' getting your letter and you are certainly a 'wonder man' to keep your word as I am afraid most men of your sex are gay deceivers but maybe you are 'different.' Any way it sure was a surprise and will gladly pay the bet if you will just tell me what it was we bet. Hope it was not money as I am a 'working girl' but if it was not more than a dollar or two will try to dig it up even if I have to 'beg, borrow or steal.'

Suppose you will think me a 'case' to make a bet and then forget what it was, but you must remember, Mr Man, that I had just met you and was 'dazzled.' Joking aside I was rather 'fussed' and will tell you why. Well, Mr Lewis, I suppose you see lots of girls like the one you told me about that you saw on the train who tried to 'get acquainted' but I want to assure you that I am not one of those kind and sincerely hope you will believe me when I tell you that you was the first man I ever spoke to meeting them like that and my friends and the people who know me would simply faint if they knew I ever spoke to a man without a 'proper introduction.'

Believe me, Mr Lewis, I am not that kind and I don't know now why I did it only that you was so 'different' looking if you know what I mean and not at all like the kind of men that usually try to force their attentions on every pretty girl they see. Lots of times I act on impulse and let my feelings run away from me and sometimes I do things on the impulse of the moment which I regret them later on, and that is what I did this time, but hope you won't give me cause to regret it and I know you won't as I know you are not that kind of a man a specially after what you told me about the girl on the train. But any way as I say, I was in a 'daze' so can't remember what it was we bet, but will try and pay it if it does not 'break' me.

Sis's train got in about ten minutes after yours had gone and when she saw me what do you think was the first thing she said? Well, Mr Lewis, she said: "Why Mibs (That is a pet name some of my friends have given me) what has happened to you? I never seen you have as much color.' So I passed it off with some remark about the heat and changed the subject as I certainly was not going to tell her that I had just been talking to a man who I had never met or she would of dropped dead from the shock. Either that or she would not of believed me as it would be hard for a person who knows me well to imagine me doing a thing like that as I have quite a reputation for 'squelching' men who try to act fresh. I don't mean anything personal by that, Mr Lewis, as am a good judge of character and could tell without you telling me that you are not that kind.

Well, Sis and I have been on the 'go' ever since she arrived as I took yesterday and today off so I could show her the 'sights' though she says she would be perfectly satisfied to just sit in the apartment and listen to me 'rattle on.' Am afraid I am a great talker, Mr Lewis, but Sis says it is as good as a show to hear me talk as I tell things in such a different way as I cannot help from seeing the humorous side of everything and she says she never gets tired of listening to me, but of course she is my sister and thinks the world of me, but she really does laugh like she enjoyed my craziness.

Maybe I told you that I have a tiny little apartment which a girl friend of mine and I have together and it is hardly big enough to turn round in, but still it is 'home' and I am a great home girl and hardly ever care to go out evenings except occasionally to the theatre or dance. But even if our 'nest' is small we are proud of it and Sis complimented us on how cozy it is and how 'homey' it looks and she said she did not see how we could afford to have everything so nice and Edith (my girl friend) said: 'Mibs deserves all the credit for that. I never knew a girl who could make a little money go a long ways like she can.' Well, of course she is my best friend and always saying nice things about me, but I do try and I hope I get results. Have always said that good taste and being careful is a whole lot more important than lots of money though it is nice to have it.

You must write and tell me how you are getting along in the 'battle of Broadway' (I laughed when I read that) and whether the publishers like your songs though I know they will. Am crazy to hear them and hear you play the piano as I love good jazz music even better than classical, though I suppose it is terrible to say such a thing. But I usually say just what I think though sometimes I wish afterwards I had not of. But still I believe it is better for a girl to be her own self and natural instead of always acting. But am afraid I will never have a chance to hear you play unless you come back to Chi and pay us a visit as my 'threat' to come to New York was just a 'threat' and I don't see any hope of ever getting there unless some rich New Yorker should fall in love with me and take me there to live. Fine chance for poor little me, eh Mr Lewis?

Well, I guess I have 'rattled on' long enough and you will think I am writing a book unless I quit and besides, Sis has asked me as a special favor to make her a pie for dinner. Maybe you don't know it, Mr Man, but I am quite famous for my pie and pastry, but I don't suppose a 'genius' is interested in common things like that.

Well, be sure and write soon and tell me what N.Y. is like and all about it and don't forget the little girlie who was 'bad' and spoke to a strange man in the station and have been blushing over it ever since.

Your friend (?)
MABELLE GILLESPIE

N.Y., Aug. 10

DEAR GIRLIE:

I bet you will think I am a fresh guy commenceing that way but Miss Gillespie is too cold and a man can not do nothing cold in this kind of weather specially in this man's town which is the hottest place I ever been in and I guess maybe the reason why New Yorkers is so bad is because they think they are all ready in H—— and can not go no worse place no matter how they behave themselves. Honest girlie I certainly envy you being where there is a breeze off the old Lake and Chi may be dirty but I never heard of nobody dying because they was dirty but four people died here yesterday on acct. of the heat and I seen two different women flop right on Broadway and had to be taken away in the ambulance and it could not of been because they was dressed too warm because it would be impossible for the women here to leave off any more cloths.

Well have not had much luck yet in the battle of Broadway as all the heads of the big music publishers is out of town on their vacation and the big boys is the only ones I will do business with as it would be silly for a man with the stuff I have got to waste my time on somebody that is just on the staff and have not got the final say. But I did play a couple of my numbers for the people up to Levy's and Goebel's and they went crazy over them in both places. So it looks like all I have to do is wait for the big boys to get back and then play my numbers for them and I will be all set. What I want is to get taken on the staff of one of the big firms as that gives a man the inside and they will plug your numbers more if you are on the staff. In the mean wile have not got nothing to worry me but am just seeing the sights of the big town as have saved up enough money to play round for a wile and any way a man that can play piano like I can don't ever have to worry about starveing. Can certainly make the old music box talk girlie and am always good for a $75 or $100 job.

Well have been here a week now and on the go every minute and I thought I would be lonesome down here but no chance of that as I have been treated fine by the people I have met and have sure met a bunch of them. One of the boys liveing in the hotel is a vaudeville actor and he is member of the Friars club and took me over there to dinner the other night and some way another the bunch got wise that I could play piano so of course I had to sit down and give them some of my numbers and everybody went crazy over them. One of the boys I met there was Paul Sears the song writer but he just writes the lyrics and has wrote a bunch of hits and when he heard some of my melodies he called me over to one side and said he would like to work with me on some numbers. How is that girlie as he is one of the biggest hit writers in N.Y.

N.Y. has got some mighty pretty girlies and I guess it would not be hard to get acquainted with them and in fact several of them has tried to make me since I been here but I always figure that a girl must be something wrong with her if she tries to make a man that she don't know nothing about so I pass them all up. But I did meet a couple of pips that a man here in the hotel went up on Riverside Drive to see them and insisted on me going along and they go on some way that I could make a piano talk so they was nothing but I must play for them so I sit down and played some of my own stuff and they went crazy over it.

One of the girls wanted I should come up and see her again, and I said I might but I think I better keep away as she acted like she wanted to vamp me and I am not the kind that likes to play round with a gal just for their company and dance with them etc. but when I see the right gal that will be a different thing and she won't have to beg me to come and see her as I will camp right on her trail till she says yes. And it won't be none of these N.Y. fly by nights neither. They are all right to look at but a man would be a sucker to get serious with them as they might take you up and next thing you know you would have a wife on your hands that don't know a dish rag from a waffle iron.

Well girlie will quit and call it a day as it is too hot to write any more and I guess I will turn on the cold water and lay in the tub a while and then turn in. Don't forget to write to

Your friend,

CHAS. F. LEWIS

Chicago, Ill., Aug. 13

DEAR MR MAN:

Hope you won't think me a 'silly Billy' for starting my letter that way but 'Mr Lewis' is so formal and 'Charles' is too much the other way and any way I would not dare call a man by their first name after only knowing them only two weeks. Though I may as well confess that Charles is my favorite name for a man and have always been crazy about it as it was my father's name. Poor old dad, he died of cancer three years ago, but left enough insurance so that mother and we girls were well provided for and do not have to do anything to support ourselves though I have been earning my own living for two years, to make things easier for mother and also because I simply can't bear to be doing nothing as I feel like a 'drone.' So I flew away from the 'home nest'

79

though mother felt bad about it as I was her favorite and she always said I was such a comfort to her as when I was in the house she never had to worry about how things would go.

But there I go gossiping about my domestic affairs just like you would be interested in them though I don't see how you could be though personally I always like to know all about my friends, but I know men are different so will try and not bore you any longer. Poor Man, I certainly feel sorry for you if New York is as hot as all that. I guess it has been very hot in Chi, too, at least everybody has been complaining about how terrible it is. Suppose you will wonder why I say 'I guess' and you will think I ought to know if it is hot. Well, sir, the reason I say 'I guess' is because I don't feel the heat like others do or at least I don't let myself feel it. That sounds crazy I know, but don't you think there is a good deal in mental suggestion and not letting yourself feel things? I believe that if a person simply won't allow themselves to be affected by disagreeable things, why such things won't bother them near as much. I know it works with me and that is the reason why I am never cross when things go wrong and 'keep smiling' no matter what happens and as far as the heat is concerned, why I just don't let myself feel it and my friends say I don't even look hot no matter if the weather is boiling and Edith, my girl friend, often says that I am like a breeze and it cools her off just to have me come in the room. Poor Edie suffers terribly during the hot weather and says it almost makes her mad at me to see how cool and unruffled I look when everybody else is perspiring and have red faces etc.

I laughed when I read what you said about New York being so hot that people thought it was the 'other place.' I can appreciate a joke, Mr Man, and that one did not go 'over my head.' Am still laughing at some of the things you said in the station though they probably struck me funnier than they would most girls as I always see the funny side and sometimes something is said and I laugh and the others wonder what I am laughing at as they cannot see anything in it themselves, but it is just the way I look at things so of course I cannot explain to them why I laughed and they think I am crazy. But I had rather part with almost anything rather than my sense of humour as it helps me over a great many rough spots.

Sis has gone back home though I would of liked to of kept her here much longer, but she had to go though she said she would of liked nothing better than to stay with me and just listen to me 'rattle on.' She always says it is just like a show to hear me talk as I always put things in such a funny way and for weeks after she has been visiting me she thinks of some of the things I said and laughs over them. Since she left Edith and I have been pretty quiet though poor Edie wants to be on the 'go' all the time and tries to make me go out with her every evening to the pictures and scolds me when I say I had rather stay home and read and calls me a 'book worm.' Well, it is true that I had rather stay home with a good book than go to some crazy old picture and the last two nights I have been reading myself to sleep with Robert W. Service's poems. Don't you love Service or don't you care for 'highbrow' writings?

Personly there is nothing I love more than to just sit and read a good book or sit and listen to somebody play the piano, I mean if they can really play and I really believe I like popular music better than the classical though I suppose that is a terrible thing to confess, but I love all kinds of music but a specially the piano when it is played by somebody who can really play.

Am glad you have not 'fallen' for the 'ladies' who have tried to make your acquaintance in New York. You are right in thinking there must be something wrong with girls who try to 'pick up' strange men as no girl with self respect would do such a thing and when I say that, Mr Man, I know you will think it is a funny thing for me to say on account of the way our friendship started, but I mean it and I assure you that was the first time I ever done such a thing in my life and would never of thought of doing it had I not known you were the right kind of a man as I flatter myself that I am a good judge of character and can tell pretty well what a person is like by just looking at them and I assure you I had made up my mind what kind of a man you were before I allowed myself to answer your opening remark. Otherwise I am the last girl in the world that would allow myself to speak to a person without being introduced to them.

When you write again you must tell me all about the girl on Riverside Drive and what she looks like and if you went to see her again and all about her. Suppose you will think I am a little old 'curiosity shop' for asking all those questions and will wonder why I want to know. Well, sir, I won't tell you why, so there, but I insist on you answering all questions and will scold you if you don't. Maybe you will think that the reason why I am so curious is because I am 'jealous' of the lady in question. Well, sir, I won't tell you whether I am or not, but will keep you 'guessing.' Now, don't you wish you knew?

Must close or you will think I am going to 'rattle on' forever or maybe you have all ready become disgusted and torn my letter up. If so all I can say is poor little me—she was a nice little girl and meant well, but the man did not appreciate her.

There! Will stop or you will think I am crazy if you do not all ready.

Yours (?)

MABELLE

N.Y., Aug. 20

DEAR GIRLIE:

Well girlie I suppose you thought I was never going to answer your letter but have been busier than a one armed paper hanger the last week as have been working on a number with Paul Sears who is one of the best lyric writers in N.Y. and has turned out as many hits as Berlin or Davis or any of them. And believe me girlie he has turned out another hit this time that is he and I have done it together. It is all done now and we are just waiting for the best chance to place it but will not place it nowheres unless we get the right kind of a deal but maybe will publish it ourselves.

The song is bound to go over big as Sears has wrote a great lyric and I have give it a great tune or at least every body that has heard it goes crazy over it and it looks like it would go over bigger than any song since Mammy and would not be surprised to see it come out the hit of the year. If it is handled right we will make a bbl. of money and Sears says it is a cinch we will clean up as much as $25000 apiece which is pretty fair for one song but this one is not like the most of them but has got a great lyric and I have wrote a melody that will knock them out of their seats. I only wish you could hear it girlie and hear it the way I play. I had to play it over and over about 50 times at the Friars last night.

I will copy down the lyric of the chorus so you can see what it is like and get the idea of the song though of course you can't tell much about it unless you hear it played and sang. The title of the song is When They're Like You and here is the chorus:

Some like them hot, some like them cold.
Some like them when they're not too darn old.
Some like them fat, some like them lean.
Some like them only at sweet sixteen.
Some like them dark, some like them light.
Some like them in the park, late at night.
Some like them fickle, some like them true,
But the time I like them is when they're like you.

How is that for a lyric and I only wish I could play my melody for you as you would go nuts over it but will send you a copy as soon as the song is published and you can get some of your friends to play it over for you and I know you will like it though it is a different melody when I play it or when somebody else plays it.

Well girlie you will see how busy I have been and am libel to keep right on being busy as we are not going to let the grass grow under our feet but as soon as we have got this number placed we will get busy on another one as a couple like that will put me on Easy st even if they don't go as big as we expect but even 25 grand is a big bunch of money and if a man could only turn out one hit a year and make that much out of it I would be on Easy st. and no more hammering on the old music box in some cabaret.

Who ever we take the song to we will make them come across with one grand for advance royaltys and that will keep me going till I can turn out another one. So the future looks bright and rosey to yours truly and I am certainly glad I come to the big town though sorry I did not do it a whole lot quicker.

This is a great old town girlie and when you have lived here a wile you wonder how you ever stood for a burg like Chi which is just a hick town along side of this besides being dirty etc. and a man is a sucker to stay there all his life specially a man in my line of work as N.Y. is the Mecca for a man that has got the musical gift. I figure that all the time I spent in Chi I was just wasteing my time and never really started to live till I come down here and I have to laugh when I think of the boys out there that is trying to make a liveing in the song writeing game and most of them starve to death all their life and the first week I am down here I meet a man like Sears and the next thing you know we have turned out a song that will make us a fortune.

Well girlie you asked me to tell you about the girlie up on the

Drive that tried to make me and asked me to come and see her again. Well I can assure you you have no reasons to be jealous in that quarter as I have not been back to see her as I figure it is wasteing my time to play round with a dame like she that wants to go out somewheres every night and if you married her she would want a house on 5th ave with a dozen servants so I have passed her up as that is not my idea of home.

What I want when I get married is a real home where a man can stay home and work and maybe have a few of his friends in once in a wile and entertain them or go to a good musical show once in a wile and have a wife that is in sympathy with you and not nag at you all the wile but be a real help mate. The girlie up on the Drive would run me ragged and have me in the poor house inside of a year even if I was makeing 25 grand out of one song. Besides she wears a make up that you would have to blast to find out what her face looks like. So I have not been back there and don't intend to see her again so what is the use of me telling you about her. And the only other girlie I have met is a sister of Paul Sears who I met up to his house wile we was working on the song but she don't hardly count as she has not got no use for the boys but treats them like dirt and Paul says she is the coldest proposition he ever seen.

Well I don't know no more to write and besides have got a date to go out to Paul's place for dinner and play some of my stuff for him so as he can see if he wants to set words to some more of my melodies. Well don't do nothing I would not do and have as good a time as you can in old Chi and will let you know how we come along with the song.

CHAS. F. LEWIS

Chicago, Ill., Aug. 23

DEAR MR MAN:

I am thrilled to death over the song and think the words awfully pretty and am crazy to hear the music which I know must be great. It must be wonderful to have the gift of writing songs and then hear people play and sing them and just think of making $25,000 in such a short time. My, how rich you will be and I certainly congratulate you though am afraid when you are rich and famous you will have no time for insignificant little me or will you be an exception and remember your 'old' friends even when you are up in the world? I sincerely hope so.

Will look forward to receiving a copy of the song and will you be sure and put your name on it? I am all ready very conceited just to think that I know a man that writes songs and makes all that money.

Seriously I wish you success with your next song and I laughed when I read your remark about being busier than a one armed paper hanger. I don't see how you think up all those comparisons and crazy things to say. The next time one of the girls asks me to go out with them I am going to tell them I can't go because I am busier than a one armed paper hanger and then they will think I made it up and say: 'The girl is clever.'

Seriously I am glad you did not go back to see the girl on the Drive and am also glad you don't like girls who makes themselves up so much as I think it is disgusting and would rather go round looking like a ghost than put artificial color on my face. Fortunately I have a complexion that does not need 'fixing' but even if my coloring was not what it is I would never think of lowering myself to 'fix' it. But I must tell you a joke that happened just the other day when Edith and I were out at lunch and there was another girl in the restaurant whom Edie knew and she introduced her to me and I noticed how this girl kept staring at me and finally she begged my pardon and asked if she could ask me a personal question and I said yes and she asked me if my complexion was really 'mine.' I assured her it was and she said: 'Well, I thought so because I did not think anybody could put it on so artistically. I certainly envy you.' Edie and I both laughed.

Well, if that girl envies me my complexion, why I envy you living in New York. Chicago is rather dirty though I don't let that part of it bother me as I bathe and change my clothing so often that the dirt does not have time to 'settle.' Edie often says she cannot see how I always keep so clean looking and says I always look like I had just stepped out of a band box. She also calls me a fish (jokingly) because I spend so much time in the water. But seriously I do love to bathe and never feel so happy as when I have just 'cleaned up' and put on fresh clothing.

Edie has just gone out to see a picture and was cross at me because I would not go with her. I told her I was going to write a letter and she wanted to know to whom and I told her and she said: 'You write to him so often that a person would almost think you was in love with him.' I just laughed and turned it off, but she does say the most embarrassing things and I would be angry if it was anybody but she that said them.

Seriously I had much rather sit here and write letters or read or just sit and dream than go out to some crazy old picture show except once in awhile I do like to go to the theater and see a good play and a specially a musical play if the music is catchy. But as a rule I am contented to just stay home and feel cozy and lots of evenings Edie and I sit here without saying hardly a word to each other though she would love to talk but she knows I had rather be quiet and she often says it is just like living with a deaf and dumb mute to live with me because I make so little noise round the apartment. I guess I was born to be a home body as I so seldom care to go 'gadding.'

Though I do love to have company once in awhile, just a few congenial friends whom I can talk to and feel at home with and play cards or have some music. My friends love to drop in here, too, as they say Edie and I always give them such nice things to eat. Though poor Edie has not much to do with it, I am afraid, as she hates anything connected with cooking which is one of the things I love best of anything and I often say that when I begin keeping house in my own home I will insist on doing most of my own work as I would take so much more interest in it than a servant, though I would want somebody to help me a little if I could afford it as I often think a woman that does all her own work is liable to get so tired that she loses interest in the bigger things of life like books and music. Though after all what bigger thing is there than home making a specially for a woman?

I am sitting in the dearest old chair that I bought yesterday at a little store on the North Side. That is my one extravagance, buying furniture and things for the house, but I always say it is economy in the long run as I will always have them and have use for them and when I can pick them up at a bargain I would be silly not to. Though heaven knows I will never be 'poor' in regards to furniture and rugs and things like that as mother's house in Toledo is full of lovely things which she says she is going to give to Sis and myself as soon as we have real homes of our own. She is going to give me the first choice as I am her favorite. She has the loveliest old things that you could not buy now for love or money including

86

lovely old rugs and a piano which Sis wanted to have a player attachment put on it but I said it would be an insult to the piano so we did not get one. I am funny about things like that, a specially old furniture and feel towards them like people whom I love.

Poor mother, I am afraid she won't live much longer to enjoy her lovely old things as she has been suffering for years from stomach trouble and the doctor says it has been worse lately instead of better and her heart is weak besides. I am going home to see her a few days this fall as it may be the last time. She is very cheerful and always says she is ready to go now as she has had enough joy out of life and all she would like would be to see her girls settled down in their own homes before she goes.

There I go, talking about my domestic affairs again and I will bet you are bored to death though personly I am never bored when my friends tell me about themselves. But I won't 'rattle on' any longer, but will say good night and don't forget to write and tell me how you come out with the song and thanks for sending me the words to it. Will you write a song about me some time? I would be thrilled to death! But I am afraid I am not the kind of girl that inspires men to write songs about them, but am just a quiet 'mouse' that loves home and am not giddy enough to be the heroine of a song.

Well, Mr Man, good night and don't wait so long before writing again to

Yours (?)

MABELLE

N.Y., Sept 8

DEAR GIRLIE:

Well girlie have not got your last letter with me so cannot answer what was in it as I have forgotten if there was anything I was supposed to answer and besides have only a little time to write as I have a date to go out on a party with the Sears. We are going to the Georgie White show and afterwards somewheres for supper. Sears is the boy who wrote the lyric to my song and it is him and his sister I am going on the party with. The sister is a cold fish that has no use for men but she is show crazy and insists on Paul takeing her to 3 or 4 of them a week.

Paul wants me to give up my room here and come and live with them as they have plenty of room and I am running a little low on money but don't know if I will do it or not as am afraid I would freeze to death in the same house with a girl like the sister as she is ice cold but she don't hang round the house much as she is always takeing trips or going to shows or somewheres.

So far we have not had no luck with the song. All the publishers we have showed it to has went crazy over it but they won't make the right kind of a deal with us and if they don't loosen up and give us a decent royalty rate we are libel to put the song out ourselves and show them up. The man up to Goebel's told us the song was O.K. and he liked it but it was more of a production number than anything else and ought to go in a show like the Follies but they won't be in N.Y. much longer and what we ought to do is hold it till next spring.

Mean wile I am working on some new numbers and also have taken a position with the orchestra at the Wilton and am going to work there starting next week. They pay good money $60 and it will keep me going.

Well girlie that is about all the news. I believe you said your father was sick and hope he is better and also hope you are getting along O.K. and take care of yourself. When you have nothing else to do write to your friend,

CHAS. F. LEWIS

Chicago, Ill., Sept. 11

DEAR MR LEWIS:

Your short note reached me yesterday and must say I was puzzled when I read it. It sounded like you was mad at me though I cannot think of any reason why you should be. If there was something I said in my last letter that offended you I wish you would tell me what it was and I will ask your pardon though I cannot remember anything I could of said that you could take offense at. But if there was something, why I assure you, Mr Lewis, that I did not mean anything by it. I certainly did not intend to offend you in any way.

Perhaps it is nothing I wrote you, but you are worried on account of the publishers not treating you fair in regards to your song and that is why your letter sounded so distant. If that is the case I hope that by this time matters have rectified themselves and the future looks brighter. But any way, Mr Lewis, don't allow yourself to worry over business cares as they will all come right in the end and I always think it is silly for people to worry themselves sick over temporary troubles, but the best way is to 'keep smiling' and look for the 'silver lining' in the cloud. That is the way I always do and no matter what happens, I manage to smile and my girl friend, Edie, calls me Sunny because I always look on the bright side.

Remember also, Mr Lewis, that $60 is a salary that a great many men would like to be getting and are living on less than that and supporting a wife and family on it. I always say that a person can get along on whatever amount they make if they manage things in the right way.

So if it is business troubles, Mr Lewis, I say don't worry, but look on the bright side. But if it is something I wrote in my last letter that offended you I wish you would tell me what it was so I can apologize as I assure you I meant nothing and would not say anything to hurt you for the world.

Please let me hear from you soon as I will not feel comfortable until I know I am not to blame for the sudden change.

Sincerely,
MABELLE GILLESPIE

N.Y., Sept. 24

DEAR MISS GILLESPIE:

Just a few lines to tell you the big news or at least it is big news to me. I am engaged to be married to Paul Sears' sister and we are going to be married early next month and live in Atlantic City where the orchestra I have been playing with has got an engagement in one of the big cabarets.

I know this will be a surprise to you as it was even a surprise to me as I did not think I would ever have the nerve to ask the girlie the big question as she was always so cold and acted like I was just in the way. But she said she supposed she would have to marry somebody some time and she did not dislike me as much as most of the other men her brother brought round and she would marry me with the understanding that she would not have to be a slave and work round the house and also I would have to take her to a show or somewheres every night and if I could not take her myself she would 'run wild' alone. Atlantic City will be O.K. for that as a lot of new shows opens down there and she will be able to see them before they get to the big town. As for her being a slave, I would hate to think of marrying a girl and then have them spend their lives in druggery round the house. We are going to live in a hotel till we find something better but will be in no hurry to start house keeping as we will have to buy all new furniture.

Betsy is some doll when she is all fixed up and believe me she knows how to fix herself up. I don't know what she uses but it is weather proof and I have been out in a rain storm with her and we both got drowned but her face stayed on. I would almost think it was real only she tells me different.

Well girlie I may write to you again once in a wile as Betsy says she don't give a damn if I write to all the girls in the world just so I don't make her read the answers but that is all I can think of to say now except good bye and good luck and may the right man come along soon and he will be a lucky man getting a girl that is such a good cook and got all that furniture etc.

But just let me give you a word of advice before I close and that is don't never speak to strange men who you don't know nothing about as they may get you wrong and think you are trying to make them. It just happened that I knew better so you was lucky in my case but the luck might not last.

Your friend,

CHAS. F. LEWIS

Chicago, Ill., Sept. 27

MY DEAR MR LEWIS:

Thanks for your advice and also thank your fiance for her generosity in allowing you to continue your correspondence with her 'rivals,' but personly I have no desire to take advantage of that generosity as I have something better to do than read letters from a man like you, a specially as I have a man friend who is not so generous as Miss Sears and would strongly object to my continuing a correspondence with another man. It is at his request that I am writing this note to tell you not to expect to hear from me again.

Allow me to congratulate you on your engagement to Miss Sears and I am sure she is to be congratulated too, though if I met the lady I would be tempted to ask her to tell me her secret, namely how she is going to 'run wild' on $60.

Sincerely,

MABELLE GILLESPIE

The Maysville Minstrel

Maysville was a town of five thousand inhabitants and its gas company served eight hundred homes, offices and stores.

The company's office force consisted of two men—Ed Hunter, trouble shooter and reader of meters, and Stephen Gale, whose title was bookkeeper, but whose job was a lot harder than that sounds.

From the first to the tenth of the month, Stephen stayed in the office, accepted checks and money from the few thrifty customers who wanted their discount of five percent, soft-soaped and argued with the many customers who thought they were being robbed, and tried to sell new stoves, plates and lamps to customers who were constantly complaining of defects in the stoves, plates and lamps they had bought fifteen or twenty years ago.

After the tenth, he kept the front door locked and went all over town calling on delinquents, many of whom were a year or more behind and had no intention of trying to catch up. This tiring, futile task usually lasted until the twenty-seventh, when Hunter started reading meters and Stephen copied the readings and made out the bills.

On the twenty-ninth, Hunter usually got drunk and Stephen had to hustle out and read the unread meters and hustle back and make out the rest of the bills.

When Townsend, the Old Man, who owned the business and five other gas businesses in larger towns, paid his semimonthly visit to Maysville, Stephen had to take a severe bawling out for failing to squeeze blood from Maysville's turnips and allowing Hunter to get drunk.

All in all, Stephen earned the $22.50 per week which he had been getting the eight years he had worked for the gas company.

He was now thirty-one. At twelve, he had been obliged to quit school and go to work as a Western Union messenger boy. His father was dead and his mother, who established herself, without

92

much profit, as a dressmaker, easily could use the few dollars Stephen drew from the telegraph company. Later on he had jobs as driver of a grocery wagon, soda clerk in a drug store and freight wrestler at the Lackawanna depot.

The $22.50 offer from the gas office was manna from somewhere; it topped his highest previous salary by seven dollars and a half.

Stephen's mother died and Stephen married Stella Nichols, to whom lack of money was no novelty. But they had a couple of children and soon fell into debt, which made Stephen less efficient than ever as a collector of the company's back bills. He couldn't blame other people for not settling when he was stalling off creditors himself.

All he could do was wish to heaven that the Old Man would come across with a substantial raise, and he knew there was as much chance of that as of Stella's swimming the English Channel with a kid under each arm.

The Gales were too poor to go to picture shows; besides, there was no one to leave the children with. So Stephen and Stella stayed at home evenings and read books from the town library. The books Stephen read were books of poetry.

And often, after Stella had gone to bed, he wrote poetry of his own.

He wrote a poem to Stella and gave it to her on one of her birthdays and she said it was great and he ought to quit the darn old gas company and write poetry for a living.

He laughed that off, remarking that he was as poor now as he cared to be.

He didn't show Stella his other poems—poems about Nature, flowers, the Lackawanna Railroad, the beauties of Maysville, et cetera—but kept them locked in a drawer of his desk at the gas office.

There was a man named Charley Roberts who traveled out of New York for an instantaneous water-heater concern. For years he had been trying to sell old Townsend, but old Townsend said the heater ate up too much gas and would make the customers squawk. They squawked enough as it was. Roberts was a determined young man and kept after Townsend in spite of the latter's discouraging attitude.

Roberts was also a wise-cracking, kidding New Yorker, who,

when at home, lunched where his heroes lunched, just to be near them, look at them and overhear some of their wise-cracks which he could repeat to his fellow drummers on the road. These heroes of his were comic-strip artists, playwrights and editors of humorous columns in the metropolitan press.

His favorite column was the one conducted by George Balch in the Standard and when he was in the small towns, he frequently clipped silly items from the local papers and sent them to George, who substituted his own captions for Charley's and pasted them up.

Charley had a tip that Old Man Townsend would be in Maysville on a certain day, and as he was in the neighborhood, he took an interurban car thither and called at the gas office. Stephen had just got back from a fruitless tour among the deadheads and was in the shop, behind the office, telling Ed Hunter that Mrs Harper's pilot-light wouldn't stay lighted.

Roberts, alone in the office, looked idly at Stephen's desk and saw a book.

It was a volume of poems by Amy Lowell. A moment later Stephen reentered from the shop.

'Hello there, Gale,' said Roberts.

'How are you, Mr Roberts?' said Stephen.

'I heard the Old Man was here,' said Roberts.

'You've missed him,' said Stephen. 'He was here yesterday afternoon and left for Haines City last night.'

'Will he be here tomorrow?'

'I couldn't tell you. He's hard to keep track of.'

'He's hard to sell, too. But I'll run over there and take a chance. I notice you've been reading highbrow poetry.'

'I got this from the library.'

'How do you like it?'

'I'm not strong for poetry that don't rhyme,' said Stephen.

'I guess it's easier to write,' said Roberts.

'I don't believe so. It isn't much trouble rhyming if you've got it in you. Look at Edgar Guest.'

'How do you know he doesn't have trouble?'

'His works don't read like it,' said Stephen, and after a pause: 'Besides, I've tried it myself.'

'Oh, so you're a poet, are you?' asked Roberts.

'I wouldn't exactly claim that, but I've written a few verses and it was more like fun than work. Maybe other people would think they were rotten, but I get pleasure writing them just the same.'

'I'd like to read them, Gale,' said Roberts eagerly.

'I don't know if I'd like you to or not. And I don't know if I've saved any. I wrote a poem to my wife on her birthday three years ago. She thought it was pretty good. I might let you read that, only I don't know if I've got a copy of it around here.'

He knew very well he had a copy of it around there.

'See if you can find it,' said Roberts.

Stephen looked in two or three drawers before he unlocked the one that contained his manuscripts.

'It's just a little thing I wrote for my wife on her birthday. You'll probably think it's rotten. It's called "To Stella." That's my wife's first name.'

Charley Roberts read the poem:

Stella you today are twenty-three years old
And yet your hair is still pure gold.
Stella they tell me your name in Latin means a star
And to me that is what you are
With your eyes and your hair so yellow
I rate myself a lucky fellow Stella.
You know I cannot afford a costly gift
As you know it costs us all I make to live
And as you know we are already in debt,
But if you will stay well and healthy
Until I am rich and wealthy
Maybe I will be more able then to give you a present
Better than I can at present.
So now Stella good-by for the present
And I hope next year I can make things more pleasant.
May you live to be old and ripe and mellow
Is my kind birthday wish for you Stella.

'Do you mean to tell me,' said Roberts, 'that it was no trouble to write that?'

'It only took me less than a half-hour,' said Stephen.

'Listen,' said Roberts. 'Let me have it.'

'What do you want with it?'

'I can get it published for you.'

'Where at?'

'In the New York Standard. I've got a friend, George Balch, who would run it in his column. He doesn't pay anything, but if this was printed and your name signed to it, it might attract attention from people who do pay for poetry. Then you could make a lot of money on the side.'

'How much do they pay?'

'Well, some of the big magazines pay as high as a dollar a line.'

'I forget how many lines there is in that.'

Roberts counted them.

'Seventeen,' he said. 'And from what I've seen of old Townsend, I bet he doesn't pay you much more a week.'

'And it only took me less than a half-hour to write,' said Stephen.

'Will you let me send it to Balch?'

'I don't know if I've got another copy.'

'Your wife must have a copy.'

'I guess maybe she has.'

He wasn't just guessing.

'I'll mail this to Balch tonight, along with a note. If he prints it, I'll send you the paper.'

'I've got one that's even longer than that,' said Stephen.

'Well, let's have it.'

'No, I guess I'd better hang onto it—if your friend don't pay for them.'

'You're absolutely right. A man's a sucker to work for nothing. You keep your other stuff till this is published and you hear from some magazine editor, as I'm sure you will. Then you can sell what you've already written, and write more, till you're making so much dough that you can buy the Maysville Gas Company from that old skinflint.'

'I don't want any gas company. I want to get out of it. I just want to write.'

'Why shouldn't you!'

'I've got to be sure of a living.'

'Living! If you can make seventeen dollars in half an hour, that's thirty-four dollars an hour, or—— How many hours do you put in here?'

'Ten.'

'Three hundred and forty dollars a day! If that isn't a living, I'm selling manicure sets to fish.'

'I couldn't keep up no such a pace. I have to wait for inspiration,' said Stephen.

'A dollar a line would be enough inspiration for me. But the times when you didn't feel like doing it yourself, you could hire somebody to do it for you.'

'That wouldn't be square, and people would know the difference anyway. It's hard to imitate another man's style. I tried once to write like Edgar Guest, but it wouldn't have fooled people that was familiar with his works.'

'Nobody can write like Guest. And you don't need to. Your own style is just as good as his and maybe better. And speaking of Guest, do you think he's starving to death? He gives away dimes to the Fords.'

Stephen was wild to tell Stella what happened, but he was afraid this Balch might not like the poem as well as Roberts had; might not think it worth publishing, and she would be disappointed.

He would wait until he actually had it in print, if ever, and then show it to her.

He didn't have to wait long. In less than a week he received by mail from New York a copy of the Standard, and in George Balch's column was his verse with his name signed to it and a caption reading 'To Stella—A Maysville Minstrel Gives His Mrs a Birthday Treat.'

For the first time in his career at the gas office, Stephen quit five minutes early and almost ran home. His wife was as excited as he had hoped she would be.

'But why does he call you a minstrel?' she asked. 'He must have heard some way about that night at the Elks.'

Stephen told her the rest of the story—how Roberts had predicted that the poem would attract the attention of magazine editors and create a demand for his verses at a dollar a line. And he confessed that he had other poems all ready to send when the call came.

He had brought two of them home from the office and he read them aloud for her approval:

'1. The Lackawanna Railroad

'The Lackawanna Railroad where does it go?
It goes from Jersey City to Buffalo.
Some of the trains stop at Maysville but they are few
Most of them go right through
Except the 8:22
Going west but the 10:12 bound for Jersey City
That is the train we like the best
As it takes you to Jersey City
Where you can take a ferry or tube for New York City.
The Lackawanna runs many freights
Sometimes they run late
But that does not make so much difference with a freight
Except the people who have to wait for their freight.
Maysville people patronize the Interurban a specially the
    farmers
So the Interurban cuts into the business of the Lackawanna,
But if you are going to New York City or Buffalo
The Lackawanna is the way to go.
Will say in conclusion that we consider it an honor
That the City of Maysville is on the Lackawanna.

'2. The Gas Business

'The Maysville Gas Co. has eight hundred meters
The biggest consumer in town is Mrs. Arnold Peters
Who owns the big house on Taylor Hill
And is always giving parties come who will.
Our collections amount to about $2600.00 per month
Five per cent discount if paid before the tenth of the month.
Mr. Townsend the owner considers people a fool
Who do not at least use gas for fuel.
As for lighting he claims it beats electricity
As electric storms often cut off the electricity
And when you have no light at night
And have to burn candles all night.
This is hardly right
A specially if you have company
Who will ask you what is the matter with the electricity.

So patronize the Gas Company which storms do not effect
And your friends will have no reason to object.'

Stella raved over both the poems, but made a very practical suggestion.

'You are cheating yourself, dear,' she said. 'The poem about the railroad, for instance, the way you have got it, it is nineteen lines, or nineteen dollars if they really pay a dollar a line. But it would be almost double the amount if you would fix the lines different.'

'How do you mean?'

She got a pencil and piece of paper and showed him:

> The Lackawanna Railroad
> Where does it go?
> It goes from Jersey City
> To Buffalo.

'You see,' she said, 'you could cut most of the lines in half and make thirty-eight dollars instead of nineteen.'

But Stephen, with one eye on profit and the other on Art, could only increase the lines of 'The Lackawanna' from nineteen to thirty and those of 'The Gas Business' from seventeen to twenty-one.

Three days later a special delivery came for Stephen.

It said:

Dear Mr. Gale:

On September second there was a poem entitled 'To Stella' in the New York Standard. The poem was signed by you. It impressed me greatly and if you have written or will write others as good, our magazine will be glad to buy them, paying you one dollar a line.

Please let me hear from you and send along any poems you may have on hand.

Sincerely,
Wallace James,
Editor, 'James's Weekly,'
New York City.

Stephen had never heard of 'James's Weekly' and did not notice that the letter was postmarked Philadelphia and written on the stationery of a Philadelphia hotel.

He rushed to his house, addressed and mailed the railroad and gas verses, and after a brief and excited conference with Stella, decided to resign his job.

Old Man Townsend, dropping into Maysville the following morning, heard the decision and was not a bit pleased. He realized he never could get anyone else to do Stephen's work at Stephen's salary.

'I'll raise you to twenty-four dollars,' he said.

'I'm not asking for a raise. I've got to quit so I can devote all my time to my poetry.'

'Your poetry!'

'Yes, sir.'

'Do you mean to say you're going to write poetry for a living?' asked the Old Man.

'Yes, sir.'

'You'll starve to death.'

'Edgar Guest is still alive.'

'I don't care if he is or not,' said the Old Man. 'It's the twelfth of the month and Hunter can tend to his job and yours both for a couple of weeks. If you want to come back at the end of that time, I'll raise you to twenty-three dollars.'

It was Stephen's intention to polish up some of his older poems and write one or two fresh ones so his supply would be ready for 'James's' demand.

But he found it next to impossible to write while the fate of the two verses he had sent in was uncertain and, deciding to leave the old manuscripts as they were, he was able to make only a feeble start on a new one:

The Delaware River

Not a great many miles from Maysville is the Delaware River
But there is no fish in this part of the River.
The upper part of the River is narrow and shallow
But they claim it is much wider near Philadelphia.

On the twentieth the envelope containing 'The Lackawanna Railroad' and 'The Gas Business' was returned from New York.

There were several inscriptions stamped and written on it, such as 'Not Found' and 'Not in Directory.'

And it dawned on Stephen that he was the victim of quite a joke.

To the accompaniment of Stella's sobs, he proceeded to tear up all his manuscripts save 'To Stella,' which she had hidden away where he couldn't find it.

'Mr Townsend came in on the eight-thirty interurban,' he said. 'I'll have to go see him.'

'All right,' said the Old Man when Stephen walked into the office. 'I'll take you back at your old salary, but don't let's have no more foolishness. Get out now and try and coax a little money out of that Harper woman. She ain't paid a nickel for eight months.'

'I wanted to speak to you about those instantaneous water-heaters,' said Stephen.

'What about them?'

'I was going to advise you not to buy them. They eat up too much gas.'

'Thanks for your advice, but I ordered some from Roberts in Haines City. I told him to send half a dozen of them here,' said the Old Man.

'Will he be here to demonstrate them?' asked Stephen grimly.

'He said he would.'

'I hope he will.'

But even as he spoke, Stephen realized there was nothing he could do about it.

Women

Young Jake uttered a few words which it would pain me to repeat.

'And what are *you* crabbin' about?' asked Mike Healy from his corner of the bench.

'Oh, nothin'!' said Jake. 'Nothin' except that I'm sick of it!'

'Sick of what?' demanded Healy.

'Of settin' here!' Jake replied.

'You!' said Mike Healy, with a short laugh. 'You've got a fine license to squawk! Why, let's see: what is it? The third of June, and your first June in the league. You ain't even *begun* to sit! Look at me! Been on this bench since catchers started wearin' a mast, or anyway it seems that long. And you never hear me crab, do you, Lefty?'

'Only when you talk,' answered the athlete addressed. 'And that's only at table or between meals.'

'But if this kid's hollerin' already,' said Mike, 'what'll he be doin' along in August or September, to say nothin' about next August and the August after that?'

'Don't worry!' said Young Jake. 'I'll either be a regular by the end of this season or I won't be on this ball club at all!'

'That-a-boy!' said Healy. 'Threaten 'em!'

'I mean what I say!' retorted Jake. 'I ain't goin' to spend my life on no bench! I come here to play baseball!'

'Oh, you did!' said Healy. 'And what do you think I come here for, to fish?'

'I ain't talkin' about you,' said Young Jake. 'I'm talkin' about myself.'

'That's a novelty in a ball player,' remarked Lefty.

'And what I'm sayin',' Jake went on, 'is that I'm sick of settin' on this bench.'

'This ain't a bad bench,' said Healy. 'They's a hell of a lot worse places you might sit.'

102

'And a hell of a lot better places!' said Jake. 'I can think of one right now. I'm lookin' right at it.'

'Where at?'

'Right up in the old stand; the third—no, the fourth row, next to the aisle, the first aisle beyond where the screen leaves off.'

'I noticed her myself!' put in Lefty. 'Damn cute! Too damn cute for a busher like you to get smoked up over.'

'Oh, I don't know!' said Young Jake. 'I didn't get along so bad with them dames down South.'

'Down South ain't here!' replied Lefty. 'Those dames in some of those swamps, they lose their head when they see a man with shoes on. But up here you've got to have something. If you pulled that Calhoun County stuff of yours on a gal like that gal in the stand she'd yell for the dog catcher. She'd——'

'They're all alike!' interrupted Mike Healy. 'South, or here, or anywheres, they're all the same, and all poison!'

'What's poison?' asked Jake.

'Women!' said Healy. 'And the more you have to do with 'em the better chance you've got of spendin' your life on this bench. Why—— That's pitchin', Joe!' he shouted when the third of the enemy batters had popped out and left a runner stranded at second base. 'You look good in there today,' he added to Joe as the big pitcher approached the dugout.

'I'm all right, I guess,' said Joe, pulling on his sweater and moving toward the water bottle. 'I wished that wind'd die down.'

The manager had come in.

'All right! Let's get at 'em!' he said. 'Nice work, Joe. Was that a fast one Meusel hit?'

'No,' said Joe. 'A hook, but it didn't break.'

'A couple of runs will beat 'em the way you're going,' said the manager, stooping over to select his bat. 'Make this fella pitch, boys,' he added. 'He was hog wild in Philly the other day.'

The half inning wore on to its close, and the noncombatants were again left in possession of the bench. Young Jake addressed Healy.

'What's women done to you, Mike?'

'Only broke me. That's all!' said Healy.

'What do you mean, broke you! The boys tells me you ain't spent nothin' but the summer since you been in the league.'

'Oh, I've got a little money,' said Healy. 'I don't throw it away. I don't go around payin' ten smackers a quart for liquid catnip. But they's more kinds of broke than money broke, a damn sight worse kinds, too. And when I say women has broke me, I mean they've made a bum out of my life; they've wrecked my—what-do-you-call-it?'

'Your career,' supplied Lefty.

'Yes, sir,' said Healy. 'And I ain't kiddin', neither. Why say, listen: Do you know where I'd be if it wasn't for a woman? Right out there in that infield, playin' that old third sack.'

'What about Smitty?' asked Young Jake.

'He'd be where I am—on this bench.'

'Aw, come on, Mike! Be yourself! You don't claim you're as good as him!' Jake remonstrated.

'I do claim it, but it don't make no difference if I am or I ain't. He shouldn't never ought to of had a chance, not on this club, anyway. You'd say the same if you knowed the facts.'

'Well, let's hear 'em.'

'It's a long story, and these boys has heard it before.'

'That's all right, Mike,' said Gephart, a spare catcher. 'We ain't listened the last twelve times.'

'Well, it was the year I come in this league, four years ago this spring. I'd been with the Toledo club a couple of years. I was the best hitter on the Toledo club. I hit .332 the first year and .354 the next year. And I led the third basemen in fieldin'.'

'It would be hard not to,' interposed Lefty. 'Anything a third baseman don't get they call it a base hit. A third baseman ought to pay to get in the park.'

Healy glanced coldly at the speaker, and resumed:

'This club had Johnnie Lambert. He was still about the best third baseman in this league, but he was thirty-five years old and had a bad knee. It had slipped out on him and cost this club the pennant. They didn't have no other third baseman. They lose sixteen out of twenty games. So that learned 'em a lesson, and they bought me. Their idear was to start Johnnie in the spring, but they didn't expect his knee to hold up. And then it was goin' to be my turn.

'But durin' the winter Johnnie got a hold of some specialist somewheres that fixed his knee, and he come South with a new least of life. He hit good and was as fast as ever on the bases. Meanwile I had been on a huntin' trip up in Michigan that winter

104

and froze my dogs, and they ailed me so that I couldn't do myself justice all spring.'

'I suppose it was some woman made you go huntin',' said Gephart, but Healy continued without replying:

'They was a gal from a town named Ligonier, Indiana, that had visited in Toledo the second year I played ball there. The people where she was visitin' was great baseball fans, and they brought her out to the game with them, and she got stuck on me.'

'Ligonier can't be a town! It must be an asylum!' said Lefty.

'She got stuck on me,' Healy repeated, 'and the people where she was stayin' asked me to their house to supper. After supper the man and his wife said how about goin' to the picture show, and the gal said she was tired and rather stay home. So the man and woman excused themselves. They said it was a picture they wanted to see and would I excuse them runnin' off and leavin' we two together. They were clubbin on me, see?

'Well, I thought to myself, I'll give this dame an unpleasant surprise, so I didn't even hold her hand all evenin'. When I got up to go she says she supposed it would be the last time she seen me as she expected to go back to Ligonier the next day. She didn't have no more intentions of goin' back the next day than crossin' Lake Erie in a hollow tooth. But she knowed if I thought it was good-by I'd kiss her. Well, I knowed it wasn't good-by, but what the hell! So that's how it started, and I went to Ligonier that fall to see her, and we got engaged to be married. At least she seemed to think so.'

'Look at that!' interrupted Young Jake, his eyes on the field of action. 'What could Sam of been thinkin'!'

'Thinkin'!' said Gephart. 'Him!'

'What would Sam do,' wondered Lefty, 'if they played baseball with only one base? He wouldn't enjoy the game if he couldn't throw to the wrong one.'

'That play's liable to cost us somethin',' said Gephart.

'I went up in Michigan on a huntin' trip with some friends of mine,' Healy continued. 'I froze my feet and was laid up all through January and February and shouldn't of never went South. It was all as I could do to wear shoes, let alone play baseball. I wasn't really myself till along the first of May. But, as I say, Johnnie Lambert had a new least of life and was lookin' better than he'd looked for years. His knee wasn't troublin' him at all.

'Well, that's how things went till around the last part of June. I didn't get no action except five or six times goin' up to hit for somebody. And I was like a young colt, crazy to be let loose. I knowed that if I once got in there and showed what I could do Judge Landis himself couldn't keep me on the bench. I used to kneel down every night and pray to God to get to work on Lambert's knee.

'The gal kept writin' me letters and I answered 'em once in a w'ile, but we hadn't saw each other since before Christmas. She hinted once or twice about when was we goin' to get married, but I told her I didn't want to even disgust the subject till I was somethin' besides a bench warmer.

'We had a serious in Chi the tail-end of June, and the first night we was there I got a long-distance call from Ligonier. It was the gal's sister, sayin' the gal was sick. She was delirious part of the time and hollerin' for me, and the doctor said if she could see me, it'd probably do her more good than medicine.

'So I said that's all right, but they ain't no off days in the schedule right now and I can't get away. But they had looked up the time table and seen where I could leave Chi after the ball game, spend the night in Ligonier and get back for the game the next day.

'So I took a train from Englewood in the evenin' and when I got off at Ligonier, there was my gal to meet me. She was the picture of health and no more delirious than usual. They said she had been just about ready to pass out when she learned I was comin' and it cured her. They didn't tell me what disease she'd had, but I suppose it was a grasshopper bite or somethin'.

'When I left next mornin', the weddin' date was set for that fall.

'Somewheres between South Bend and Laporte, the train stopped and liked it so well that we stayed there over three hours. We hit Englewood after four o'clock and I got to the park just in time to see them loadin' Lambert into a machine to take him away. His knee had broke down on him in the first innin's. He ain't never played ball since. And Smitty, who's always been a natural second baseman, he had my job.'

'He's filled it pretty good,' said Lefty.

'That's either here or there,' retorted Healy. 'If I'd been around, nobody'd ever knowed if he could play third base or not. And the worst of him is,' he added, 'that he never gets hurt.'

106

'Maybe you ain't prayed for him like you done for Lambert,' said Young Jake. 'What happened to the gal? Did you give her the air?'

'No, I didn't,' said Healy. 'When I give my word, I keep it. I simply wrote and told her that I'd agreed to marry her and I wouldn't go back on it. But that my feelin's towards her was the same as if she was an advanced case of spinal meningitis. She never answered the letter, so I don't know if we're still engaged or not.'

The inning was over and the boys were coming in.

'Joe was lucky to get out of that with only two runs,' remarked Lefty. 'But of course it was Sam that put him in bad.'

'I'm goin' to see if he'll leave me get up on the lines,' said Young Jake, 'so I can get a better look at that dame.'

The manager waited for Sam to catch up.

'What the hell was the matter with you, Sam?' he demanded.

Sam looked silly.

'I thought——'

'That's where you make your mistake!' the manager broke in. 'Tough luck, Joe! But two runs are nothing. We'll get 'em back.'

'Shall I go up on the lines?' asked Young Jake, hopefully.

'You? No!' said the manager. 'You, Mike,' turning to Healy, 'go over and coach at third base. You brought us luck yesterday.'

So it was Mike who was held partly responsible a few moments later when Smitty, who had tripled, was caught napping off the bag.

'Nice coachin', Mike!' said Lefty, as Healy came back to the bench.

'Why don't he watch hisself!' growled Mike. 'And besides, I did yell at him!'

'You're a liar!' said Lefty. 'Your back was to the ball game. You were lookin' up in the stand.'

'Why would I be lookin' at the stand!' demanded Healy.

But nobody answered him. There was silence for a time. The boys were depressed; in their own language, their dauber was down. Finally Young Jake spoke.

'She's starin' right over this way!' he said.

'Who?' asked Gephart.

'That dame I pointed out. In the tan suit. 'Way over behind third base, the other side of the screen, in the fourth row.'

107

'I see her. Not bad!'

'I'll say she's not bad!' said Jake.

'Women!' said Healy. 'You better get your mind on baseball or you'll be back in that silo league, jumpin' from town to town in a w'eelbarrow.'

'I don't see why you should be off all women just because one of them brought you a little hard luck.'

'She wasn't the only one! Why, say, if it wasn't for women I'd be playin' regular third base for McGraw right now and cuttin' in on the big money every fall.'

'I didn't know you was ever with McGraw.'

'I wasn't,' said Healy, 'but I ought to been, and would of been only for a woman. It was when I was playin' with the Dayton club; my first year in baseball. Boy, I was fast as a streak! I was peggin' bunts to first base before the guy could drop his bat. I covered so much ground to my left that I was always knockin' the shortstop down and bumpin' heads with the right fielder. Everybody was marvelin' at me. Some of the old timers said I reminded them of Bill Bradley at his best, only that I made Bradley look like he was out of the game for a few days.

'Baldy Pierce was umpirin' in our league that year. He wasn't a bad umps, but he never left business interfere with pleasure. Many's the time he called the last fella out in the last innin's when the fella was safer than a hot chocolate at the Elks' convention— just because Baldy was hungry for supper.

'He was so homely that dogs wouldn't live in the same town, and his friends used to try and make him wear his mask off the field as well as on. And yet he grabbed some of the prettiest gals you ever see. He said to me once, he said, "Mike," he said, "you tell me I'm homelier than Railroad Street, but I can cop more pips than you can with all your good looks!" '

At this point there were unprintable comments by Lefty, Gephart, and other occupants of the bench.

'One of these gals of his,' Healy went on, 'was a gal named Helen Buck from Hamilton, Ohio. She was visitin' in Dayton and come out to the ball game. The first day she was there a lot of the boys was hit in the face by thrown balls, and every time a foul went to the stand the whole infield run in to shag it. But she wouldn't look at nobody but Pierce.

'Well, McGraw had heard about me, and he sent a fella named

McDonald, that was scoutin' for him, to look me over. It was in September and we was just about through. How the games come out didn't make no difference, but I knowed this McDonald was there and what he was there for, so I wanted to make a showin'. He had came intendin' to stay two days, but he'd overlooked a skip in the schedule that left us without no game the second day, so he said one game would have to be enough, as he had to go somewheres else.

'We was playin' the Springfield club. I had a good day in the field, but Bill Hutton, who started pitchin' for them, he was hog wild and walked me the first two times up. The third time they was a man on third and I had to follow orders and squeeze him home. So I hadn't had no chance to really show what I could do up there at the plate.

'Well, we come into the ninth innin's with the score tied and it was gettin' pretty dark. We got two of them out, and then their first baseman, Jansen, he got a base on balls. Bill Boone caught a hold of one just right and cracked it to the fence and it looked like Jansen would score, but he was a slow runner. Davy Shaw, our shortstop, thought he must of scored and when the ball was thrown to him he throwed it to me to get Boone, who was tryin' for three bases.

'Well, I had took in the situation at a glance; I seen that Jansen hadn't scored and if I put the ball on Boone quick enough, why the run wouldn't count. So I lunged at Boone and tagged him before Jansen had crossed the plate. But Pierce said the score counted and that Boone wasn't out because I'd missed him. Missed him! Say, I bet that where I tagged him they had to take stitches!

'Anyway, that give 'em a one run lead, and when the first two fellas got out in our half everybody thought it was over. But Davy Shaw hit one to right center that a man like I could of ran around twice on it, but they held Davy at third base. And it was up to me to bring him in.

'By this time Jim Preston was pitchin' for Springfield, and Jim was always a mark for me. I left the first one go by, as it was outside, but Pierce called it a strike. Then they was a couple of balls that hc couldn't call strikes. I cracked the next one over the leftfield fence, but it was a few inches foul. That made it two and two, and the next ball he throwed, well, if I hadn't ducked my head just when I did they'd of been brains scattered all over

Montgomery County. And what does Pierce do but yell "Batter out!" and run for the clubhouse!

'Well, I run after him and asked him what the hell, and here is what he said. He said, "Mike," he said, "these games don't mean nothin', but if this here game had of wound up a tie it would of meant a game tomorrow, when we got a off day. And I made a date for tomorrow to go on a picnic with my little gal in Hamilton. You wouldn't want me to miss that, would you?" '

'Why,' inquired Young Jake, 'didn't you break his nose or bust him in the chin?'

'His nose was already broke,' said Healy, 'and he didn't have no chin. I tried to get a hold of McDonald, the fella that was there scoutin' me. I was goin' to explain the thing to him. But he'd left before I could catch him. It seems, though, that he'd set over to the side where he couldn't see what a lousy strike it was and he told a friend of mine that he couldn't recommend a man that would take a third strike when a base hit would of tied up the game; that on top of me "missin' " Boone at third——'

Another half inning was over and Healy started for the third-base coaching line without waiting for the manager to reach the bench. His teammates were not in a position to see the glance he threw at a certain spot in the stand as he walked to his 'work.' When the side was retired scoreless and he had returned to his corner of the dugout he looked more desolate than ever.

'Women!' he said. 'Why, if it wasn't for women I'd be playin' third base for Huggins; I'd have Joe Dugan's job; I'd be livin' right here in the capital of the world.'

'How do you make that out?' asked Young Jake.

'It's a long story,' said Healy, 'but I can tell you in a few words. We was playin' the New York Club out home. Frank Baker had began to slip and Huggins was lookin' for a good young fella to take his place. He was crazy to get me, but he had heard that I didn't want to play in New York. This had came from me kiddin' with some of the boys on the New York Club, tellin' 'em I wouldn't play here if they give me the town. So Huggins wanted to make sure before he started a trade. And he didn't want no one to see him talkin' to me. So he came around one night to the hotel where I was livin' at the time. I was up in my room waitin' for the phone gal to be off duty. She was stuck on me and I had a date to take her for a drive. So when Huggins come to see me she said I was out. She was afraid her date was goin' to be interfered with. So Huggins went away and his club left town that night.'

'What did you do to her?' asked Jake.

'Oh, I couldn't do nothin' to her,' said Healy. 'She claimed she didn't know who it was.'

'Didn't he give his name?'

'No.'

'Then how do you know it was Huggins?'

'She said it was a little fella.'

'He ain't the only little fella.'

'He's the littlest fella I know,' said Healy.

'But you ain't sure what he wanted to see you for.'

'What *would* Huggins want to see me for—to scratch my back? But as I say, she didn't know who it was, so I couldn't do nothin' to her except ignore her from then on, and they couldn't of been no worse punishment as far as she was concerned.'

'All and all,' summed up Lefty, 'if it wasn't for women, you'd of been playin' third base for McGraw and Huggins and this club, all at the same time.'

'Yes,' said Healy, 'and with Washin'ton, too. Why——'

'Mike Healy!' interrupted the voice of Dick Trude, veteran usher. 'Here's a mash note and it wants an answer.'

Healy read the note and crumpled it in his hand.

'Who is she?' he asked.

'Look where I point,' said Trude. 'It's that good-lookin' dame in the tan suit, in the fourth row, back of third base. There! She asked me who you was when you was out there coachin'. So I told her, and she give me that note. She said you could answer yes or no.'

'Make it "yes," ' said Healy, and Trude went away.

Healy threw the crumpled note under the water bottle and addressed Young Jake.

'What I want you to get through your head, boy——'

'Oh, for God's sakes, shut up!' said Young Jake.

111

Ex Parte

Most always when a man leaves his wife, there's no excuse in the world for him. She may have made whoop-whoop-whoopee with the whole ten commandments, but if he shows his disapproval to the extent of walking out on her, he will thereafter be a total stranger to all his friends excepting the two or three bums who will tour the night clubs with him so long as he sticks to his habits of paying for everything.

When a woman leaves her husband, she must have good and sufficient reasons. He drinks all the time, or he runs around, or he doesn't give her any money, or he uses her as the heavy bag in his home gymnasium work. No more is he invited to his former playmates' houses for dinner and bridge. He is an outcast just the same as if he had done the deserting. Whichever way it happens, it's his fault. He can state his side of the case if he wants to, but there is nobody around listening.

Now I claim to have a little chivalry in me, as well as a little pride. So in spite of the fact that Florence had broadcast her grievances over the red and blue network both, I intend to keep mine to myself till death do me part.

But after I'm gone, I want some of my old pals to know that this thing wasn't as lopsided as she has made out, so I will write the true story, put it in an envelope with my will and appoint Ed Osborne executor. He used to be my best friend and would be yet if his wife would let him. He'll have to read all my papers, including this, and he'll tell everybody else about it and maybe they'll be a little sorry that they treated me like an open manhole.

(Ed, please don't consider this an attempt to be literary. You know I haven't written for publication since our days on 'The Crimson and White,' and I wasn't so hot then. Just look on it as a statement of facts. If I were still alive, I'd take a bible oath that

112

nothing herein is exaggerated. And whatever else may have been my imperfections, I never lied save to shield a woman or myself.)

Well, a year ago last May I had to go to New York. I called up Joe Paxton and he asked me out to dinner. I went, and met Florence. She and Marjorie Paxton had been at school together and she was there for a visit. We fell in love with each other and got engaged. I stopped off in Chicago on the way home, to see her people. They liked me all right, but they hated to have Florence marry a man who lived so far away. They wanted to postpone her leaving home as long as possible and they made us wait till April this year.

I had a room at the Belden and Florence and I agreed that when we were married, we would stay there awhile and take our time about picking out a house. But the last day of March, two weeks before the date of our wedding, I ran into Jeff Cooper and he told me his news, that the Standard Oil was sending him to China in some big job that looked permanent.

'I'm perfectly willing to go,' he said. 'So is Bess. It's a lot more money and we think it will be an interesting experience. But here I am with a brand-new place on my hands that cost me $45,000, including the furniture, and no chance to sell it in a hurry except at a loss. We were just beginning to feel settled. Otherwise we would have no regrets about leaving this town. Bess hasn't any real friends here and you're the only one I can claim.'

'How much would you take for your house, furniture and all?' I asked him.

'I'd take a loss of $5,000,' he said. 'I'd take $40,000 with the buyer assuming my mortgage of $15,000, held by the Phillips Trust and Mortgage Company in Seattle.'

I asked him if he would show me the place. They had only been living there a month and I hadn't had time to call. He said, what did I want to look at it for and I told him I would buy it if it looked O.K. Then I confessed that I was going to be married; you know I had kept it a secret around here.

Well, he took me home with him and he and Bess showed me everything, all new and shiny and a bargain if you ever saw one. In the first place, there's the location, on the best residential street in town, handy to my office and yet with a whole acre of ground, and a bed of cannas coming up in the front yard that Bess had planted

113

when they bought the property last fall. As for the house, I always like stucco, and this one is *built*! You could depend on old Jeff to see to that.

But the furniture was what decided me. Jeff had done the smart thing and ordered the whole works from Wolfe Brothers, taking their advice on most of the stuff, as neither he nor Bess knew much about it. Their total bill, furnishing the entire place, rugs, beds, tables, chairs, everything, was only $8,500, including a mahogany upright player-piano that they ordered from Seattle. I had my mother's old mahogany piano in storage and I kind of hoped Jeff wouldn't want me to buy this, but it was all or nothing, and with a bargain like that staring me in the face, I didn't stop to argue, not when I looked over the rest of the furniture and saw what I was getting.

The living-room had, and still has, three big easy chairs and a couch, all over-stuffed, as they call it, to say nothing of an Oriental rug that alone had cost $500. There was a long mahogany table behind the couch, with lamps at both ends in case you wanted to lie down and read. The dining-room set was solid mahogany—a table and eight chairs that had separated Jeff from $1,000.

The floors downstairs were all oak parquet. Also he had blown himself to an oak mantelpiece and oak woodwork that must have run into heavy dough. Jeff told me what it cost him extra, but I don't recall the amount.

The Coopers were strong for mahogany and wanted another set for their bedroom, but Jake Wolfe told them it would get monotonous if there was too much of it. So he sold them five pieces—a bed, two chairs, a chiffonier and a dresser—of some kind of wood tinted green, with flowers painted on it. This was $1,000 more, but it certainly was worth it. You never saw anything prettier than that bed when the lace spreads were on.

Well, we closed the deal and at first I thought I wouldn't tell Florence, but would let her believe we were going to live at the Belden and then give her a surprise by taking her right from the train to our own home. When I got to Chicago, though, I couldn't keep my mouth shut. I gave it away and it was I, not she, that had the surprise.

Instead of acting tickled to death, as I figured she would, she just looked kind of funny and said she hoped I had as good taste in houses as I had in clothes. She tried to make me describe the house and the furniture to her, but I wouldn't do it. To appreciate a layout like that, you have to see it for yourself.

We were married and stopped in Yellowstone for a week on our way here. That was the only really happy week we had together. From the minute we arrived home till she left for good, she was a different woman than the one I thought I knew. She never smiled and several times I caught her crying. She wouldn't tell me what ailed her and when I asked if she was just homesick, she said no and choked up and cried some more.

You can imagine that things were not as I expected they would be. In New York and in Chicago and Yellowstone, she had had more *life* than any girl I ever met. Now she acted all the while as if she were playing the title rôle at a funeral.

One night late in May the telephone rang. It was Mrs Dwan and she wanted Florence. If I had known what this was going to mean, I would have slapped the receiver back on the hook and let her keep on wanting.

I had met Dwan a couple of times and had heard about their place out on the Turnpike. But I had never seen it or his wife either.

Well, it developed that Mildred Dwan had gone to school with Florence and Marjorie Paxton, and she had just learned from Marjorie that Florence was my wife and living here. She said she and her husband would be in town and call on us the next Sunday afternoon.

Florence didn't seem to like the idea and kind of discouraged it. She said we would drive out and call on them instead. Mrs Dwan said no, that Florence was the newcomer and it was her (Mrs Dwan's) first move. So Florence gave in.

They came and they hadn't been in the house more than a minute when Florence began to cry. Mrs Dwan cried, too, and Dwan and I stood there first on one foot and then the other, trying to pretend we didn't know the girls were crying. Finally, to relieve the tension, I invited him to come and see the rest of the place. I showed him all over and he was quite enthusiastic. When we returned to the living-room, the girls had dried their eyes and were back in school together.

Florence accepted an invitation for one-o'clock dinner a week from that day. I told her, after they had left, that I would go along

115

only on condition that she and our hostess would both control their tear-ducts. I was so accustomed to solo sobbing that I didn't mind it any more, but I couldn't stand a duet of it either in harmony or unison.

Well, when we got out there and had driven down their private lane through the trees and caught a glimpse of their house, which people around town had been talking about as something wonderful, I laughed harder than any time since I was single. It looked just like what it was, a reorganized barn. Florence asked me what was funny, and when I told her, she pulled even a longer face than usual.

'I think it's beautiful,' she said.

Tie that!

I insisted on her going up the steps alone. I was afraid if the two of us stood on the porch at once, we'd fall through and maybe founder before help came. I warned her not to smack the knocker too hard or the door might crash in and frighten the horses.

'If you make jokes like that in front of the Dwans,' she said, 'I'll never speak to you again.'

'I'd forgotten you ever did,' said I.

I was expecting a hostler to let us in, but Mrs Dwan came in person.

'Are we late?' said Florence.

'A little,' said Mrs Dwan, 'but so is dinner. Helga didn't get home from church till half past twelve.'

'I'm glad of it,' said Florence. 'I want you to take me all through this beautiful, beautiful house right this minute.'

Mrs Dwan called her husband and insisted that he stop in the middle of mixing a cocktail so he could join us in a tour of the beautiful, beautiful house.

'You wouldn't guess it,' said Mrs Dwan, 'But it used to be a barn.'

I was going to say I had guessed it. Florence gave me a look that changed my mind.

'When Jim and I first came here,' said Mrs Dwan, 'we lived in an ugly little rented house on Oliver Street. It was only temporary, of course; we were just waiting till we found what we really wanted. We used to drive around the country Saturday afternoons and Sundays, hoping we would run across the right sort of thing. It was in the late fall when we first saw this place. The leaves were off the trees and it was visible from the Turnpike.

'Oh, Jim!' I exclaimed. "Look at that simply gorgeous old barn! With those wide shingles! And I'll bet you it's got hand-hewn beams in that middle, main section." Jim bet me I was wrong, so we left the car, walked up the driveway, found the door open and came brazenly in. I won my bet as you can see.'

She pointed to some dirty old rotten beams that ran across the living-room ceiling and looked as if five or six generations of rats had used them for gnawing practise.

'They're beautiful!' said Florence.

'The instant I saw them,' said Mrs Dwan, 'I knew this was going to be our home!'

'I can imagine!' said Florence.

'We made inquiries and learned that the place belonged to a family named Taylor,' said Mrs Dwan. 'The house had burned down and they had moved away. It was suspected that they had started the fire themselves, as they were terribly hard up and it was insured. Jim wrote to old Mr Taylor in Seattle and asked him to set a price on the barn and the land, which is about four acres. They exchanged several letters and finally Mr Taylor accepted Jim's offer. We got it for a song.'

'Wonderful!' said Florence.

'And then, of course,' Mrs Dwan continued, 'we engaged a house-wrecking company to tear down the other four sections of the barn—the stalls, the cow-shed, the tool-shed, and so forth—and take them away, leaving us just this one room. We had a man from Seattle come and put in these old pine walls and the flooring, and plaster the ceiling. He was recommended by a friend of Jim's and he certainly knew his business.'

'I can see he did,' said Florence.

'He made the hay-loft over for us, too, and we got the wings built by day-labor, with Jim and me supervising. It was so much fun that I was honestly sorry when it was finished.'

'I can imagine!' said Florence.

Well, I am not very well up in Early American, which was the name they had for pretty nearly everything in the place, but for the benefit of those who are not on terms with the Dwans I will try and describe from memory the *objets d'art* they bragged of the most and which brought forth the loudest squeals from Florence.

The living-room walls were brown bare boards without a

picture or scrap of wall-paper. On the floor were two or three 'hooked rugs,' whatever that means, but they needed five or six more of them, or one big carpet, to cover up all the knots in the wood. There was a maple 'low-boy'; a 'dough-trough' table they didn't have space for in the kitchen; a pine 'stretcher' table with sticks connecting the four legs near the bottom so you couldn't put your feet anywhere; a 'Dutch' chest that looked as if it had been ordered from the undertaker by one of Singer's Midgets, but he got well; and some 'Windsor' chairs in which the only position you could get comfortable was to stand up behind them and lean your elbows on their back.

Not one piece that matched another, and not one piece of mahogany anywhere. And the ceiling, between the beams, had apparently been plastered by a workman who was that way, too.

'Some day soon I hope to have a piano,' said Mrs Dwan. 'I can't live much longer without one. But so far I haven't been able to find one that would fit in.'

'Listen,' I said. 'I've got a piano in storage that belonged to my mother. It's a mahogany upright and not so big that it wouldn't fit in this room, especially when you get that "trough" table out. It isn't doing me any good and I'll sell it to you for $250. Mother paid $1,250 for it new.'

'Oh, I couldn't think of taking it!' said Mrs Dwan.

'I'll make it $200 even just because you're a friend of Florence's,' I said.

'Really, I couldn't!' said Mrs. Dwan.

'You wouldn't have to pay for it all at once,' I said.

'Don't you see,' said Florence, 'that a mahogany upright piano would be a perfect horror in here? Mildred wouldn't have it as a gift, let alone buy it. It isn't in the period.'

'She could get it tuned,' I said.

The answer to this was, 'I'll show you the up-stairs now and we can look at the dining-room later on.'

We were led to the guest-chamber. The bed was a maple four-poster, with pineapple posts, and a 'tester' running from pillar to post. You would think a 'tester' might be a man that went around trying out beds, but it's really a kind of frame that holds a canopy over the bed in case it rains and the roof leaks. There was a quilt made by Mrs Dwan's great-grandmother, Mrs Anthony Adams, in 1859, at Lowell, Mass. How is that for a memory?

'This used to be the hay-loft,' said Mrs Dwan.

'You ought to have left some of the hay so the guests could hit it,' I said.

The dressers, chests of drawers, and the chairs were all made of maple. And the same in the Dwans' own room; everything maple.

'If you had maple in one room and mahogany in the other,' I said, 'people wouldn't get confused when you told them that so and so was up in Maple's room.'

Dwan laughed, but the women didn't.

The maid hollered up that dinner was ready.

'The cocktails aren't ready,' said Dwan.

'You will have to go without them,' said Mrs Dwan. 'The soup will be cold.'

This put me in a great mood to admire the 'sawbuck' table and the 'slatback' chairs, which were evidently the *chef-d'œuvre* and the *pièce de résistance* of the *chez Dwan*.

'It came all the way from Pennsylvania,' said Mildred, when Florence's outcries, brought on by her first look at the table, had died down. 'Mother picked it up at a little place near Stroudsburg and sent it to me. It only cost $550, and the chairs were $45 apiece.'

'How reasonable!' exclaimed Florence.

That was before she had sat in one of them. Only one thing was more unreasonable than the chairs, and that was the table itself, consisting of big planks nailed together and laid onto a railroad tie, supported underneath by a whole forest of cross-pieces and beams. The surface was as smooth on top as the trip to Catalina Island and all around the edges, great big divots had been taken out with some blunt instrument, probably a bayonet. There were stains and scorch marks that Florence fairly crowed over, but when I tried to add to the general ensemble by laying a lighted cigarette right down beside my soup-plate, she and both the Dwans yelled murder and made me take it off.

They planted me in an end seat, a location just right for a man who had stretched himself across a railway track and had both legs cut off at the abdomen. Not being that kind of man, I had to sit so far back that very few of my comestibles carried more than half-way to their target.

After dinner I was all ready to go home and get something to eat, but it had been darkening up outdoors for half an hour and

119

now such a storm broke that I knew it was useless trying to persuade Florence to make a start.

'We'll play some bridge,' said Dwan, and to my surprise he produced a card-table that was nowhere near 'in the period.'

At my house there was a big center chandelier that lighted up a bridge game no matter in what part of the room the table was put. But here we had to waste forty minutes moving lamps and wires and stands and when they were all fixed, you could tell a red suit from a black suit, but not a spade from a club. Aside from that and the granite-bottomed 'Windsor' chairs and the fact that we played 'families' for a cent a point and Florence and I won $12 and didn't get paid, it was one of the pleasantest afternoons I ever spent gambling.

The rain stopped at five o'clock and as we splashed through the puddles of Dwan's driveway, I remarked to Florence that I had never known she was such a kidder.

'What do you mean?' she asked me.

'Why, your pretending to admire all that junk,' I said.

'Junk!' said Florence. 'That is one of the most beautifully furnished homes I have ever seen!'

And so far as I can recall, that was her last utterance in my presence for six nights and five days.

At lunch on Saturday I said: 'You know I like the silent drama one evening a week, but not twenty-four hours a day every day. What's the matter with you? If it's laryngitis, you might write me notes.'

'I'll tell you what's the matter!' she burst out. 'I hate this house and everything in it! It's too new! Everything shines! I loathe new things! I want a home like Mildred's, with things in it that I can look at without blushing for shame. I can't invite anyone here. It's too hideous. And I'll never be happy here a single minute as long as I live!'

Well, I don't mind telling that this kind of got under my skin. As if I hadn't intended to give her a pleasant surprise! As if Wolfe Brothers, in business thirty years, didn't know how to furnish a home complete! I was pretty badly hurt, but I choked it down and said, as calmly as I could:

'If you'll be a little patient, I'll try to sell this house and its contents for what I paid for it and them. It oughtn't to be much trouble; there are plenty of people around who know a bargain.

120

But it's too bad you didn't confess your barn complex to me long ago. Only last February, old Ken Garrett had to sell his establishment and the men who bought it turned it into a garage. It was a livery-stable which I could have got for the introduction of a song, or maybe just the vamp. And we wouldn't have had to spend a nickel to make it as nice and comfortable and homey as your friend Mildred's dump.'

Florence was on her way upstairs before I had finished my speech.

I went down to Earl Benham's to see if my new suit was ready. It was and I put it on and left the old one to be cleaned and pressed.

On the street I met Harry Cross.

'Come up to my office,' he said. 'There's something in my desk that may interest you.'

I accepted his invitation and from three different drawers he pulled out three different quart bottles of Early American rye.

Just before six o'clock I dropped in Kane's store and bought myself a pair of shears, a blow torch and an ax. I started home, but stopped among the trees inside my front gate and cut big holes in my coat and trousers. Alongside the path to the house was a sizable mud puddle. I waded in it. And I bathed my gray felt hat.

Florence was sitting on the floor of the living-room, reading. She seemed a little upset by my appearance.

'Good heavens! What's happened?'

'Nothing much,' said I. 'I just didn't want to look too new.'

'What are those things you're carrying?'

'Just a pair of shears, a blow torch and an ax. I'm going to try and antique this place and think I'll begin on the dining-room table.'

Florence went into her scream, dashed upstairs and locked herself in. I went about my work and had the dinner-table looking pretty Early when the maid smelled fire and rushed in. She rushed out again and came back with a pitcher of water. But using my vest as a snuffer, I had had the flames under control all the while and there was nothing for her to do.

'I'll just nick it up a little with this ax,' I told her, 'and by the time I'm through, dinner ought to be ready.'

'It will never be ready as far as I'm concerned,' she said. 'I'm leaving just as soon as I can pack.'

And Florence had the same idea—vindicating the old adage about great minds.

I heard the front door slam and the back door slam, and I felt kind of tired and sleepy, so I knocked off work and went up to bed.

That's my side of the story, Eddie, and it's true so help me my bootlegger. Which reminds me that the man who sold Harry the rye makes this town once a week, or did when this was written. He's at the Belden every Tuesday from nine to six and his name is Mike Farrell.

Nora

'Mr Hazlett, shake hands with Jerry Morris and Frank Moon. I guess you've heard of the both of them.'

The speaker was Louis Brock, producer of musical shows, who had cleared over half a million dollars in two years through the popularity of 'Jersey Jane,' tunes by Morris and lyrics by Moon.

They were in Brock's inner office, the walls of which were adorned with autographed pictures of six or seven of the more celebrated musical comedy stars and a too-perfect likeness of Brock's wife, whom he had evidently married in a dense fog.

'Mr Hazlett,' continued Brock, 'has got a book which he wrote as a straight play, but it struck me right off that it was great material for a musical, especially with you two fellas to do the numbers. It's a brand-new idear, entirely opposite from most of these here musical comedy books that's all the same thing and the public must be getting sick of them by this time. Don't you think so, Jerry?'

'I certainly do,' the tunesmith replied. 'Give us a good novelty story, and with what I and Frank can throw in there to jazz it up, we'll run till the theatre falls down.'

'Well, Mr Hazlett,' said Brock, 'suppose you read us the book and we'll see what the boys thinks of it.'

Hazlett was quite nervous in spite of Brock's approval of his work and the fact that friends to whom he had shown it had given it high praise and congratulated him on his good fortune in getting a chance to collaborate with Morris and Moon—Morris, who had set a new style in melodies and rhythms and whose tunes made up sixty percent of all dance programs, and Moon, the ideal lyricist who could fit Jerry's fast triplets with such cute-sounding three-syllable rhymes that no one ever went to the considerable trouble of trying to find out what they meant.

'I've tried to stay away from the stereotyped Cinderella theme,' said Hazlett. 'In my story, the girl starts out just moderately well off and winds up poor. She sacrifices everything for love and the end finds her alone with her lover, impoverished but happy. She——'

'Let's hear the book,' said the producer.

Hazlett, with trembling fingers, opened to the first page of his script.

'Well,' he began, 'the title is "Nora" and the first scene——'

'Excuse me a minute,' Morris interrupted. 'I promised a fella that I'd come over and look at a big second-hand Trinidad Twelve. Only eight grand and a bargain if there ever was one, hey, Frank?'

'I'll say it's a bargain,' Moon agreed.

'The fella is going to hold it for me till half-past three and its nearly three o'clock now. So if you don't mind, Mr Hazlett, I wish that instead of reading the book clear through, you'd kind of give us a kind of a synopsis and it will save time and we can tell just as good, hey, Frank?'

'Just as good,' said Moon.

'All right, Mr Hazlett,' Brock put in. 'Suppose you tell the story in your own way, with just the main idear and the situations.'

'Well,' said Hazlett, 'of course, as a straight play, I wrote it in three acts, but when Mr Brock suggested that I make a musical show out of it, I cut it to two. To start with, the old man, the girl's uncle, is an Irishman who came to this country when he was about twenty years old. He worked hard and he was thrifty and finally he got into the building business for himself. He's pretty well-to-do, but he's avaricious and not satisfied with the three or four hundred thousand he's saved up. He meets another Irish immigrant about his own age, a politician who has a lot to say about the letting of big city building contracts. This man, Collins, had a handsome young son, John, twenty-three or twenty-four.

'The old man, the girl's uncle—their name is Crowley—he tries his hardest to get in strong with old Collins so Collins will land him some of the city contracts, but Collins, though he's very friendly all the while, he doesn't do Crowley a bit of good in a business way.

'Well, Crowley gives a party at his house for a crowd of his Irish friends in New York, young people and people his own age, and during the party young John Collins sees a picture of Crowley's beautiful niece, Nora. She's still in Ireland and has never been to this country. Young Collins asks Crowley who it is and he tells him and young Collins says she is the only girl he will ever marry.

'Crowley then figures to himself that if he can connect up with the Collinses by having his niece marry young John, he can land just about all the good contracts there are. So he cables for Nora to come over and pay him a visit. She comes and things happen just as Crowley planned—John and Nora fall in love.

'Now there's a big dinner and dance in honor of the Mayor and one of the guests is Dick Percival, a transplanted Englishman who has made fifty million dollars in the sugar business. He also falls in love with Nora and confesses it to her uncle. Old Crowley has always hated Englishmen, but his avarice is so strong that he decides Nora must get rid of John and marry Dick. Nora refuses to do this, saying John is "her man" and that she will marry him or nobody.

'Crowley forbids her to see John, but she meets him whenever she can get out. The uncle and niece had a long, stubborn battle of wills, neither yielding an inch. Finally John's father, old Collins, is caught red-handed in a big bribery scandal and sent to the penitentiary. It is also found out that he has gambled away all his money and John is left without a dime.

'Crowley, of course, thinks this settles the argument, that Nora won't have anything more to do with a man whose father is a crook and broke besides, and he gets up a party to announce the engagement between her and Dick. Nora doesn't interfere at all, but insists that young John Collins be invited. When the announcement is made, Nora says her uncle has got the name of her fiancé wrong; she has been engaged to John Collins since the first day she came to the United States, and if he will still have her, she is his. Then she and John walk out alone into the world, leaving Dick disappointed and Crowley in a good old-fashioned Irish rage.'

'Well, boys,' said Brock, after a pause, 'What do you think of it?'

The 'boys' were silent.

'You see,' said Brock, 'for natural ensembles, you got the first party at What's-his-name's, the scene on the pier when the gal lands from Ireland, the Mayor's party at some hotel maybe, and another party at What's-his-name's, only this time it's outdoors at

125

his country place. You can have the boy sing a love-song to the picture before he ever sees the gal; you can make that the melody you want to carry clear through. You can have love duets between she and the boy and she and the Englishman. You can write a song like "East Side, West Side" for the Mayor's party.

'You can write a corking good number for the pier scene, where the people of all nationalities are meeting their relatives and friends. And you can run wild with all the good Irish tunes in the world.'

'Where's your comic?' inquired Morris.

'Mr Hazlett forgot to mention the comic,' Brock said. 'He's an old Irishman, a pal of What's-his-name's, a kind of a Jiggs.'

'People don't want an Irish comic these days,' said Morris. 'Can't you make him a Wop or a Heeb?'

'I'd have to rewrite the part,' said Hazlett.

'No you wouldn't,' said Morris. 'Give him the same lines with a different twist to them.'

'It really would be better,' Brock put in, 'if you could change him to a Heeb or even a Dutchman. I've got to have a spot for Joe Stein and he'd be a terrible flop as a Turkey.'

'And listen,' said Morris. 'What are you going to do with Enriqueta?'

'Gosh! I'd forgot her entirely!' said Brock. 'Of course we'll have to make room for her.'

'Who is she?' Hazlett inquired.

'The best gal in Spain,' said Brock. 'I brought her over here and I'm paying her two thousand dollars every week, with nothing for her to do. You'll have to write in a part for her.'

'Write in a part!' exclaimed Morris. 'She'll play the lead or she won't play.'

'But how is a Spanish girl going to play Nora Crowley?' asked Hazlett.

'Why does your dame have to be Nora Crowley?' Morris retorted. 'Why does she have to be Irish at all?'

'Because her uncle is Irish.'

'Make him a Spaniard, too.'

'Yes, and listen,' said Moon. 'While you're making the gal and her uncle Spaniards, make your boy a Wop. If you do that, I and Jerry have got a number that'll put your troupe over with a bang! Play it for them, Jerry.'

126

Morris went to the piano and played some introductory chords.

'This is a great break of luck,' said Moon, 'to have a number already written that fits right into the picture. Of course, I'll polish the lyric up a little more and I want to explain that the boy sings part of the lines, the gal the rest. But here's about how it is. Let's go, Jerry!'

Morris repeated his introduction and Moon began to sing:

'Somewhere in the old world
You and I belong.
It will be a gold world,
Full of light and song.
Why not let's divide our time
Between your native land and mine?
Move from Italy to Spain,
Then back to Italy again?

'In sunny Italy,
My Spanish queen,
You'll fit so prettily
In that glorious scene.
You will sing me 'La Paloma';
I will sing you 'Cara Roma';
We will build a little home, a
Bungalow serene.
Then in the Pyrenees,
Somewhere in Spain,
We'll rest our weary knees
Down in Lovers' Lane,
And when the breakers roll a-
Cross the azure sea,
Espanola, Gorgonzola;
Spain and Italy.'

'A wow!' cried Brock. 'Congratulations, Jerry! You, too, Frank! What do you think of that one, Mr Hazlett?'

'Very nice,' said Hazlett. 'The tune sounds like "Sole Mio" and "La Paloma." '

'It sounds like them both and it's better than either,' said the composer.

'That one number makes our troupe, Jerry,' said Brock. 'You don't need anything else.'

'But we've got something else, hey, Frank?'

'You mean "Montgomery"?' said Moon.

'Yeh.'

'Let's hear it,' requested Brock.

'It'll take a dinge comic to sing it.'

'Well, Joe Stein can do a dinge.'

'I'll say he can! I like him best in blackface. And he's just the boy to put over a number like this.'

Morris played another introduction, strains that Hazlett was sure he had heard a hundred times before, and Moon was off again:

'I want to go to Alabam'.
That's where my lovin' sweetheart am,
And won't she shout and dance for joy
To see once more her lovin' boy!
I've got enough saved up, I guess,
To buy her shoes and a bran'-new dress.
She's black as coal, and yet I think
When I walk in, she'll be tickled pink.

'Take me to Montgomery
Where it's always summery.
New York's just a mummery.
Give me life that's real.
New York fields are rotten fields.
Give me those forgotten fields;
I mean those there cotton fields,
Selma and Mobile
I done been away so long;
Never thought I'd stay so long.
Train, you'd better race along
To my honey lamb.
Train, you make it snappy till
('Cause I won't be happy till)
I am in the capital,
Montgomery, Alabam'.'

'Another knock-out!' said Brock enthusiastically. 'Boys, either one of those numbers are better than anything in "Jersey Jane." Either one of them will put our troupe over. And the two of them together in one show! Well, it's in!'

Hazlett mustered all his courage.

'They're a couple of mighty good songs,' he said. 'But I don't exactly see how they'll fit.'

'Mr Hazlett,' said Jerry Morris. 'I understand this is your first experience with a musical comedy. I've had five successes in four years and could have had five more if I wanted to work that hard. I know the game backwards and I hope you won't take offense if I tell you a little something about it.'

'I'm always glad to learn,' said Hazlett.

'Well, then,' said Morris, 'you've got a great book there, with a good novelty idear, but it won't go without a few changes, changes that you can make in a half-hour and not detract anything from the novelty. In fact, they will add to it. While you were telling your story, I was thinking of it from the practical angle, the angle of show business, and I believe I can put my finger right on the spots that have got to be fixed.

'In the first place, as Louie has told you, he's got a contract with Enriqueta and she won't play any secondary parts. That means your heroine must be Spanish. Well, why not make her uncle her father and have him a Spaniard, running a Spanish restaurant somewhere down-town? It's a small restaurant and he just gets by. He has to use her as cashier and she sits in the window where the people going past can see her.

'One day the boy, who is really an Italian count—we'll call him Count Pizzola—he is riding alone in a taxi and he happens to look in the window and see the gal. He falls in love with her at first sight, orders the driver to stop and gets out and goes in the restaurant. He sits down and has his lunch, and while he is eating we can put in a novelty dance number with the boys and gals from the offices that are also lunching in this place.

'When the number is over, I'd have a comedy scene between Stein, who plays a dinge waiter, and, say, a German customer who isn't satisfied with the food or the check or something. Louie, who would you suggest for that part?'

'How about Charlie Williams?' said Brock.

'Great!' said Morris. 'Well, they have this argument and the dinge throws the waiter out. The scrap amuses Pizzola and the gal, too, and they both laugh and that brings them together. He doesn't tell her he is a count, but she likes him pretty near as well as he likes her. They gab a while and then go into the Spanish number I just played for you.

'Now, in your story, you've got a boat scene where the gal is landing from Ireland. You'd better forget that scene. There was a boat scene in "Hit the Deck," and a lot of other troupes. We don't want anything that isn't our own. But Pizzola is anxious to take the gal out somewhere and let's see—Frank, where can he take her?'

'Why not a yacht?' suggested Moon.

'Great! He invites her out on a yacht, but he's got to pretend it isn't his own yacht. He borrowed it from a friend. She refuses at first, saying she hasn't anything to wear. She's poor, see? So he tells her his sister has got some sport clothes that will fit her. He gets the clothes for her and then we have a scene in her room where she is putting them on with a bunch of girl friends helping her. We'll write a number for that.

'Now the clothes he gave her are really his sister's clothes and the sister has carelessly left a beautiful brooch pinned in them. We go to the yacht and the Spanish dame knocks everybody dead. They put on an amateur show. That will give Enriqueta a chance for a couple more numbers. She and Pizzola are getting more and more stuck on each other and they repeat the Spanish song on the yacht, in the moonlight.

'There's a Frenchman along on the party who is greatly attracted by Enriqueta's looks. The Frenchman hates Pizzola. He has found out in some way that Enriqueta is wearing Pizzola's sister's clothes and he notices the diamond brooch. He figures that if he can steal it off of her, why, suspicion will be cast on the gal herself on account of her being poor, and Pizzola, thinking her a thief, won't have anything more to do with her and he, the Frenchman, can have her. So, during a dance, he manages to steal the brooch and he puts it in his pocket.

'Of course Pizzola's sister is also on the yachting party. All of a sudden she misses her brooch. She recalls having left it in the clothes she lent to Enriqueta. She goes to Enriqueta and asks her for it and the poor Spanish dame can't find it. Then Pizzola's sister calls her a thief and Pizzola himself can't help thinking she is one.

'They demand that she be searched, but rather than submit to that indignity, she bribes a sailor to take her off the yacht in a small launch and the last we see of her she's climbing overboard to get into the launch while the rest of the party are all abusing her. That's your first act curtain.

'I'd open the second act with a paddock scene at the Saratoga race-track. We'll write a jockey number and have about eight boys and maybe twenty-four gals in jockey suits. Enriqueta's father has gone broke in the restaurant business and he's up here looking for a job as assistant trainer or something. He used to train horses for the bull-fights in Spain.

'The gal is along with him and they run into the Frenchman that stole the brooch. The Frenchman tries to make love to the gal, but she won't have anything to do with him. While they are talking, who should come up but Pizzola! He is willing to make up with Enriqueta even though he still thinks her a thief. She won't meet his advances.

'He asks the Frenchman for a light. The Frenchman has a patent lighter and in pulling it out of his pocket, he pulls the brooch out, too. Then Pizzola realizes what an injustice he has done the gal and he pretty near goes down on his knees to her, but she has been badly hurt and won't forgive him yet.

'Now we have a scene in the café in the club-house and Stein is one of the waiters there. He sings the Montgomery number with a chorus of waiters and lunchers and at the end of the number he and the Spanish gal are alone on the stage.

'She asks him if he is really going to Montgomery and he says yes, and she says she and her father will go with him. She is anxious to go some place where there is no danger of running into the Frenchman or Pizzola.

'The third scene in the second act ought to be a plantation in Alabama. Stein is working there and the negroes are having a celebration or revival of some kind. Louie, you can get a male quartet to sing us some spirituals.

'Enriqueta's father has landed a job as cook at the plantation and she is helping with the housework. Pizzola and his sister follow her to Montgomery and come out to see her at the plantation.

'They are about to go up on the porch and inquire for her when they hear her singing the Spanish number. This proves to Pizzola that she still loves him and he finally gets his sister to plead with her for forgiveness. She forgives him. He tells her who he really is and how much dough he's got. And that pretty near washes us up.'

'But how about our Japanese number?' said Moon.

'That's right,' Morris said. 'We'll have to send them to Japan before we end it. I've got a cherry-blossom number that must have the right setting. But that's easy to fix. You make these few changes I've suggested, Mr Hazlett, and I feel that we've got a hit.

'And I want to say that your book is a whole lot better than most of the books they hand us. About the fella falling in love with the gal's picture—that's a novelty idear.'

Hazlett said good-by to his producer and collaborators, went home by taxi and called up his bootlegger.

'Harry,' he said, 'what kind of whiskey have you got?'

'Well, Mr Hazlett, I can sell you some good Scotch, but I ain't so sure of the rye. In fact, I'm kind of scared of it.'

'How soon can you bring me a case?'

'Right off quick. It's the Scotch you want, ain't it?'

'No,' said Hazlett. 'I want the rye.'

The Facts

I

The engagement was broken off before it was announced. So only a thousand or so of the intimate friends and relatives of the parties knew anything about it. What they knew was that there had been an engagement and that there was one no longer. The cause of the breach they merely guessed, and most of the guesses were, in most particulars, wrong.

Each intimate and relative had a fragment of the truth. It remained for me to piece the fragments together. It was a difficult job, but I did it. Part of my evidence is hearsay; the major portion is fully corroborated. And not one of my witnesses had anything to gain through perjury.

So I am positive that I have at my tongue's end the facts, and I believe that in justice to everybody concerned I should make them public.

Ellen McDonald had lived on the North Side of Chicago for twenty-one years. Billy Bowen had been a South-Sider for seven years longer. But neither knew of the other's existence until they met in New York, the night before the Army-Navy game.

Billy, sitting with a business acquaintance at a neighboring table in Tonio's, was spotted by a male member of Ellen's party, a Chicagoan, too. He was urged to come on over. He did, and was introduced. The business acquaintance was also urged, came, was introduced and forgotten; forgotten, that is, by every one but the waiter, who observed that he danced not nor told stories, and figured that his function must be to pay. The business acquaintance had been Billy's guest. Now he became host, and without seeking the office.

It was not that Billy and Miss McDonald's male friends were niggards. But unfortunately for the b.a., the checks always happened to arrive when everybody else was dancing or so hysterical over Billy's repartee as to be potentially insolvent.

133

Billy was somewhere between his fourteenth and twenty-first highball; in other words, at his best, from the audience's standpoint. His dialogue was simply screaming and his dancing just heavenly. He was Frank Tinney doubling as Vernon Castle. On the floor he tried and accomplished twinkles that would have spelled catastrophe if attempted under the fourteen mark, or over the twenty-one. And he said the cutest things—one right after the other.

II

You can be charmed by a man's dancing, but you can't fall in love with his funniness. If you're going to fall in love with him at all, you'll do it when you catch him in a serious mood.

Miss McDonald caught Billy Bowen in one at the game next day. Entirely by accident or a decree of fate, her party and his sat in adjoining boxes. Not by accident, Miss McDonald sat in the chair that was nearest Billy's. She sat there first to be amused; she stayed to be conquered.

Here was a different Billy from the Billy of Tonio's. Here was a Billy who trained his gun on your heart and let your risibles alone. Here was a dreamy Billy, a Billy of romance.

How calm he remained through the excitement! How indifferent to the thrills of the game! There was depth to him. He was a man. Her escort and the others round her were children, screaming with delight at the puerile deeds of pseudo heroes. Football was a great sport, but a sport. It wasn't Life. Would the world be better or worse for that nine-yard gain that Elephant or Oliphant, or whatever his name was, had just made? She knew it wouldn't. Billy knew, too, for Billy was deep. He was thinking man's thoughts. She could tell by his silence, by his inattention to the scene before him. She scarcely could believe that here was the same person who, last night, had kept his own, yes, and the neighboring tables, roaring with laughter. What a complex character his!

In sooth, Mr Bowen was thinking man's thoughts. He was thinking that if this pretty Miss McDowell, or Donnelly, were elsewhere, he could go to sleep. And that if he could remember which team he had bet on and could tell which team was which, he would have a better idea of whether he was likely to win or lose.

When, after the game, they parted, Billy rallied to the extent of asking permission to call. Ellen, it seemed, would be very glad to have him, but she couldn't tell exactly when she would have to be back in Chicago; she still had three more places to visit in the East. Could she possibly let him know when she did get back? Yes, she could and would; if he really wanted her to, she would drop him a note. He certainly wanted her to.

This, thought Billy, was the best possible arrangement. Her note would tell him her name and address, and save him the trouble of 'phoning to all the McConnells, McDowells, and Donnellys on the North Side. He did want to see her again; she was pretty, and, judging from last night, full of pep. And she had fallen for him; he knew it from that look.

He watched her until she was lost in the crowd. Then he hunted round for his pals and the car that had brought them up. At length he gave up the search and wearily climbed the elevated stairs. His hotel was on Broadway, near Forty-fourth. He left the train at Forty-second, the third time it stopped there.

'I guess you've rode far enough,' said the guard. 'Fifteen cents' worth for a nickel. I guess we ought to have a Pullman on these here trains.'

'I guess,' said Billy, 'I guess——'

But the repartee well was dry. He stumbled down-stairs and hurried towards Broadway to replenish it.

III

Ellen McDonald's three more places to visit in the East must have been deadly dull. Anyway, on the sixth of December, scarcely more than a week after his parting with her in New York, Billy Bowen received the promised note. It informed him merely that her name was Ellen McDonald, that she lived at so-and-so Walton Place, and that she was back in Chicago.

That day, if you'll remember, was Monday. Miss McDonald's parents had tickets for the opera. But Ellen was honestly just worn out, and would they be mad at her if she stayed home and went to bed? They wouldn't. They would take Aunt Mary in her place.

On Tuesday morning, Paul Potter called up and wanted to know if she would go with him that night to 'The Follies.' She was horribly sorry, but she'd made an engagement. The engagement,

135

evidently, was to study, and the subject was harmony, with Berlin, Kern, and Van Alstyne as instructors. She sat on the piano-bench from half-past seven till quarter after nine, and then went to her room vowing that she would accept any and all invitations for the following evening.

Fortunately, no invitations arrived, for at a quarter of nine Wednesday night, Mr Bowen did. And in a brand-new mood. He was a bit shy and listened more than he talked. But when he talked, he talked well, though the sparkling wit of the night at Tonio's was lacking. Lacking, too, was the preoccupied air of the day at the football game. There was no problem to keep his mind busy, but even if the Army and Navy had been playing football in this very room, he could have told at a glance which was which. Vision and brain were perfectly clear. And he had been getting his old eight hours, and, like the railroad hen, sometimes nine and sometimes ten, every night since his arrival home from Gotham, N.Y. Mr Bowen was on the wagon.

They talked of the East, of Tonio's, of the game (this was where Billy did most of his listening), of the war, of theaters, of books, of college, of automobiles, of the market. They talked, too, of their immediate families. Billy's, consisting of one married sister in South Bend, was soon exhausted. He had two cousins here in town whom he saw frequently, two cousins and their wives, but they were people who simply couldn't stay home nights. As for himself, he preferred his rooms and a good book to the so-called gay life. Ellen should think that a man who danced so well would want to be doing it all the time. It was nice of her to say that he danced well, but really he didn't, you know. Oh, yes, he did. She guessed she could tell. Well, anyway, the giddy whirl made no appeal to him, unless, of course, he was in particularly charming company. His avowed love for home and quiet surprised Ellen a little. It surprised Mr. Bowen a great deal. Only last night, he remembered, he had been driven almost desperate by that quiet of which he was now so fond; he had been on the point of busting loose, but had checked himself in time. He had played Canfield till ten, though the book-shelves were groaning with their load.

Ellen's family kept them busy for an hour and a half. It was a dear family and she wished he could meet it. Mother and father were out playing bridge somewhere to-night. Aunt Mary had gone to bed. Aunts Louise and Harriet lived in the next block.

Sisters Edith and Wilma would be home from Northampton for the holidays about the twentieth. Brother Bob and his wife had built the cutest house; in Evanston. Her younger brother, Walter, was a case! He was away to-night, had gone out right after dinner. He'd better be in before mother and father came. He had a new love-affair every week, and sixteen years old last August. Mother and father really didn't care how many girls he was interested in, so long as they kept him too busy to run round with those crazy schoolmates of his. The latter were older than he; just the age when it seems smart to drink beer and play cards for money. Father said if he ever found out that Walter was doing those things, he'd take him out of school and lock him up somewhere.

Aunts Louise and Mary and Harriet did a lot of settlement work. They met all sorts of queer people, people you'd never believe existed. The three aunts were unmarried.

Brother Bob's wife was dear, but absolutely without a sense of humor. Bob was full of fun, but they got along just beautifully together. You never saw a couple so much in love.

Edith was on the basket-ball team at college and terribly popular. Wilma was horribly clever and everybody said she'd make Phi Beta Kappa.

Ellen, so she averred, had been just nothing in school; not bright; not athletic, and, of course, not popular.

'Oh, of course not,' said Billy, smiling.

'Honestly,' fibbed Ellen.

'You never could make me believe it,' said Billy.

Whereat Ellen blushed, and Billy's unbelief strengthened.

At this crisis, the Case burst into the room with his hat on. He removed it at sight of the caller and awkwardly advanced to be introduced.

'I'm going to bed,' he announced, after the formality.

'I hoped,' said Ellen, 'you'd tell us about the latest. Who is it now? Beth?'

'Beth nothing!' scoffed the Case. 'We split up the day of the Keewatin game.'

'What was the matter?' asked his sister.

'I'm going to bed,' said the Case. 'It's pretty near midnight.'

'By George, it is!' exclaimed Billy. 'I didn't dream it was that late!'

137

'No,' said Walter. 'That's what I tell dad—the clock goes along some when you're having a good time.'

Billy and Ellen looked shyly at each other, and then laughed; laughed harder, it seemed to Walter, than the joke warranted. In fact, he hadn't thought of it as a joke. If it was that good, he'd spring it on Kathryn to-morrow night. It would just about clinch her.

The Case, carrying out his repeated threat, went to bed and dreamed of Kathryn. Fifteen minutes later Ellen retired to dream of Billy. And an hour later than that, Billy was dreaming of Ellen, who had become suddenly popular with him, even if she hadn't been so at Northampton, which he didn't believe.

IV

They saw 'The Follies' Friday night. A criticism of the show by either would have been the greatest folly of all. It is doubtful that they could have told what theater they'd been to ten minutes after they'd left it. From wherever it was, they walked to a dancing place and danced. Ellen was so far gone that she failed to note the change in Billy's trotting. Foxes would have blushed for shame at its awkwardness and lack of variety. If Billy was a splendid dancer, he certainly did not prove it this night. All he knew or cared to know was that he was with the girl he wanted. And she knew only that she was with Billy, and happy.

On the drive home, the usual superfluous words were spoken. They were repeated inside the storm-door at Ellen's father's house, while the taxi driver, waiting, wondered audibly why them suckers of explorers beat it to the Pole to freeze when the North Side was so damn handy.

Ellen's father was out of town. So in the morning she broke the news to mother and Aunt Mary, and then sat down and wrote it to Edith and Wilma. Next she called up Bob's wife in Evanston, and after that she hurried to the next block and sprang it on Aunts Louise and Harriet. It was decided that Walter had better not be told. He didn't know how to keep a secret. Walter, therefore, was in ignorance till he got home from school. The only person he confided in the same evening was Kathryn, who was the only person he saw.

Bob and his wife and Aunts Louise and Harriet came to Sunday dinner, but were chased home early in the afternoon. Mr McDonald was back and Billy was coming to talk to him. It would embarrass Billy to death to find such a crowd in the house. They'd all meet him soon, never fear, and when they met him, they'd be crazy about him. Bob and Aunt Mary and mother would like him because he was so bright and said such screaming things, and the rest would like him because he was so well-read and sensible, and so horribly good-looking.

Billy, I said, was coming to talk to Mr McDonald. When he came, he did very little of the talking. He stated the purpose of his visit, told what business he was in and affirmed his ability to support a wife. Then he assumed the rôle of audience while Ellen's father delivered an hour's lecture. The speaker did not express his opinion of Tyrus Cobb or the Kaiser, but they were the only subjects he overlooked. Sobriety and industry were words frequently used.

'I don't care,' he prevaricated, in conclusion, 'how much money a man is making if he is sober and industrious. You attended college, and I presume you did all the fool things college boys do. Some men recover from their college education, others don't. I hope you're one of the former.'

The Sunday-night supper, just cold scraps you might say, was partaken of by the happy but embarrassed pair, the trying-to-look happy but unembarrassed parents, and Aunt Mary. Walter, the Case, was out. He had stayed home the previous evening.

'He'll be here to-morrow night and the rest of the week, or I'll know the reason why,' said Mr McDonald.

'He won't, and I'll tell you the reason why,' said Ellen.

'He's a real boy, Sam,' put in the real boy's mother. 'You can't expect him to stay home every minute.'

'I can't expect anything of him,' said the father. 'You and the girls and Mary here have let him have his own way so long that he's past managing. When I was his age, I was in my bed at nine o' clock.'

'Morning or night?' asked Ellen.

Her father scowled. It was evident he could not take a joke, not even a good one.

After the cold scraps had been ruined, Mr McDonald drew Billy into the smoking-room and offered him a cigar. The prospective son-in-law was about to refuse and express a preference

139

for cigarettes when something told him not to. A moment later he was deeply grateful to the something.

'I smoke three cigars a day,' said the oracle, 'one after each meal. That amount of smoking will hurt nobody. More than that is too much. I used to smoke to excess, four or five cigars per day, and maybe a pipe or two. I found it was affecting my health, and I cut down. Thank heaven, no one in my family ever got the cigarette habit; disease, rather. How any sane, clean-minded man can start on those things is beyond me.'

'Me, too,' agreed Billy, taking the proffered cigar with one hand and making sure with the other that his silver pill-case was as deep down in his pockets as it would go.

'Cigarettes, gambling, and drinking go hand in hand,' continued the man of the house. 'I couldn't trust a cigarette fiend with a nickel.'

'There are only two or three kinds he could get for that,' said Billy.

'What say?' demanded Mr McDonald, but before Billy was obliged to wriggle out of it, Aunt Mary came in and reminded her brother-in-law that it was nearly church time.

Mr McDonald and Aunt Mary went to church. Mrs McDonald, pleading weariness, stayed home with 'the children.' She wanted a chance to get acquainted with this pleasant-faced boy who was going to rob her of one of her five dearest treasures.

The three were no sooner settled in front of the fireplace than Ellen adroitly brought up the subject of auction bridge, knowing that it would relieve Billy of the conversational burden.

'Mother is really quite a shark, aren't you, mother?' she said.

'I don't fancy being called a fish,' said the mother.

'She's written two books on it, and she and father have won so many prizes that they may have to lease a warehouse. If they'd only play for money, just think how rich we'd all be!'

'The game is fascinating enough without adding to it the excitements and evils of gambling,' said Mrs McDonald.

'It is a fascinating game,' agreed Billy.

'It is,' said Mrs McDonald, and away she went.

Before father and Aunt Mary got home from church, Mr Bowen was a strong disciple of conservativeness in bidding and thoroughly convinced that all the rules that had been taught were dead wrong. He saw the shark's points so quickly and agreed so

140

whole-heartedly with her arguments that he impressed her as one of the most intelligent young men she had ever talked to. It was too bad it was Sunday night, but some evening soon he must come over for a game.

'I'd like awfully well to read your books,' said Billy.

'The first one's usefulness died with the changes in the rules,' replied Mrs McDonald. 'But I think I have one of the new ones in the house, and I'll be glad to have you take it.'

'I don't like to have you give me your only copy.'

'Oh, I believe we have two.'

She knew perfectly well she had two dozen.

Aunt Mary announced that Walter had been seen in church with Kathryn. He had made it his business to be seen. He and the lady had come early and had manœuvred into the third row from the back, on the aisle leading to the McDonald family pew. He had nudged his aunt as she passed on the way to her seat, and she had turned and spoken to him. She could not know that he and Kathryn had 'ducked' before the end of the processional.

After reporting favorably on the Case, Aunt Mary launched into a description of the service. About seventy had turned out. The music had been good, but not quite as good as in the morning. Mr Pratt had sung 'Fear Ye Not, O Israel!' for the offertory. Dr Gish was still sick and a lay reader had served. She had heard from Allie French that Dr Gish expected to be out by the middle of the week and certainly would be able to preach next Sunday morning. The church had been cold at first, but very comfortable finally.

Ellen rose and said she and Billy would go out in the kitchen and make some fudge.

'I was afraid Aunt Mary would bore you to death,' she told Billy, when they had kissed for the first time since five o'clock. 'She just lives for the church and can talk on no other subject.'

'I wouldn't hold that against her,' said Billy charitably.

The fudge was a failure, as it was bound to be. But the Case, who came in just as it was being passed round, was the only one rude enough to say so.

'Is this a new stunt?' he inquired, when he had tested it.

'Is what a new stunt?' asked Ellen.

'Using cheese instead of chocolate.'

'That will do, Walter,' said his father. 'You can go to bed.'

Walter got up and started for the hall. At the threshold he stopped.

'I don't suppose there'll be any of that fudge left,' he said. 'But if there should be, you'd better put it in the mouse trap.'

Billy called a taxi and departed soon after Walter's exit. When he got out at his South Side abode, the floor of the tonneau was littered with recent cigarettes.

And that night he dreamed that he was president of the anti-cigarette league; that Dr Gish was vice-president, and that the motto of the organization was 'No trump.'

Billy Bowen's business took him out of town the second week in December, and it was not until the twentieth that he returned. He had been East and had ridden home from Buffalo on the same train with Wilma and Edith McDonald. But he didn't know it and neither did they. They could not be expected to recognize him from Ellen's description—that he was horribly good-looking. The dining-car conductor was all of that.

Ellen had further written them that he (not the dining-car conductor) was a man of many moods; that sometimes he was just nice and deep, and sometimes he was screamingly funny, and sometimes so serious and silent that she was almost afraid of him.

They were wild to see him and the journey through Ohio and Indiana would not have been half so long in his company. Edith, the athletic, would have revelled in his wit. Wilma would gleefully have fathomed his depths. They would both have been proud to flaunt his looks before the hundreds of their kind aboard the train. Their loss was greater than Billy's, for he, smoking cigarettes as fast as he could light them and playing bridge that would have brought tears of compassion to the shark's eyes, enjoyed the trip, every minute of it.

Ellen and her father were at the station to meet the girls. His arrival on this train had not been heralded, and it added greatly to the hysterics of the occasion.

Wilma and Edith upbraided him for not knowing by instinct who they were. He accused them of recognizing him and purposely avoiding him. Much more of it was pulled in the same light vein, pro and con.

He was permitted at length to depart for his office. On the way he congratulated himself on the improbability of his ever being obliged to play basket-ball versus Edith. She must be a whizz in condition. Chances were she'd train down to a hundred and ninety-five before the big games. The other one, Wilma, was a splinter if he ever saw one. You had to keep your eyes peeled or you'd miss her entirely. But suppose you did miss her; what then! If she won her Phi Beta Kappa pin, he thought, it would make her a dandy belt.

These two, he thought, were a misdeal. They should be re-shuffled and cut nearer the middle of the deck. Lots of other funny things he thought about these two.

Just before he had left Chicago on this trip, his stenographer had quit him to marry an elevator-starter named Felix Bond. He had 'phoned one of his cousins and asked him to be on the lookout for a live stenographer who wasn't likely to take the eye of an elevator-starter. The cousin had had one in mind.

Here was her card on Billy's desk when he reached the office. It was not a business-card visiting-card, at $3 per hundred. 'Miss Violet Moore,' the engraved part said. Above was written: 'Mr Bowen: Call me up any night after seven. Calumet 2678.'

Billy stowed the card in his pocket and plunged into a pile of uninteresting letters.

On the night of the twenty-second there was a family dinner at McDonald's, and Billy was in on it. At the function he met the rest of them—Bob and his wife, and Aunt Harriet and Aunt Louise.

Bob and his wife, despite the former's alleged sense of humor, spooned every time they were contiguous. That they were in love with each other, as Ellen had said, was easy to see. The wherefore was more of a puzzle.

Bob's hirsute adornment having been disturbed by his spouse's digits during one of the orgies, he went up-stairs ten minutes before dinner time to effect repairs. Mrs Bob was left alone on the davenport. In performance of his social duties, Billy went over and sat down beside her. She was not, like Miss Muffet, fright-ened away, but terror or some other fiend rendered her tempor-arily dumb. The game Mr Bowen was making his fifth attempt to pry open a conversation when Bob came back.

To the impartial observer the scene on the davenport appeared heartless enough. There was a generous neutral zone between Billy and Flo, that being an abbreviation of Mrs Bob's given name, which, as a few may suspect, was Florence. Billy was working hard and his face was flushed with the effort. The flush may have aroused Bob's suspicions. At any rate, he strode across the room, scowling almost audibly, shot a glance at Billy that would have made the Kaiser wince, halted magnificently in front of his wife, and commanded her to accompany him to the hall.

Billy's flush became ace high. He was about to get up and break a chair when a look from Ellen stopped him. She was at his side before the pair of Bobs had skidded out of the room.

'Please don't mind,' she begged. 'He's crazy. I forgot to tell you that he's insanely jealous.'

'Did I understand you to say he had a sense of humor?'

'It doesn't work where Flo's concerned. If he sees her talking to a man he goes wild.'

'With astonishment, probably,' said Billy.

'You're a nice boy,' said Ellen irrelevantly.

Dinner was announced and Mr Bowen was glad to observe that Flo's terrestrial body was still intact. He was glad, too, to note that Bob was no longer frothing. He learned for the first time that the Case and Kathryn were of the party. Mrs McDonald had wanted to make sure of Walter's presence; hence the presence of his crush.

Kathryn giggled when she was presented to Billy. It made him uncomfortable and he thought for a moment that a couple of studs had fallen out. He soon discovered, however, that the giggle was permanent, just as much a part of Kathryn as her fraction of a nose. He looked forward with new interest to the soup course, but was disappointed to find that she could negotiate it without disturbing the giggle or the linen.

He next centred his attention on Wilma and Edith. Another disappointment was in store. There were as many and as large oysters in Wilma's soup as in any one's. She ate them all, and, so far as appearances went, was the same Wilma. He had expected that Edith would either diet or plunge. But Edith was as prosaic in her consumption of victuals as Ellen, for instance, or Aunt Louise.

He must content himself for the present with Aunt Louise. She was sitting directly opposite and he had an unobstructed view of the widest part he had ever seen in woman's hair.

'Ogden Avenue,' he said to himself.

Aunt Louise was telling about her experiences and Aunt Harriet's among the heathen of Peoria Street.

'You never would would dream there were such people!' said she.

'I suppose most of them are foreign born,' supposed her brother, who was Mr McDonald.

'Practically all of them,' said Aunt Louise.

Billy wanted to ask her whether she had ever missionaried among the Indians. He thought possibly an attempt to scalp her had failed by a narrow margin.

Between courses Edith worked hard to draw out his predicated comicality and Wilma worked as hard to make him sound his low notes. Their labors were in vain. He was not sleepy enough to be deep, and he was fourteen highballs shy of comedy.

In disgust, perhaps, at her failure to be amused, the major portion of the misdeal capsized her cocoa just before the close of the meal and drew a frown from her father, whom she could have thrown in ten minutes, straight falls, any style.

'She'll never miss that ounce,' thought Billy.

When they got up from the table and started for the living-room, Mr Bowen found himself walking beside Aunt Harriet, who had been so silent during dinner that he had all but forgotten her.

'Well, Miss McDonald,' he said, 'it's certainly a big family, isn't it?'

'Well, young man,' said Aunt Harriet, 'it ain't no small family, that's sure.'

'I should say not,' repeated Billy.

Walter and his giggling crush intercepted him.

'What do you think of Aunt Harriet's grammar?' demanded Walter.

'I didn't notice it,' lied Billy.

'No, I s'pose not. "Ain't no small family." I s'pose you didn't notice it. She isn't a real aunt like Aunt Louise and Aunt Mary. She's just an adopted aunt. She kept house for dad and Aunt Louise after their mother died, and when dad got married, she just kept on living with Aunt Louise.'

'Oh,' was Billy's fresh comment, and it brought forth a fresh supply of giggles from Kathryn.

Ellen had already been made aware of Billy's disgusting plans. He had to catch a night train for St Louis, and he would be there all day to-morrow, and he'd be back Friday, but he wouldn't have

145

time to see her, and he'd surely call her up. And Friday afternoon he was going to South Bend to spend Christmas Day with his married sister, because it was probably the last Christmas he'd be able to spend with her.

'But I'll hustle home from South Bend Sunday morning,' he said. 'And don't you dare make any engagement for the afternoon.'

'I do wish you could be with us Christmas Eve. The tree won't be a bit of fun without you.'

'You know I wish I could. But you see how it is.'

'I think your sister's mean.'

Billy didn't deny it.

'Who's going to be here Christmas Eve?'

'Just the people we had to-night, except Kathryn and you. Why?'

'Oh, nothing,' said Billy.

'Look here, sir,' said his betrothed. 'Don't you do anything foolish. You're not supposed to buy presents for the whole family. Just a little, tiny one for me, if you want to, but you mustn't spend much on it. And if you get anything for any one else in this house, I'll be mad.'

'I'd like to see you mad,' said Billy.

'You'd wish you hadn't,' Ellen retorted.

When Billy had gone, Ellen returned to the living-room and faced the assembled company.

'Well,' she said, 'now that you've all seen him, what's the verdict?'

The verdict seemed to be unanimously in his favor.

'But,' said Bob, 'I thought you said he was so screamingly funny.'

'Yes,' said Edith, 'you told me that, too.'

'Give him a chance,' said Ellen. 'Wait till he's in a funny mood. You'll simply die laughing!'

V

It is a compound fracture of the rules to have so important a character as Tommy Richards appear in only one chapter. But remember, this isn't a regular story, but a simple statement of what occurred when it occurred. During Chapter Four, Tommy

146

had been on his way home from the Pacific Coast, where business had kept him all fall. His business out there and what he said en route to Chicago are collateral.

Tommy had been Billy's pal at college. Tommy's home was in Minnesota, and Billy was his most intimate, practically his only friend in the so-called metropolis of the Middle West. So Tommy, not knowing that Billy had gone to St Louis, looked forward to a few pleasant hours with him between the time of the coast train's arrival and the Minnesota train's departure.

The coast train reached Chicago about noon. It was Thursday noon, the twenty-third. Tommy hustled from the station to Billy's office, and then learned of the St Louis trip. Disappointed, he roamed the streets a while and at length dropped into the downtown ticket office of his favorite Minnesota road. He was told that everything for the night was sold out. Big Christmas business. Tommy pondered.

'How about to-morrow night?' he inquired.

'I can give you a lower to-morrow night on the six-thirty,' replied Leslie Painter, that being the clerk's name.

'I'll take it,' said Tommy.

He did so, and the clerk took $10.05.

'I'll see old Bill after all,' said Tommy.

Leslie Painter made no reply.

In the afternoon Tommy sat through a vaudeville show, and at night he looped the loop. He retired early, for the next day promised to be a big one.

Billy got in from St Louis at seven Friday morning and had been in his office an hour when Tommy appeared. I have no details of the meeting.

At half-past eight Tommy suggested that they'd better go out and h'ist one.

'Still on it, eh?' said Billy.

'What do you mean?'

'I mean that I'm off of it.'

'Good Lord! For how long?'

'The last day of November.'

'Too long! You look sick already.'

'I feel great,' averred Billy.

'Well, I don't. So come along and bathe in vichy.'

On the way 'along' Billy told Tommy about Ellen. Tommy's

147

congratulations were physical and jarred Billy from head to heels.

'Good stuff!' cried Tommy so loudly that three pedestrians jumped sideways. 'Old Bill hooked! And do you think you're going to celebrate this occasion with water?'

'I think I am,' was Billy's firm reply.

'You think you are! What odds?'

'A good lunch against a red hot.'

'You're on!' said Tommy. 'And I'm going to be mighty hungry at one o'clock.

'You'll be hungry and alone.'

'What's the idea? If you've got a lunch date with the future, I'm in on it.'

'I haven't,' said Billy. 'But I'm going to South Bend on the one-forty, and between now and then I have nothing to do but clean up my mail and buy a dozen Christmas presents.'

They turned in somewhere.

'Don't you see the girl at all to-day?' asked Tommy.

'Not to-day. All I do is call her up.'

'Well, then, if you get outside of a couple, who'll be hurt? Just for old time's sake.'

'If you need lunch money, I'll give it to you.'

'No, no. That bet's off.'

'It's not off. I won't call it off.'

'Suit yourself,' said Tommy graciously.

At half-past nine, it was officially decided that Billy had lost the bet. At half-past twelve, Billy said it was time to pay it.

'I'm not hungry enough,' said Tommy.

'Hungry or no hungry,' said Billy, 'I buy your lunch now or I don't buy it. See? Hungry or no hungry.'

'What's the hurry?' asked Tommy.

'I guess you know what's the hurry. Me for South Bend on the one-forty, and I got to go to the office first. Hurry or no hurry.'

'Listen to reason, Bill. How are you going to eat lunch, go to the office, buy a dozen Christmas presents and catch the one-forty?'

'Christmas presents! I forgot 'em! What do you think of that? I forgot 'em. Good night!'

'What are you going to do?'

'Do! What can I do? You got me into this mess. Get me out!'

'Sure, I'll get you out if you'll listen to reason!' said Tommy. 'Has this one-forty train got anything on you? Are you under

148

obligations to it? Is the engineer your girl's uncle?'

'I guess you know better than that. I guess you know I'm not engaged to a girl who's got an uncle for an engineer.'

'Well, then, what's the next train?'

'That's the boy, Tommy! That fixes it! I'll go on the next train.'

'You're sure there is one?' asked Tommy.

'Is one! Say, where do you think South Bend is? In Europe?'

'I wouldn't mind,' said Tommy.

'South Bend's only a two-hour run. Where did you think it was? Europe?'

'I don't care where it is. The question is, what's the next train after one-forty?'

'Maybe you think I don't know,' said Billy. He called the gentleman with the apron. 'What do you know about this, Charley? Here's an old pal of mine who thinks I don't know the time-table to South Bend.'

'He's mistaken, isn't he?' said Charley.

'Is he mistaken? Say, Charley, if you knew as much as I do about the time-table to South Bend, you wouldn't be here.'

'No, sir,' said Charley. 'I'd be an announcer over in the station.'

'There!' said Billy triumphantly. 'How's that, Tommy? Do I know the time-table or don't I?'

'I guess you do,' said Tommy. 'But I don't think you ought to have secrets from an old friend.'

'There's no secrets about it, Charley.'

'My name is Tommy,' corrected his friend.

'I know that. I know your name as well as my own, better'n my own. I know your name as well as I know the time-table.'

'If you'd just tell me the time of that train, we'd all be better off.'

'I'll tell you, Tommy. I wouldn't hold out anything on you, old boy. It's five twenty-five.'

'You're sure?'

'Sure! Say, I've taken it a hundred times if I've taken it once.'

'All right,' said Tommy. 'That fixes it. We'll go in and have lunch and be through by half-past one. That'll give you four hours to do your shopping, get to your office and make your train.'

'Where you going while I shop?'

'Don't bother about me.'

'You go along with me.'

'Nothing doing.'

'Yes, you do.'

'No, I don't.'

But this argument was won by Mr Bowen. At ten minutes of three, when they at last called for the check, Mr Richards looked on the shopping expedition in an entirely different light. Two hours before, it had not appealed to him at all. Now he could think of nothing that would afford more real entertainment. Mr. Richards was at a stage corresponding to Billy's twenty-one. Billy was far past it.

'What we better do,' said Tommy, 'is write down a list of all the people so we won't forget anybody.'

'That's the stuff!' said Billy. 'I'll name 'em, you write 'em.'

So Tommy produced a pencil and took dictation on the back of a menu-card.

'First, girl's father, Sam'l McDonald.'

'Samuel McDonald,' repeated Tommy. 'Maybe you'd better give me some dope on each one, so if we're shy of time, we can both be buying at once.'

'All right,' said Billy. 'First, Sam'l McDonal'. He's an ol' crab. Raves about cig'rettes.'

'Like 'em?'

'No. Hates 'em.'

'Sam'l McDonald, cigarettes,' wrote Tommy. 'Old crab,' he added.

When the important preliminary arrangement had at last been completed, the two old college chums went out into the air.

'Where do we shop?' asked Tommy.

'Marsh's,' said Billy. ' 'S only place I got charge account.'

'Maybe we better take a taxi and save time,' suggested Tommy. So they waited five minutes for a taxi and were driven to Marsh's, two blocks away.

'We'll start on the first floor and work up,' said Tommy, who had evidently appointed himself captain.

They found themselves among the jewelry and silverware.

'You might get something for the girl here,' suggested Tommy.

'Don't worry 'bout her,' said Billy. 'Leave her till las'.'

'What's the limit on the others?'

'I don't care,' said Billy. 'Dollar, two dollars, three dollars.'

'Well, come on,' said Tommy. 'We got to make it snappy.'

But Billy hung back.

'Say, ol' boy,' he wheedled. 'You're my ol'st frien'. Is that right?'

'That's right,' agreed Tommy.

'Well, say, ol' frien', I'm pretty near all in.'

'Go home, then, if you want to. I can pull this all right alone.'

'Nothin' doin'. But if I could jus' li'l nap, ten, fifteen minutes—you could get couple things here on fir' floor and then come get me.'

'Where?'

'Third floor waitin'-room.'

'Go ahead. But wait a minute. Give me some of your cards. And will I have any trouble charging things?'

'Not a bit. Tell 'em you're me.'

It was thus that Tommy Richards was left alone in a large store, with Billy Bowen's charge account, Billy Bowen's list, and Billy Bowen's cards.

He glanced at the list.

' "Samuel McDonald, cigarettes. Old crab," ' he read.

He approached a floor-walker.

'Say, old pal,' he said. 'I'm doing some shopping and I'm in a big hurry. Where'd I find something for an old cigarette fiend?'

'Cigarette-cases, two aisles down and an aisle to your left,' said Old Pal.

Tommy raised the limit on the cigarette-case he picked out for Samuel McDonald. It was $3.75.

'I'll cut down somewhere else,' he thought. 'The father-in-law ought to be favored a little.'

'Charge,' he said in response to a query. 'William Bowen, Bowen and Company, 18 South La Salle. And here's a card for it. That go out to-night sure?'

He looked again at the list.

'Mrs Samuel McDonald, bridge bug. Miss Harriet McDonald, reverse English. Miss Louise McDonald, thin hair. Miss Mary Carey, church stuff. Bob and Wife, "The Man Who Married a Dumb Wife" and gets mysteriously jealous. Walter McDonald, real kid. Edith, fat lady. Wilma, a splinter.'

He consulted Old Pal once more. Old Pal's advice was to go to the third floor and look over the books. The advice proved sound. On the third floor Tommy found for Mother 'The First Principles of Auction Bridge,' and for Aunt Harriet an English grammar. He also bumped into a counter laden with hymnals, chant books, and Books of Common Prayer.

'Aunt Mary!' he exclaimed. And to the clerk: 'How much are your medium prayer-books?'

'What denomination?' asked the clerk, whose name was Freda Swanson.

'One or two dollars,' said Tommy.

'What church, I mean?' inquired Freda.

'How would I know?' said Tommy. 'Are there different books for different churches?'

'Sure. Catholic, Presbyterian, Episcopal, Lutheran——'

'Let's see. McDonald, Carey. How much are the Catholic ones?'

'Here's one at a dollar and a half. In Latin, too.'

'That's it. That'll give her something to work on.'

Tommy figured on the back of his list.

'Good work, Tommy!' he thought. 'Four and a half under the top limit for those three. Walter's next.'

He plunged on Walter. A nice poker set, discovered on the fourth floor, came to five eleven. Tommy wished he could keep it for himself. He also wished constantly that the women shoppers had taken a course in dodging. He was almost as badly battered as the day he played guard against the Indians.

'Three left besides the queen herself,' he observed. 'Lord, no. I forgot Bob and his missus.'

He moved down-stairs again to the books.

'Have you got "The Man Who Married A Dumb Wife"?' he queried.

Anna Henderson looked, but could not find it.

'Never mind!' said Tommy. 'Here's one that'll do.'

And he ordered 'The Green-Eyed Monster' for the cooing doves in Evanston.

'Now,' he figured, 'there's just Wilma and Edith and Aunt Louise.' Once more he started away from the books, but a title caught his eye: 'Eat and Grow Thin.'

'Great!' exclaimed Tommy. 'It'll do for Edith. By George! It'll do for both of them. "Eat" for Wilma and the "Grow Thin" for Edith. I guess that's doubling up some! And now for Aunt Louise.'

The nearest floor-walker told him, in response to his query, that switches would be found on the second floor.

'I ought to have a switch-engine to take me round,' said

Tommy, who never had felt better in his life. But the floor-walker did not laugh, possibly because he was tired.

'Have you anything to match it with?' asked the lady in the switch-yard.

'No, I haven't.'

'Can you give me an idea of the color?'

'What colors have you got?' demanded Tommy.

'Everything there is. I'll show them all to you, if you've got the time.'

'Never mind,' said Tommy. 'What's your favorite color in hair?'

The girl laughed.

'Golden,' she said.

'You're satisfied, aren't you?' said Tommy, for the girl had chosen the shade of her own shaggy mane. 'All right, make it golden. And a merry Christmas to you.'

He forgot to ask the price of switches. He added up the rest and found that the total was $16.25.

'About seventy-five cents for the hair,' he guessed. 'That will make it seventeen even. I'm some shopper. And all done in an hour and thirteen minutes.'

He discovered Billy asleep in the waiting-room and it took him three precious minutes to bring him to.

'Everybody's fixed but the girl herself,' he boasted. 'I got books for most of 'em.'

'Where you been?' asked Billy. 'What time is it?'

'You've got about thirty-three minutes to get a present for your lady love and grab your train. You'll have to pass up the office.'

'What time is it? Where you been?'

'Don't bother about that. Come on.'

On the ride down, Billy begged every one in the elevator to tell him the time, but no one seemed to know. Tommy hurried him out of the store and into a taxi.

'There's a flock of stores round the station,' said Tommy. 'You can find something there for the dame.'

But the progress of the cab through the packed down-town streets was painfully slow and the station clock, when at last they got in sight of it, registered 5.17.

'You can't wait!' said Tommy. 'Give me some money and tell me what to get.'

153

Billy fumbled clumsily in seven pockets before he located his pocketbook. In it were two fives and a ten.

'I gotta have a feevee,' he said.

'All right. I'll get something for fifteen. What'll it be?'

'Make it a wrist-watch.'

'Sure she has none?'

'She's got one. That's for other wris'.'

'I used your last card. Have you got another?'

'Pocketbook,' said Billy.

Tommy hastily searched and found a card. He pushed Billy toward the station entrance.

'Good-by and merry Christmas,' said Tommy.

'Goo'-by and God bless you!' said Billy, but he was talking to a large policeman.

'Where are you trying to go?' asked the latter.

'Souse Ben',' said Billy.

'Hurry up, then. You've only got a minute.'

The minute and six more were spent in the purchase of a ticket. And when Billy reached the gate, the 5.25 had gone and the 5.30 was about to chase it.

'Where to?' inquired the gateman.

'Souse Ben',' said Billy.

'Run then,' said the gateman.

Billy ran. He ran to the first open vestibule of the Rock Island train, bound for St Joe, Missouri.

'Where to?' asked a porter.

'Souse,' said Billy.

'Ah can see that,' said the porter. 'But where you goin'?'

The train began to move and Billy, one foot dragging on the station platform, moved with it. The porter dexterously pulled him aboard. And he was allowed to ride to Englewood.

Walking down Van Buren Street, it suddenly occurred to the genial Mr Richards that he would have to go some himself to get his baggage and catch the 6.30 for the northwest. He thought of it in front of a Van Buren jewelry shop. He stopped and went in.

Three-quarters of an hour later, a messenger-boy delivered a particularly ugly and frankly inexpensive wrist-watch at the McDonald home. The parcel was addressed to Miss McDonald and the accompanying card read:

'Mr Bowen: Call me up any night after seven. Calumet 2678. Miss Violet Moore.'

There was no good-will toward men in the McDonald home this Christmas. Ellen spent the day in bed and the orders were that she must not be disturbed.

Down-stairs, one person smiled. It was Walter. He smiled in spite of the fact that his father had tossed his brand-new five-dollar poker set into the open fireplace. He smiled in spite of the fact that he was not allowed to leave the house, not even to take Kathryn to church.

'Gee!' he thought, between smiles, 'Billy sure had nerve!'

Bob walked round among his relatives seeking to dispel the gloom with a remark that he thought apt and nifty:

'Be grateful,' was the remark, 'that he had one of his screamingly funny moods before it was too late.'

But no one but Bob seemed to think much of the remark, and no one seemed grateful.

Those are the facts, and it was quite a job to dig them up. But I did it.

A Day with Conrad Green

Conrad Green woke up depressed and, for a moment, could not think why. Then he remembered. Herman Plant was dead; Herman Plant, who had been his confidential secretary ever since he had begun producing; who had been much more than a secretary—his champion, votary, shield, bodyguard, tool, occasional lackey, and the butt of his heavy jokes and nasty temper. For forty-five dollars a week.

Herman Plant was dead, and this Lewis, recommended by Ezra Peebles, a fellow entrepreneur, had not, yesterday, made a good first impression. Lewis was apparently impervious to hints. You had to tell him things right out, and when he did understand he looked at you as if you were a boob. And insisted on a salary of sixty dollars right at the start. Perhaps Peebles, who, Green knew, hated him almost enough to make it fifty-fifty, was doing him another dirty trick dressed up as a favor.

After ten o'clock, and still Green had not had enough sleep. It had been nearly three when his young wife and he had left the Bryant-Walkers'. Mrs Green, the former Marjorie Manning of the Vanities chorus, had driven home to Long Island, while he had stayed in the rooms he always kept at the Ambassador.

Marjorie had wanted to leave a good deal earlier; through no lack of effort on her part she had been almost entirely ignored by her aristocratic host and hostess and most of the guests. She had confided to her husband more than once that she was sick of the whole such-and-such bunch of so-and-so's. As far as she was concerned, they could all go to hell and stay there! But Green had been rushed by the pretty and stage-struck Joyce Brainard, wife of the international polo star, and had successfully combated his own wife's importunities till the Brainards themselves had gone.

Yes, he could have used a little more sleep, but the memory of

156

the party cheered him. Mrs Brainard, excited by his theatrical aura and several highballs, had been almost affectionate. She had promised to come to his office some time and talk over a stage career which both knew was impossible so long as Brainard lived. But, best of all, Mr and Mrs Green would be listed in the papers as among those present at the Bryant-Walkers', along with the Vanderbecks, the Suttons, and the Schuylers, and that would just about be the death of Peebles and other social sycophants of 'show business.' He would order all the papers now and look for his name. No; he was late and must get to his office. No telling what a mess things were in without Herman Plant. And, by the way, he mustn't forget Plant's funeral this afternoon.

He bathed, telephoned for his breakfast, and his favorite barber, dressed in a symphony of purple and gray, and set out for Broadway, pretending not to hear the 'There's Conrad Green!' spoken in awed tones by two flappers and a Westchester realtor whom he passed en route.

Green let himself into his private office, an office of luxurious, exotic furnishings, its walls adorned with expensive landscapes and a Zuloaga portrait of his wife. He took off his twenty-five dollar velour hat, approved of himself in the large mirror, sat down at his desk, and rang for Miss Jackson.

'All the morning papers,' he ordered, 'and tell Lewis to come in.'

'I'll have to send out for the papers,' said Miss Jackson, a tired-looking woman of forty-five or fifty.

'What do you mean, send out? I thought we had an arrangement with that boy to leave them every morning.'

'We did. But the boy says he can't leave them any more till we've paid up to date.'

'What do we owe?'

'Sixty-five dollars.'

'Sixty-five dollars! He's crazy! Haven't you been paying him by the week?'

'No. You told me not to.'

'I told you nothing of the kind! Sixty-five dollars! He's trying to rob us!'

'I don't believe so, Mr Green,' said Miss Jackson. 'He showed me his book. It's more than thirty weeks since he began, and you know we've never paid him.'

'But hell! There isn't sixty-five dollars' worth of newspapers ever been printed! Tell him to sue us! And now send out for the papers and do it quick! After this we'll get them down at the corner every morning and pay for them. Tell Lewis to bring me the mail.'

Miss Jackson left him, and presently the new secretary came in. He was a man under thirty, whom one would have taken for a high school teacher rather than a theatrical general's aide-de-camp.

'Good-morning, Mr Green,' he said.

His employer disregarded the greeting.

'Anything in the mail?' he asked.

'Not much of importance. I've already answered most of it. Here are a few things from your clipping bureau and a sort of dunning letter from some jeweler in Philadelphia.'

'What did you open that for?' demanded Green, crossly. 'Wasn't it marked personal?'

'Look here, Mr Green,' said Lewis quietly: 'I was told you had a habit of being rough with your employees. I want to warn you that I am not used to that sort of treatment and don't intend to get used to it. If you are decent with me, I'll work for you. Otherwise I'll resign.'

'I don't know what you're talking about, Lewis. I didn't mean to be rough. It's just my way of speaking. Let's forget it and I'll try not to give you any more cause to complain.'

'All right, Mr Green. You told me to open all your mail except the letters with that one little mark on them——'

'Yes, I know. Now let's have the clippings.'

Lewis laid them on the desk.

'I threw away about ten of them that were all the same—the announcement that you had signed Bonnie Blue for next season. There's one there that speaks of a possible partnership between you and Sam Stein——'

'What a nerve he's got, giving out a statement like that. Fine chance of me mixing myself up with a crook like Stein! Peebles says he's a full stepbrother to the James boys. So is Peebles himself, for that matter. What's this long one about?'

'It's about that young composer, Casper Ettelson. It's by Deems Taylor of the World. There's just a mention of you down at the bottom.'

'Read it to me, will you? I've overstrained my eyes lately.'

The dead Herman Plant had first heard of that recent eye strain twenty years ago. It amounted to almost total blindness where words of over two syllables were concerned.

'So far,' Lewis read, 'Ettelson has not had a book worthy of his imaginative, whimsical music. How we would revel in an Ettelson score with a Barrie libretto and a Conrad Green production.'

'Who is this Barrie?' asked Green.

'I suppose it's James M. Barrie,' replied Lewis, 'the man who wrote Peter Pan.'

'I thought that was written by a fella over in England,' said Green.

'I guess he does live in England. He was born in Scotland. I don't know where he is now.'

'Well, find out if he's in New York, and, if he is, get a hold of him. Maybe he'll do a couple of scenes for our next show. Come in, Miss Jackson. Oh, the papers!'

Miss Jackson handed them to him and went out. Green turned first to the society page of the *Herald Tribune*. His eye trouble was not so severe as to prevent his finding that page. And he could read his name when it was there to be read.

Three paragraphs were devoted to the Bryant-Walker affair, two of them being lists of names. And Mr and Mrs Conrad Green were left out.

'——!' commented Green, and grabbed the other papers. The *World* and *Times* were searched with the same hideous result. And the others did not mention the party at all.

'——!' repeated Green. 'I'll get somebody for this!' Then, to Lewis: 'Here! Take this telegram. Send it to the managing editors of all the morning papers; you'll find their names pasted on Plant's desk. Now: "Ask your society editor why my name was not on list of guests at Bryant-Walker dinner Wednesday night. Makes no difference to me, as am not seeking and do not need publicity, but it looks like conspiracy, and thought you ought to be informed, as have always been good friend of your paper, as well as steady advertiser." I guess that's enough.'

'If you'll pardon a suggestion,' said Lewis, 'I'm afraid a telegram like this would just be laughed at.'

'You send the telegram; I'm not going to have a bunch of cheap reporters make a fool of me!'

159

'I don't believe you can blame the reporters. There probably weren't reporters there. The list of guests is generally given out by the people who give the party.'

'But listen——' Green paused and thought. 'All right. Don't send the telegram. But if the Bryant-Walkers are ashamed of me, why the hell did they invite me? I certainly didn't want to go and they weren't under obligation to me. I never——'

As if it had been waiting for its cue, the telephone rang at this instant, and Kate, the switchboard girl, announced that the Bryant-Walkers' secretary was on the wire.

'I am speaking for Mrs Bryant-Walker,' said a female voice. 'She is chairman of the committee on entertainment for the Women's Progress Bazaar. The bazaar is to open on the third of next month and wind up on the evening of the fifth with a sort of vaudeville entertainment. She wanted me to ask you——'

Green hung up with an oath.

'That's the answer!' he said. 'The damn grafters!'

Miss Jackson came in again.

'Mr Robert Blair is waiting to see you.'

'Who is he?'

'You know. He tried to write some things for one of the shows last year.'

'Oh, yes. Say, did you send flowers to Plant's house?'

'I did,' replied Miss Jackson. 'I sent some beautiful roses.'

'How much?'

'Forty-five dollars,' said Miss Jackson.

'Forty-five dollars for roses! And the man hated flowers even when he was alive! Well, send in this Blair.'

Robert Blair was an ambitious young free lance who had long been trying to write for the stage, but with little success.

'Sit down, Blair,' said Green. 'What's on your mind?'

'Well, Mr Green, my stuff didn't seem to suit you last year, but this time I think I've got a scene that can't miss.'

'All right. If you want to leave it here, I'll read it over.'

'I haven't written it out. I thought I'd tell you the idea first.'

'Well, go ahead, but cut it short; I've got a lot of things to do today. Got to go to old Plant's funeral for one thing.'

'I bet you miss him, don't you?' said Blair, sympathetically.

'Miss him! I should say I do! A lovable character and'—with a

160

glance at Lewis—'the best secretary I'll ever have. But let's hear your scene.'

'Well,' said Blair, 'it may not sound like much the way I tell it, but I think it'll work out great. Well, the police get a report that a woman has been murdered in her home, and they go there and find her husband, who is acting very nervous. They give him the third degree, and he finally breaks down and admits he killed her. They ask him why, and he tells them he is very fond of beans, and on the preceding evening he came home to dinner and asked her what there was to eat, and she told him she had lamb chops, mashed potatoes, spinach, and apple pie. So he says, "No beans?" and she says, "No beans." So he shoots her dead. Of course, the scene between the husband and wife is acted out on the stage. Then——'

'It's no good!' said Conrad Green. 'In the first place, it takes too many people, all those policemen and everybody.'

'Why, all you need is two policemen and the man and his wife. And wait till I tell you the rest of it.'

'I don't like it; it's no good. Come back again when you've got something.'

When Blair had gone Green turned to Lewis.

'That's all for just now,' he said, 'but on your way out tell Miss Jackson to get a hold of Martin and say I want him to drop in here as soon as he can.'

'What Martin?' asked Lewis.

'She'll know—Joe Martin, the man that writes most of our librettos.'

Alone, Conrad Green crossed the room to his safe, opened it, and took out a box on which was inscribed the name of a Philadelphia jeweler. From the box he removed a beautiful rope of matched pearls and was gazing at them in admiration when Miss Jackson came in; whereupon he hastily replaced them in their case and closed the safe.

'That man is here again,' said Miss Jackson, 'That man Hawley from *Gay New York*.'

'Tell him I'm not in.'

'I did, but he says he saw you come in and he's going to wait till you'll talk to him. Really, Mr Green, I think it would be best in the long run to see him. He's awfully persistent.'

'All right; send him in,' said Green, impatiently, 'though I have no idea what he can possibly want of me.'

161

Mr Hawley, dapper and eternally smiling, insisted on shaking hands with his unwilling host, who had again sat down at his desk.

'I think,' he said, 'we've met before.'

'Not that I know of,' Green replied shortly.

'Well, it makes no difference, but I'm sure you've read our little paper, *Gay New York*.'

'No,' said Green. 'All I have time to read is manuscripts.'

'You don't know what you're missing,' said Hawley. 'It's really a growing paper, with a big New York circulation, and a circulation that is important from your standpoint.'

'Are you soliciting subscriptions?' asked Green.

'No. Advertising.'

'Well, frankly, Mr Hawley, I don't believe I need any advertising. I believe that even the advertising I put in the regular daily papers is a waste of money.'

'Just the same,' said Hawley, 'I think you'd be making a mistake not to take a page in *Gay New York*. It's only a matter of fifteen hundred dollars.'

'Fifteen hundred dollars! That's a joke! Nobody's going to hold *me* up!'

'Nobody's trying to, Mr Green. But I might as well tell you that one of our reporters came in with a story the other day—well, it was about a little gambling affair in which some of the losers sort of forgot to settle, and—well, my partner was all for printing it, but I said I had always felt friendly toward you and why not give you a chance to state your side of it?'

'I don't know what you're talking about. If your reporter has got my name mixed up in a gambling story he's crazy.'

'No. He's perfectly sane and very, very careful. We make a specialty of careful reporters and we're always sure of our facts.'

Conrad Green was silent for a long, long time. Then he said:

'I tell you, I don't know what gambling business you refer to, and, furthermore, fifteen hundred dollars is a hell of a price for a page in a paper like yours. But still, as you say, you've got the kind of circulation that might do me good. So if you'll cut down the price——'

'I'm sorry, Mr Green, but we never do that.'

'Well, then, of course you'll have to give me a few days to get my ad fixed up. Say you come back here next Monday afternoon.'

'That's perfectly satisfactory, Mr Green,' said Hawley, 'and I assure you that you're not making a mistake. And now I won't keep you any longer from your work.'

He extended his hand, but it was ignored, and he went out, his smile a little broader than when he had come in. Green remained at his desk, staring straight ahead of him and making semi-audible references to certain kinds of dogs as well as personages referred to in the Old and New Testaments. He was interrupted by the entrance of Lewis.

'Mr Green,' said the new secretary, 'I have found a check for forty-five dollars made out to Herman Plant. I imagine it is for his final week's pay. Would you like to have me change it and make it out to his widow?'

'Yes,' said Green. 'But no; wait a minute. Tear it up and I'll make out my personal check to her and add something to it.'

'All right,' said Lewis, and left.

'Forty-five dollars' worth of flowers,' said Green to himself, and smiled for the first time that morning.

He looked at his watch and got up and put on his beautiful hat.

'I'm going to lunch,' he told Miss Jackson on his way through the outer office. 'If Peebles or anybody important calls up, tell them I'll be here all afternoon.'

'You're not forgetting Mr Plant's funeral?'

'Oh, that's right. Well, I'll be here from one-thirty to about three.'

A head waiter at the Astor bowed to him obsequiously and escorted him to a table near a window, while the occupants of several other tables gazed at him spellbound and whispered, 'Conrad Green.'

A luncheon of clams, sweetbreads, spinach, strawberry ice cream, and small coffee seemed to satisfy him. He signed his check and then tipped his own waiter and the head waiter a dollar apiece, the two tips falling just short of the cost of the meal.

Joe Martin, his chief librettist, was waiting when he got back to his office.

'Oh, hello, Joe!' he said, cordially. 'Come right inside. I think I've got something for you.'

Martin followed him in and sat down without waiting for an invitation. Green seated himself at his desk and drew out his cigarette case.

163

'Have one, Joe?'

'Not that kind!' said Martin, lighting one of his own. 'You've gotten rotten taste in everything but gals.'

'And librettists,' replied Green, smiling.

'But here's what I wanted to talk about. I couldn't sleep last night, and I just laid there and an idea came to me for a comedy scene. I'll give you the bare idea and you can work it out. It'll take a girl and one of the comics, maybe Fraser, and a couple of other men that can play.

'Well, the idea is that the comic is married to the girl. In the first place, I'd better mention that the comic is crazy about beans. Well, one night the comic—no, wait a minute. The police get word that the comic's wife has been murdered and two policemen come to the comic's apartment to investigate. They examine the corpse and find out she's been shot through the head. They ask the comic if he knows who did it and he says no, but they keep after him, and finally he breaks down and admits that he did it himself.

'But he says, "Gentlemen, if you'll let me explain the circumstances, I don't believe you'll arrest me." So they tell him to explain, and he says that he came home from work and he was very hungry and he asked his wife what they were going to have for dinner. So she tells him—clams and sweetbreads and spinach and strawberry ice cream and coffee. So he asks her if she isn't going to have any beans and she says no, and he shoots her. What do you think you could do with that idea?'

'Listen, Connie,' said Martin: 'You've only got half the scene, and you've got that half wrong. In the second place, it was played a whole season in the Music Box and it was written by Bert Kalmar and Harry Ruby. Otherwise I can do a whole lot with it.'

'Are you sure you're right?'

'I certainly am!'

'Why, that damn little thief! He told me it was his!'

'Who?' asked Martin.

'Why, that Blair, that tried to butt in here last year. I'll fix him!'

'I thought you said it was your own idea.'

'Hell, no! Do you think I'd be stealing stuff, especially if it was a year old?'

'Well,' said Martin, 'when you get another inspiration like this, give me a ring and I'll come around. Now I've got to hurry up to the old Stadium and see what the old Babe does in the first inning.'

'I'm sorry, Joe. I thought it was perfectly all right.'

'Never mind! You didn't waste much of my time. But after this you'd better leave the ideas to me. So long!'

'Good-by, Joe; and thanks for coming in.'

Martin went and Green pressed the button for Miss Jackson.

'Miss Jackson, don't ever let that young Blair in here again. He's a faker!'

'All right, Mr Green. But don't you think it's about time you were starting for the funeral? It's twenty minutes of three.'

'Yes. But let's see: where is Plant's house?'

'It's up on One Hundred and Sixtieth street, just off Broadway.'

'My God! Imagine living there! Wait a minute, Miss Jackson. Send Lewis here.'

'Lewis,' he said, when the new secretary appeared, 'I ate something this noon that disagreed with me. I wanted to go up to Plant's funeral, but I really think it would be dangerous to try it. Will you go up there, let them know who you are, and kind of represent me? Miss Jackson will give you the address.'

'Yes, sir,' said Lewis, and went out.

Almost immediately the sanctum door opened again and the beautiful Marjorie Green, née Manning, entered unannounced. Green's face registered not altogether pleasant surprise.

'Why, hello, dear!' he said. 'I didn't know you were coming to town today.'

'I never told you I wasn't,' his wife replied.

They exchanged the usual connubial salutations.

'I supposed you noticed,' said Mrs. Green, 'that our names were not on the list of guests at the party.'

'No; I haven't had time to look at the papers. But what's the difference?'

'No difference at all, of course. But do you know what I think? I think we were invited just because those people want to get something out of you, for some benefit or something.'

'A fine chance! I hope they try it!'

'However, that's not what I came to talk about.'

'Well, dear, what is it?'

'I thought maybe you'd remember something.'

'What, honey?'

'Why—oh, well, there's no use talking about it if you've forgotten.'

Green's forehead wrinkled in deep thought; then suddenly his face brightened.

'Of course I haven't forgotten! It's your birthday!'

'You just thought of it now!'

'No such a thing! I've been thinking of it for weeks!'

'I don't believe you! If you had been, you'd have said something, and'—his wife was on the verge of tears—'you'd have given me some little thing, just any little thing.'

Once more Green frowned, and once more brightened up.

'I'll prove it to you,' he said, and walked rapidly to the safe.

In a moment he had placed in her hands the jewel box from Philadelphia. In another moment she had opened it, gasped at the beauty of its contents, and thrown her arms around his neck.

'Oh dearest!' she cried. 'Can you ever forgive me for doubting you?'

She put the pearls to her mouth as if she would eat them.

'But haven't you been terribly extravagant?'

'I don't consider anything too extravagant for you.'

'You're the best husband a girl ever had!'

'I'm glad you're pleased,' said Green.

'Pleased! I'm overwhelmed. And to think I imagined you'd forgotten! But I'm not going to break up your whole day. I know you want to get out to poor old Plant's funeral. So I'll run along. And maybe you'll take me to dinner somewhere tonight.'

'I certainly will! You be at the Ambassador about six-thirty and we'll have a little birthday party. But don't you want to leave the pearls here now?'

'I should say not! They're going to stay with me forever! Anyone that tries to take them will do it over my dead body!'

'Well, good-by, then, dear.'

'Till half past six.'

Green, alone again, kicked shut the door of his safe and returned to his desk, saying in loud tones things which are not ordinarily considered appropriate to the birthday of a loved one. The hubbub must have been audible to Miss Jackson outside, but perhaps she was accustomed to it. It ceased at another unannounced entrance, that of a girl even more beautiful than the one who had just gone out. She looked at Green and laughed.

'My God! You look happy!' she said.

'Rose!'

166

'Yes, it's Rose. But what's the matter with you?'

'I've had a bad day.'

'But isn't it better now?'

'I didn't think you were coming till to-morrow.'

'But aren't you glad I came today?'

'You bet I am!' said Green. 'And if you'll come here and kiss me I'll be all the gladder.'

'No. Let's get our business transacted first.'

'What business?'

'You know perfectly well! Last time I saw you you insisted that I must give up everybody else but you. And I promised you it would be all off between Harry and I if——Well, you know. There was a little matter of some pearls.'

'I meant everything I said.'

'Well, where are they?'

'They're all bought and all ready for you. But I bought them in Philadelphia and for some damned reason they haven't got here yet.'

'Got here yet! Were they so heavy you couldn't bring them with you?'

'Honest, dear, they'll be here day after tomorrow at the latest.'

' "Honest" is a good word for you to use! Do you think I'm dumb? Or is it that you're so used to lying that you can't help it?'

'If you'll let me explain——'

'Explain hell! We made a bargain and you haven't kept your end of it. And now——'

'But listen——'

'I'll listen to nothing! You know where to reach me and when you've kept your promise you can call me up. Till then—Well, Harry isn't such bad company.'

'Wait a minute, Rose!'

'You've heard all I've got to say. Good-by!'

And she was gone before he could intercept her.

Conrad Green sat as if stunned. For fifteen minutes he was so silent and motionless that one might have thought him dead. Then he shivered as if with cold and said aloud:

'I'm not going to worry about them any more. To hell with all of them!'

He drew the telephone to him and took off the receiver.

'Get me Mrs Bryant-Walker.'

And after a pause:

'Is this Mrs Bryant-Walker? No, I want to speak to her personally. This is Conrad Green. Oh, hello, Mrs Walker. Your secretary called me up this morning, but we were cut off. She was saying something about a benefit. Why, yes, certainly, I'll be glad to. As many of them as you want. If you'll just leave it all in my hands I'll guarantee you a pretty good entertainment. It's no bother at all. It's a pleasure. Thank you. Good-by.'

Lewis came in.

'Well, Lewis, did you get to the funeral?'

'Yes, Mr Green, and I saw Mrs Plant and explained the circumstances to her. She said you had always been very kind to her husband. She said that during the week of his illness he talked of you nearly all the time and expressed confidence that if he died you would attend his funeral. So she wished you had been there.'

'Good God! So do I!' said Conrad Green.

The Love Nest

'I'll tell you what I'm going to do with you, Mr Bartlett,' said the great man. 'I'm going to take you right out to my home and have you meet the wife and family; stay to dinner and all night. We've got plenty of room and extra pajamas, if you don't mind them silk. I mean that'll give you a chance to see us just as we are. I mean you can get more that way than if you sat here a whole week, asking me questions.'

'But I don't want to put you to a lot of trouble,' said Bartlett.

'Trouble!' The great man laughed. 'There's no trouble about it. I've got a house that's like a hotel. I mean a big house with lots of servants. But anyway I'm always glad to do anything I can for a writing man, especially a man that works for Ralph Doane. I'm very fond of Ralph. I mean I like him personally besides being a great editor. I mean I've known him for years and when there's anything I can do for him, I'm glad to do it. I mean it'll be a pleasure to have you. So if you want to notify your family——'

'I haven't any family,' said Bartlett.

'Well, I'm sorry for you! And I bet when you see mine, you'll wish you had one of your own. But I'm glad you can come and we'll start now so as to get there before the kiddies are put away for the night. I mean I want you to be sure and see the kiddies. I've got three.'

'I've seen their pictures,' said Bartlett. 'You must be very proud of them. They're all girls, aren't they?'

'Yes, sir; three girls. I wouldn't have a boy. I mean I always wanted girls. I mean girls have got a lot more zip to them. I mean they're a lot zippier. But let's go! The Rolls is downstairs and if we start now we'll get there before dark. I mean I want you to see the place while it's still daylight.'

The great man—Lou Gregg, president of Modern Pictures, Inc.—escorted his visitor from the magnificent office by a private door and down a private stairway to the avenue, where the glittering car with its glittering chauffeur waited.

'My wife was in town today,' said Gregg as they glided north-ward, 'and I hoped we could ride out together, but she called up about two and asked would I mind if she went on home in the Pierce. She was through with her shopping and she hates to be away from the house and the kiddies any longer than she can help. Celia's a great home girl. You'd never know she was the same girl now as the girl I married seven years ago. I mean she's different. I mean she's not the same. I mean her marriage and being a mother has developed her. Did you ever see her? I mean in pictures?'

'I think I did once,' replied Bartlett. 'Didn't she play the young sister in "The Cad"?'

'Yes, with Harold Hodgson and Marie Blythe.'

'I thought I'd seen her. I remember her as very pretty and vivacious.'

'She certainly was! And she is yet! I mean she's even prettier, but of course she ain't a kid, though she looks it. I mean she was only seventeen in that picture and that was ten years ago. I mean she's twenty-seven years old now. But I never met a girl with as much zip as she had in those days. It's remarkable how marriage changes them. I mean nobody would ever thought Celia Sayles would turn out to be a sit-by-the-fire. I mean she still likes a good time, but her home and kiddies come first. I mean her home and kiddies come first.'

'I see what you mean,' said Bartlett.

An hour's drive brought them to Ardsley-on-Hudson and the great man's home.

'A wonderful place!' Bartlett exclaimed with a heroic sem-blance of enthusiasm as the car turned in at an *arc de triomphe* of a gateway and approached a white house that might have been mistaken for the Yale Bowl.

'It ought to be!' said Gregg. 'I mean I've spent enough on it. I mean these things cost money.'

He indicated with a gesture the huge house and Urbanesque landscaping.

'But no amount of money is too much to spend on home. I mean it's a good investment if it tends to make your family proud and satisfied with their home. I mean every nickel I've spent here is like

170

so much insurance; it insures me of a happy wife and family. And what more can a man ask!'

Bartlett didn't know, but the topic was forgotten in the business of leaving the resplendent Rolls and entering the even more resplendent reception hall.

'Forbes will take your things,' said Gregg. 'And, Forbes, you may tell Dennis that Mr Bartlett will spend the night.' He faced the wide stairway and raised his voice. 'Sweetheart!' he called.

From above came the reply in contralto: 'Hello, sweetheart!'

'Come down, sweetheart. I've brought you a visitor.'

'All right, sweetheart, in just a minute.'

Gregg led Bartlett into a living-room that was five laps to the mile and suggestive of an Atlantic City auction sale.

'Sit there,' said the host, pointing to a balloon-stuffed easy chair, 'and I'll see if we can get a drink. I've got some real old Bourbon that I'd like you to try. You know I come from Chicago and I always liked Bourbon better than Scotch. I mean I always preferred it to Scotch. Forbes,' he addressed the servant, 'we want a drink. You'll find a full bottle of that Bourbon in the cupboard.'

'It's only half full, sir,' said Forbes.

'Half full! That's funny! I mean I opened it last night and just took one drink. I mean it ought to be full.'

'It's only half full,' repeated Forbes, and went to fetch it.

'I'll have to investigate,' Gregg told his guest. 'I mean this ain't the first time lately that some of my good stuff has disappeared. When you keep so many servants, it's hard to get all honest ones. But here's Celia!'

Bartlett rose to greet the striking brunette who at this moment made an entrance so Delsarte as to be almost painful. With never a glance at him, she minced across the room to her husband and took a half interest in a convincing kiss.

'Well, sweetheart,' she said when it was at last over.

'This is Mr Bartlett, sweetheart,' said her husband. 'Mr Bartlett, meet Mrs Gregg.'

Bartlett shook his hostess's proffered two fingers.

'I'm so pleased!' said Celia in a voice reminiscent of Miss Claire's imitation of Miss Barrymore.

'Mr Bartlett,' Gregg went on, 'is with Mankind, Ralph Doane's magazine. He is going to write me up; I mean us.'

'No, you mean you,' said Celia. 'I'm sure the public is not interested in great men's wives.'

'I am sure you are mistaken, Mrs Gregg,' said Bartlett politely. 'In this case at least. You are worth writing up aside from being a great man's wife.'

'I'm afraid you're a flatterer, Mr Bartlett,' she returned. 'I have been out of the limelight so long that I doubt if anybody remembers me. I'm no longer an artist; merely a happy wife and mother.'

'And I claim, sweetheart,' said Gregg, 'that it takes an artist to be that.'

'Oh, no, sweetheart!' said Celia. 'Not when they have you for a husband!'

The exchange of hosannahs was interrupted by the arrival of Forbes with the tray.

'Will you take yours straight or in a high-ball?' Gregg inquired of his guest. 'Personally I like good whisky straight. I mean mixing it with water spoils the flavor. I mean whisky like this, it seems like a crime to mix it with water.'

'I'll have mine straight,' said Bartlett, who would have preferred a high-ball.

While the drinks were being prepared, he observed his hostess more closely and thought how much more charming she would be if she had used finesse in improving on nature. Her cheeks, her mouth, her eyes, and lashes had been, he guessed, far above the average in beauty before she had begun experimenting with them. And her experiments had been clumsy. She was handsome in spite of her efforts to be handsomer.

'Listen, sweetheart,' said her husband. 'One of the servants has been helping himself to this Bourbon. I mean it was a full bottle last night and I only had one little drink out of it. And now it's less than half full. Who do you suppose has been at it?'

'How do I know, sweetheart? Maybe the groceryman or the iceman or somebody.'

'But you and I and Forbes are the only ones that have a key. I mean it was locked up.'

'Maybe you forgot to lock it.'

'I never do. Well, anyway, Bartlett, here's a go!'

'Doesn't Mrs Gregg indulge?' asked Bartlett.

'Only a cocktail before dinner,' said Celia. 'Lou objects to me drinking whisky, and I don't like it much anyway.'

172

'I don't object to you drinking whisky, sweetheart. I just object to you drinking to excess. I mean I think it coarsens a woman to drink. I mean it makes them coarse.'

'Well, there's no argument, sweetheart. As I say, I don't care whether I have it or not.'

'It certainly is great Bourbon!' said Bartlett, smacking his lips and putting his glass back on the tray.

'You bet it is!' Gregg agreed. 'I mean you can't buy that kind of stuff any more. I mean it's real stuff. You help yourself when you want another. Mr Bartlett is going to stay all night, sweetheart. I told him he could get a whole lot more of a line on us that way than just interviewing me in the office. I mean I'm tongue-tied when it comes to talking about my work and my success. I mean it's better to see me out here as I am, in my home, with my family. I mean my home life speaks for itself without me saying a word.'

'But, sweetheart,' said his wife, 'what about Mr Latham?'

'Gosh! I forgot all about him! I must phone and see if I can call it off. That's terrible! You see,' he explained to Bartlett, 'I made a date to go up to Tarrytown tonight, to K.L. Latham's, the sugar people. We're going to talk over the new club. We're going to have a golf club that will make the rest of them look like a toy. I mean a real golf club! They want me to kind of run it. And I was to go up there tonight and talk it over. I'll phone and see if I can postpone it.'

'Oh, don't postpone it on my account!' urged Bartlett. 'I can come out again some other time, or I can see you in town.'

'I don't see how you *can* postpone it, sweetheart,' said Celia. 'Didn't he say old Mr King was coming over from White Plains? They'll be mad at you if you don't go.'

'I'm afraid they would resent it, sweetheart. Well, I'll tell you. You can entertain Mr Bartlett and I'll go there right after dinner and come back as soon as I can. And Bartlett and I can talk when I get back. I mean we can talk when I get back. How is that?'

'That suits me,' said Bartlett.

'I'll be as entertaining as I can,' said Celia, 'but I'm afraid that isn't very entertaining. However, if I'm too much of a bore, there's plenty to read.'

'No danger of my being bored,' said Bartlett.

'Well, that's all fixed then,' said the relieved host. 'I hope you'll excuse me running away. But I don't see how I can get out of it. I

173

mean with old King coming over from White Plains. I mean he's
and old man. But listen, sweetheart—where are the kiddies? Mr
Bartlett wants to see them.'

'Yes, indeed!' agreed the visitor.

'Of course you'd say so!' Celia said. 'But we *are* proud of them!
I suppose all parents are the same. They all think their own
children are the only children in the world. Isn't that so, Mr
Bartlett? Or haven't you any children?'

'I'm sorry to say I'm not married.'

'Oh, you poor thing! We pity him, don't we, sweetheart? But
why aren't you, Mr Bartlett? Don't tell me you're a woman
hater!'

'Not now, anyway,' said the gallant Bartlett.

'Do you get that, sweetheart? He's paying you a pretty
compliment.'

'I heard it, sweetheart. And now I'm sure he's a flatterer. But I
must hurry and get the children before Hortense puts them to
bed.'

'Well,' said Gregg when his wife had left the room, 'would you
say she's changed?'

'A little, and for the better. She's more than fulfilled her early
promise.'

'I think so,' said Gregg. 'I mean I think she was a beautiful girl
and now she's an even more beautiful woman. I mean wifehood
and maternity have given her a kind of a—well, you know—I
mean a kind of a pose. I mean a pose. How about another drink?'

They were emptying their glasses when Celia returned with two
of her little girls.

'The baby's in bed and I was afraid to ask Hortense to get her up
again. But you'll see her in the morning. This is Norma and this is
Grace. Girls, this is Mr Bartlett.'

The girls received this news calmly.

'Well, girls,' said Bartlett.

'What do you think of them, Bartlett?' demanded their father. 'I
mean what do you think of them?'

'They're great!' replied the guest with creditable warmth.

'I mean aren't they pretty?'

'I should say they are!'

'There, girls! Why don't you thank Mr Bartlett?'

'Thanks,' murmured Norma.

'How old are you, Norma?' asked Bartlett.

'Six,' said Norma.

'Well,' said Bartlett. 'And how old is Grace?'

'Four,' replied Norma.

'Well,' said Bartlett. 'And how old is baby sister?'

'One and a half,' answered Norma.

'Well,' said Bartlett.

As this seemed to be final, 'Come girls,' said their mother. 'Kiss daddy good night and I'll take you back to Hortense.'

'I'll take them,' said Gregg. 'I'm going up-stairs anyway. And you can show Bartlett around. I mean before it gets any darker.'

'Good night, girls,' said Bartlett, and the children murmured a good night.

'I'll come and see you before you're asleep,' Celia told them. And after Gregg had led them out, 'Do you really think they're pretty?' she asked Bartlett.

'I certainly do. Especially Norma. She's the image of you,' said Bartlett.

'She looks a little like I used to,' Celia admitted. 'But I hope she doesn't look like me now. I'm too old looking.'

'You look remarkably young!' said Bartlett. 'No one would believe you were the mother of three children.'

'Oh, Mr Bartlett! But I mustn't forget I'm to "show you around." Lou is so proud of our home!'

'And with reason,' said Bartlett.

'It *is* wonderful! I call it our love nest. Quite a big nest, don't you think? Mother says it's too big to be cosy; she says she can't think of it as a home. But I always say a place is whatever one makes of it. A woman can be happy in a tent if they love each other. And miserable in a royal palace without love. Don't you think so, Mr Bartlett?'

'Yes, indeed.'

'Is this really such wonderful Bourbon? I think I'll just take a sip of it and see what it's like. It can't hurt me if it's so good. Do you think so, Mr Bartlett?'

'I don't believe so.'

'Well then, I'm going to taste it and if it hurts me it's your fault.'

Celia poured a whisky glass two-thirds full and drained it at a gulp.

'It *is* good, isn't it?' she said. 'Of course I'm not much of a judge

175

as I don't care for whisky and Lou won't let me drink it. But he's raved so about this Bourbon that I did want to see what it was like. You won't tell on me, will you, Mr Bartlett?'

'Not I!'

'I wonder how it would be in a high-ball. Let's you and I have just one. But I'm forgetting I'm supposed to show you the place. We won't have time to drink a high-ball and see the place too before Lou comes down. Are you so crazy to see the place?'

'Not very.'

'Well, then, what do you say if we have a high-ball? And it'll be a secret between you and I.'

They drank in silence and Celia pressed a button by the door.

'You may take the bottle and tray,' she told Forbes. 'And now,' she said to Bartlett, 'we'll go out on the porch and see as much as we can see. You'll have to guess the rest.'

Gregg, having changed his shirt and collar, joined them.

'Well,' he said to Bartlett, 'have you seen everything?'

'I guess I have, Mr Gregg,' lied the guest readily. 'It's a wonderful place!'

'We like it. I mean it suits us. I mean it's my idear of a real home. And Celia calls it her love nest.'

'So she told me,' said Bartlett.

'She'll always be sentimental,' said her husband.

He put his hand on her shoulder, but she drew away.

'I must run up and dress,' she said.

'Dress!' exclaimed Bartlett, who had been dazzled by her flowered green chiffon.

'Oh, I'm not going to really dress,' she said. 'But I couldn't wear this thing for dinner!'

'Perhaps you'd like to clean up a little, Bartlett,' said Gregg. 'I mean Forbes will show you your room if you want to go up.'

'It might be best,' said Bartlett.

Celia, in a black lace dinner gown, was rather quiet during the elaborate meal. Three or four times when Gregg addressed her, she seemed to be thinking of something else and had to ask, 'What did you say, sweetheart?' Her face was red and Bartlett imagined that she had 'sneaked' a drink or two besides the two helpings of Bourbon and the cocktail that had preceded dinner.

'Well, I'll leave you,' said Gregg when they were in the living-room once more. 'I mean the sooner I get started, the sooner I'll be back. Sweetheart, try and keep your guest awake and don't let him die of thirst. *Au revoir*, Bartlett. I'm sorry, but it can't be helped. There's a fresh bottle of the Bourbon, so go to it. I mean help yourself. It's too bad you have to drink alone.'

'It *is* too bad, Mr Bartlett,' said Celia when Gregg had gone.

'What's too bad?' asked Bartlett.

'That you have to drink alone. I feel like I wasn't being a good hostess to let you do it. In fact, I refuse to let you do it. I'll join you in just a little wee sip.'

'But it's so soon after dinner!'

'It's never too soon! I'm going to have a drink myself and if you don't join me, you're a quitter.'

She mixed two life-sized high-balls and handed one to her guest.

'Now we'll turn on the radio and see if we can't stir things up. There! No, no! Who cares about the old baseball! Now! This is better! Let's dance.'

'I'm sorry, Mrs Gregg, but I don't dance.'

'Well, you're an old cheese! To make me dance alone! "All alone, yes, I'm all alone." '

There was no affectation in her voice now and Bartlett was amazed at her unlabored grace as she glided around the big room.

'But it's no fun alone,' she complained. 'Let's shut the damn thing off and talk.'

'I love to watch you dance,' said Bartlett.

'Yes, but I'm no Pavlowa,' said Celia as she silenced the radio. 'And besides, it's time for a drink.'

'I've still got more than half of mine.'

'Well, you had that wine at dinner, so I'll have to catch up with you.'

She poured herself another high-ball and went at the task of 'catching up.'

'The trouble with you, Mr—now isn't that a scream! I can't think of your name.'

'Bartlett.'

'The trouble with you, Barker—do you know what's the trouble with you? You're too sober. See? You're too damn sober! That's the whole trouble, see? If you weren't so sober, we'd be better off. See? What I can't understand is how you can be so sober and me so high.'

'You're not used to it.'

'Not used to it! That's the cat's pajamas! Say, I'm like this half the time, see? If I wasn't, I'd die!'

'What does your husband say?'

'He don't say because he don't know. See, Barker? There's nights when he's out and there's a few nights when I'm out myself. And there's other nights when we're both in and I pretend I'm sleepy and I go up-stairs. See? But I don't go to bed. See? I have a little party all by myself. See? If I didn't, I'd die!'

'What do you mean, you'd die?'

'You're dumb, Barker! You may be sober, but you're dumb! Did you fall for all that apple sauce about the happy home and the contented wife? Listen, Barker—I'd give anything in the world to be out of this mess. I'd give anything to never see him again.'

'Don't you love him any more? Doesn't he love you? Or what?'

'Love! I never did love him! I didn't know what love was! And all his love is for himself!'

'How did you happen to get married?'

'I was a kid; that's the answer. A kid and ambitious. See? He was a director then and he got stuck on me and I thought he'd make me a star. See, Barker? I married him to get myself a chance. And now look at me!'

'I'd say you were fairly well off.'

'Well off, am I? I'd change places with the scum of the earth just to be free! See, Barker? And I could have been a star without any help if I'd only realized it. I had the looks and I had the talent. I've got it yet. I could be a Swanson and get myself a marquis; maybe a prince! And look what I did get! A self-satisfied, self-centered——! I thought he'd *make* me! See, Barker! Well, he's made me all right; he's made me a chronic mother and it's a wonder I've got any looks left.

'I fought at first. I told him marriage didn't mean giving up my art, my life work. But it was no use. He wanted a beautiful wife and beautiful children for his beautiful home. Just to show us off. See? I'm part of his chattels. See, Barker? I'm just like his big diamond or his cars or his horses. And he wouldn't stand for his wife "lowering" herself to act in pictures. Just as if pictures hadn't made him!

'You go back to your magazine tomorrow and write about our love nest. See, Barker? And be sure and don't get mixed and call it

178

a baby ranch. Babies! You thought little Norma was pretty. Well, she is. And what is it going to get her? A rich —— of a husband that treats her like a ——! That's what it'll get er if I don't interfere. I hope I don't last long enough to see her grow up, but if I do, I'm going to advise her to run away from home and live her own life. And *be* somebody! Not a *thing* like I am! See, Barker?'

'Did you ever think of a divorce?'

'Did I ever think of one! Listen—but there's no chance. I've got nothing on him, and no matter what he had on me, he'd never let the world know it. He'd keep me here and torture me like he does now, only worse. But I haven't done anything wrong, see? The men I might care for, they're all scared of him and his money and power. See, Barker? And the others are just as bad as him. Like fat old Morris, the hotel man, that everybody thinks he's a model husband. The reason he don't step out more is because he's too stingy. But I could have him if I wanted him. Every time he gets near enough to me, he squeezes my hand. I guess he thinks it's a nickel, the tight old——! But come on, Barker. Let's have a drink. I'm running down.'

'I think it's about time you were running up—up-stairs,' said Bartlett. 'If I were you, I'd try to be in bed and asleep when Gregg gets home.'

'You're all right, Barker. And after this drink I'm going to do just as you say. Only I thought of it before you did, see? I think of it lots of nights. And tonight you can help me out by telling him I had a bad headache.'

Left alone, Bartlett thought a while, then read, and finally dozed off. He was dozing when Gregg returned.

'Well, well, Bartlett,' said the great man, 'did Celia desert you?'

'It was perfectly all right, Mr. Gregg. She had a headache and I told her to go to bed.'

'She's had a lot of headaches lately; reads too much, I guess. Well, I'm sorry I had this date. It was about a new golf club and I had to be there. I mean I'm going to be president of it. I see you consoled yourself with some of the Bourbon. I mean the bottle doesn't look as full as it did.'

'I hope you'll forgive me for helping myself so generously,' said Bartlett. 'I don't get stuff like that every day!'

'Well, what do you say if we turn in? We can talk on the way to town tomorrow. Though I guess you won't have much to ask me.

I guess you know all about us. I mean you know all about us now.'

'Yes, indeed, Mr Gregg. I've got plenty of material if I can just handle it.'

Celia had not put in an appearance when Gregg and his guest were ready to leave the house next day.

'She always sleeps late,' said Gregg. 'I mean she never wakes up very early. But she's later than usual this morning. Sweetheart!' he called up the stairs.

'Yes, sweetheart,' came the reply.

'Mr Bartlett's leaving now. I mean he's going.'

'Oh, good-by, Mr Bartlett. Please forgive me for not being down to see you off.'

'You're forgiven, Mrs Gregg. And thanks for your hospitality.'

'Good-by, sweetheart!'

'Good-by, sweetheart!'

The Golden Honeymoon

Mother says that when I start talking I never know when to stop.
But I tell her the only time I get a chance is when she ain't around,
so I have to make the most of it. I guess the fact is neither one of us
would be welcome in a Quaker meeting, but as I tell Mother, what
did God give us tongues for if He didn't want we should use them?
Only she says He didn't give them to us to say the same thing over
and over again, like I do, and repeat myself. But I say:

'Well, Mother,' I say, 'when people is like you and I and been
married fifty years, do you expect everything I say will be something you ain't heard me say before? But it may be new to others,
as they ain't nobody else lived with me as long as you have.'

So she says:

'You can bet they ain't, as they couldn't nobody else stand you
that long.'

'Well,' I tell her, 'you look pretty healthy.'

'Maybe I do,' she will say, 'but I looked even healthier before I
married you.'

You can't get ahead of Mother.

Yes, sir, we was married just fifty years ago the seventeenth day
of last December and my daughter and son-in-law was over from
Trenton to help us celebrate the Golden Wedding. My son-in-law
is John H. Kramer, the real estate man. He made $12,000 one year
and is pretty well thought of around Trenton; a good, steady,
hard worker. The Rotarians was after him a long time to join, but
he kept telling them his home was his club. But Edie finally made
him join. That's my daughter.

Well, anyway, they come over to help us celebrate the Golden
Wedding and it was pretty crimpy weather and the furnace don't
seem to heat up no more like it used to and Mother made the
remark that she hoped this winter wouldn't be as cold as the last,
referring to the winter previous. So Edie said if she was us, and

nothing to keep us home, she certainly wouldn't spend no more winters up here and why didn't we just shut off the water and close up the house and go down to Tampa, Florida? You know we was there four winters ago and staid five weeks, but it cost us over three hundred and fifty dollars for hotel bill alone. So Mother said we wasn't going no place to be robbed. So my son-in-law spoke up and said that Tampa wasn't the only place in the South, and besides we didn't have to stop at no high price hotel but could rent us a couple of rooms and board out somewheres, and he had heard that St Petersburg, Florida, was *the* spot and if we said the word he would write down there and make inquiries.

Well, to make a long story short, we decided to do it and Edie said it would be our Golden Honeymoon and for a present my son-in-law paid the difference between a section and a compartment so as we could have a compartment and have more privatecy. In a compartment you have an upper and lower berth just like the regular sleeper, but it is a shut in room by itself and got a wash bowl. The car we went in was all compartments and no regular berths at all. It was all compartments.

We went to Trenton the night before and staid at my daughter and son-in-law and we left Trenton the next afternoon at 3.23 p.m.

This was the twelfth day of January. Mother set facing the front of the train, as it makes her giddy to ride backwards. I set facing her, which does not affect me. We reached North Philadelphia at 4.03 p.m. and we reached West Philadelphia at 4.14, but did not go into Broad Street. We reached Baltimore at 6.30 and Washington, D.C., at 7.25. Our train laid over in Washington two hours till another train come along to pick us up and I got out and strolled up the platform and into the Union Station. When I come back, our car had been switched on to another track, but I remembered the name of it, the La Belle, as I had once visited my aunt out in Oconomowoc, Wisconsin, where there was a lake of that name, so I had no difficulty in getting located. But Mother had nearly fretted herself sick for fear I would be left.

'Well,' I said, 'I would of followed you on the next train.'

'You could of,' said Mother, and she pointed out that she had the money.

'Well,' I said, 'we are in Washington and I could of borrowed from the United States Treasury. I would of pretended I was an Englishman.'

Mother caught the point and laughed heartily.

Our train pulled out of Washington at 9.40 p.m. and Mother and I turned in early, I taking the upper. During the night we passed through the green fields of old Virginia, though it was too dark to tell if they was green or what color. When we got up in the morning, we was at Fayetteville, North Carolina. We had breakfast in the dining car and after breakfast I got in conversation with the man in the next compartment to ours. He was from Lebanon, New Hampshire, and a man about eighty years of age. His wife was with him, and two unmarried daughters and I made the remark that I should think the four of them would be crowded in one compartment, but he said they had made the trip every winter for fifteen years and knowed how to keep out of each other's way. He said they was bound for Tarpon Springs.

We reached Charleston, South Carolina, at 12.50 p.m. and arrived at Savannah, Georgia, at 4.20. We reached Jacksonville, Florida, at 8.45 p.m. and had an hour and a quarter to lay over there, but Mother made a fuss about me getting off the train, so we had the darky make up our berths and retired before we left Jacksonville. I didn't sleep good as the train done a lot of hemming and hawing, and Mother never sleeps good on a train as she says she is always worrying that I will fall out. She says she would rather have the upper herself, as then she would not have to worry about me, but I tell her I can't take the risk of having it get out that I allowed my wife to sleep in an upper berth. It would make talk.

We was up in the morning in time to see our friends from New Hampshire get off at Tarpon Springs, which we reached at 6.53 a.m.

Several of our fellow passengers got off at Clearwater and some at Belleair, where the train backs right up to the door of the mammoth hotel. Belleair is the winter headquarters for the golf dudes and everybody that got off there had their bag of sticks, as many as ten and twelve in a bag. Women and all. When I was a young man we called it shinny and only needed one club to play with and about one game of it would of been a-plenty for some of these dudes, the way we played it.

The train pulled into St Petersburg at 8.20 and when we got off the train you would think they was a riot, what with all the darkies barking for the different hotels.

I said to Mother, I said:

'It is a good thing we have got a place picked out to go to and don't have to choose a hotel, as it would be hard to choose amongst them if every one of them is the best.'

She laughed.

We found a jitney and I give him the address of the room my son-in-law had got for us and soon we was there and introduced ourselves to the lady that owns the house, a young widow about forty-eight years of age. She showed us our room, which was light and airy with a comfortable bed and bureau and washstand. It was twelve dollars a week, but the location was good, only three blocks from Williams Park.

St Pete is what folks call the town, though they also call it the Sunshine City, as they claim they's no other place in the country where they's fewer days when Old Sol don't smile down on Mother Earth, and one of the newspapers gives away all their copies free every day when the sun don't shine. They claim to of only give them away some sixty-odd times in the last eleven years. Another nickname they have got for the town is 'the Poor Man's Palm Beach,' but I guess they's men that comes there that could borrow as much from the bank as some of the Willie boys over to the other Palm Beach.

During our stay we paid a visit to the Lewis Tent City, which is the headquarters for the Tin Can Tourists. But maybe you ain't heard about them. Well, they are an organization that takes their vacation trips by auto and carries everything with them. That is, they bring along their tents to sleep in and cook in and they don't patronize no hotels or cafeterias, but they have got to be bona fide auto campers or they can't belong to the organization.

They tell me they's over 200,000 members to it and they call themselves the Tin Canners on account of most of their food being put up in tin cans. One couple we seen in the Tent City was a couple from Brady, Texas, named Mr and Mrs Pence, which the old man is over eighty years of age and they had come in their auto all the way from home, a distance of 1,641 miles. They took five weeks for the trip, Mr Pence driving the entire distance.

The Tin Canners hails from every State in the Union and in the summer time they visit places like New England and the Great Lakes region, but in the winter the most of them comes to Florida and scatters all over the State. While we was down there, they was a national convention of them at Gainesville, Florida, and they elected a Fredonia, New York, man as their president. His title is Royal Tin Can Opener of the World. They have got a song wrote up which everybody has got to learn it before they are a member:

The tin can forever! Hurrah, boys! Hurrah!
Up with the tin can! Down with the foe!
We will rally round the campfire, we'll rally once again,
Shouting, 'We auto camp forever!'

That is something like it. And the members has also got to have a tin can fastened on to the front of their machine.

I asked Mother how she would like to travel around that way and she said:

'Fine, but not with an old rattle brain like you driving.'

'Well,' I said, 'I am eight years younger than this Mr Pence who drove here from Texas.'

'Yes,' she said, 'but he is old enough to not be skittish.'

You can't get ahead of Mother.

Well, one of the first things we done in St Petersburg was to go to the Chamber of Commerce and register our names and where we was from as they's a great rivalry amongst the different States in regards to the number of their citizens visiting in town and of course our little State don't stand much of a show, but still every little bit helps, as the fella says. All and all, the man told us, they was eleven thousand names registered, Ohio leading with some fifteen hundred-odd and New York State next with twelve hundred. Then come Michigan, Pennsylvania and so on down, with one man each from Cuba and Nevada.

The first night we was there, they was a meeting of the New York–New Jersey Society at the Congregational Church and a man from Ogdensburg, New York State, made the talk. His subject was Rainbow Chasing. He is a Rotarian and a very convicting speaker, though I forget his name.

Our first business, of course, was to find a place to eat and after trying several places we run on to a cafeteria on Central Avenue that suited us up and down. We eat pretty near all our meals there and it averaged about two dollars per day for the two of us, but the food was well cooked and everything nice and clean. A man

185

don't mind paying the price if things is clean and well cooked.

On the third day of February, which is Mother's birthday, we spread ourselves and eat supper at the Poinsettia Hotel and they charged us seventy-five cents for a sirloin steak that wasn't hardly big enough for one.

I said to Mother: 'Well,' I said, 'I guess it's a good thing every day ain't your birthday or we would be in the poorhouse.'

'No,' says Mother, 'because if every day was my birthday, I would be old enough by this time to of been in my grave long ago.'

You can't get ahead of Mother.

In the hotel they had a card-room where they was several men and ladies playing five hundred and this new fangled whist bridge. We also seen a place where they was dancing, so I asked Mother would she like to trip the light fantastic toe and she said no, she was too old to squirm like you have got to do now days. We watched some of the young folks at it awhile till Mother got disgusted and said we would have to see a good movie to take the taste out of our mouth. Mother is a great movie heroyne and we go twice a week here at home.

But I want to tell you about the Park. The second day we was there we visited the Park, which is a good deal like the one in Tampa, only bigger, and they's more fun goes on here every day than you could shake a stick at. In the middle they's a big band-stand and chairs for the folks to set and listen to the concerts, which they give you music for all tastes, from Dixie up to classical pieces like Hearts and Flowers.

Then all around they's places marked off for different sports and games—chess and checkers and dominoes for folks that enjoys those kind of games, and roque and horse-shoes for the nimbler ones. I used to pitch a pretty fair shoe myself, but ain't done much of it in the last twenty years.

Well, anyway, we bought a membership ticket in the club which costs one dollar for the season, and they tell me that up to a couple years ago it was fifty cents, but they had to raise it to keep out the riffraff.

Well, Mother and I put in a great day watching the pitchers and she wanted I should get in the game, but I told her I was all out of practice and would make a fool of myself, though I seen several men pitching who I guess I could take their measure without no practice. However, they was some good pitchers, too, and one

186

boy from Akron, Ohio, who could certainly throw a pretty shoe. They told me it looked like he would win the championship of the United States in the February tournament. We come away a few days before they held that and I never did hear if he win. I forget his name, but he was a clean cut young fella and he has got a brother in Cleveland that's a Rotarian.

Well, we just stood around and watched the different games for two or three days and finally I set down in a checker game with a man named Weaver from Danville, Illinois. He was a pretty fair checker player, but he wasn't no match for me, and I hope that don't sound like bragging. But I always could hold my own on a checker-board and the folks around here will tell you the same thing. I played with his Weaver pretty near all morning for two or three mornings and he beat me one game and the only other time it looked like he had a chance, the noon whistle blowed and we had to quit and go to dinner.

While I was playing checkers, Mother would set and listen to the band, as she loves music, classical or no matter what kind, but anyway she was setting there one day and between selections the woman next to her opened up a conversation. She was a woman about Mother's own age, seventy or seventy-one, and finally she asked Mother's name and Mother told her her name and where she was from and Mother asked her the same question, and who do you think the woman was?

Well, sir, it was the wife of Frank M. Hartsell, the man who was engaged to Mother till I stepped in and cut him out, fifty-two years ago!

Yes, sir!

You can imagine Mother's surprise! and Mrs Hartsell was surprised, too, when Mother told her she had once been friends with her husband, though Mother didn't say how close friends they had been, or that Mother and I was the cause of Hartsell going out West. But that's what we was. Hartsell left his town a month after the engagement was broke off and ain't never been back since. He had went out to Michigan and become a veterinary, and that is where he had settled down, in Hillsdale, Michigan, and finally married his wife.

Well, Mother screwed up her courage to ask if Frank was still living and Mrs Hartsell took her over to where they was pitching horse-shoes and there was old Frank, waiting his turn. And he knowed Mother as soon as he seen her, though it was over fifty years. He said he knowed her by her eyes.

'Why, it's Lucy Frost!' he says, and he throwed down his shoes and quit the game.

Then they come over and hunted me up and I will confess I wouldn't of knowed him. Him and I is the same age to the month, but he seems to show it more, some way. He is balder for one thing. And his beard is all white, where mine has still got a streak of brown in it. The very first thing I said to him, I said:

'Well, Frank, that beard of yours makes me feel like I was back north. It looks like a regular blizzard.'

'Well,' he said, 'I guess yourn would be just as white if you had it dry cleaned.'

But Mother wouldn't stand that.

'Is that so!' she said to Frank. 'Well, Charley ain't had no tobacco in his mouth for over ten years!'

And I ain't!

Well, I excused myself from the checker game and it was pretty close to noon, so we decided to all have dinner together and they was nothing for it only we must try their cafeteria on Third Avenue. It was a little more expensive than ours and not near as good, I thought. I and Mother had about the same dinner we had been having every day and our bill was $1.10. Frank's check was $1.20 for he and his wife. The same meal wouldn't of cost them more than a dollar at our place.

After dinner we made them come up to our house and we all set in the parlor, which the young woman had give us the use of to entertain company. We begun talking over old times and Mother said she was a-scared Mrs Hartsell would find it tiresome listening to we three talk over old times, but as it turned out they wasn't much chance for nobody else to talk with Mrs Hartsell in the company. I have heard lots of women that could go it, but Hartsell's wife takes the cake of all the women I ever seen. She told us the family history of everybody in the State of Michigan and bragged for a half hour about her son, who she said is in the drug business in Grand Rapids, and a Rotarian.

When I and Hartsell could get a word in edgeways we joked one another back and forth and I chafed him about being a horse doctor.

'Well, Frank,' I said, 'you look pretty prosperous, so I suppose

188

they's been plenty of glanders around Hillsdale.'

'Well,' he said, 'I've managed to make more than a fair living. But I've worked pretty hard.'

'Yes,' I said, 'and I suppose you get called out all hours of the night to attend births and so on.'

Mother made me shut up.

Well, I thought they wouldn't never go home and I and Mother was in misery trying to keep awake, as the both of us generally always takes a nap after dinner. Finally they went, after we had made an engagement to meet them in the Park the next morning, and Mrs Hartsell also invited us to come to their place the next night and play five hundred. But she had forgot that they was a meeting of the Michigan Society that evening, so it was not till two evenings later that we had our first card game.

Hartsell and his wife lived in a house on Third Avenue North and had a private setting room besides their bedroom. Mrs. Hartsell couldn't quit talking about their private setting room like it was something wonderful. We played cards with them, with Mother and Hartsell partners against his wife and I. Mrs. Hartsell is a miserable card player and we certainly got the worst of it.

After the game she brought out a dish of oranges and we had to pretend it was just what we wanted, though oranges down there is like a young man's whiskers; you enjoy them at first, but they get to be a pesky nuisance.

We played cards again the next night at our place with the same partners and I and Mrs. Hartsell was beat again. Mother and Hartsell was full of compliments for each other on what a good team they made, but the both of them knowed well enough where the secret of their success laid. I guess all and all we must of played ten different evenings and they was only one night when Mrs. Hartsell and I come out ahead. And that one night wasn't no fault of hern.

When we had been down there about two weeks, we spent one evening as their guest in the Congregational Church, at a social give by the Michigan Society. A talk was made by a man named Bitting of Detroit, Michigan, on How I was Cured of Story Telling. He is a big man in the Rotarians and give a witty talk.

A woman named Mrs Oxford rendered some selections which Mrs Hartsell said was grand opera music, but whatever they was

189

my daughter Edie could of give her cards and spades and not made such a hullaballoo about it neither.

Then they was a ventriloquist from Grand Rapids and a young woman about forty-five of age that mimicked different kinds of birds. I whispered to Mother that they all sounded like a chicken, but she nudged me to shut up.

After the show we stopped in a drug store and I set up the refreshments and it was pretty close to ten o'clock before we finally turned in. Mother and I would of preferred tending the movies, but Mother said we mustn't offend Mrs Hartsell, though I asked her had we came to Florida to enjoy ourselves or to just not offend an old chatter-box from Michigan.

I felt sorry for Hartsell one morning. The women folks both had an engagement down to the chiropodist's and I run across Hartsell in the Park and he foolishly offered to play me checkers.

It was him that suggested it, not me, and I guess he repented himself before we had played one game. But he was too stubborn to give up and set there while I beat him game after game and the worst part of it was that a crowd of folks had got in the habit of watching me play and there they all was, looking on, and finally they seen what a fool Frank was making of himself, and they began to chafe him and pass remarks. Like one of them said:

'Who ever told you you was a checker player!'

And:

'You might maybe be good for tiddle-de-winks, but not checkers!'

I almost felt like letting him beat me a couple games. But the crowd would of knowed it was a put up job.

Well, the women folks joined us in the Park and I wasn't going to mention our little game, but Hartsell told about it himself and admitted he wasn't no match for me.

'Well,' said Mrs Hartsell, 'checkers ain't much of a game anyway, is it?' She said: 'It's more of a children's game, ain't it? At least, I know my boy's children used to play it a good deal.'

'Yes, ma'am,' I said. 'It's a children's game the way your husband plays it, too.'

Mother wanted to smooth things over, so she said:

'Maybe they's other games where Frank can beat you.'

'Yes,' said Mrs Hartsell, 'and I bet he could beat you pitching horse-shoes.'

190

'Well,' I said, 'I would give him a chance to try, only I ain't pitched a shoe in over sixteen years.'

'Well,' said Hartsell, 'I ain't played checkers in twenty years.'

'You ain't never played it,' I said.

'Anyway,' says Frank, 'Lucy and I is your master at five hundred.'

Well, I could of told him why that was, but had decency enough to hold my tongue.

It had got so now that he wanted to play cards every night and when I or Mother wanted to go to a movie, any one of us would have to pretend we had a headache and then trust to goodness that they wouldn't see us sneak into the theater. I don't mind playing cards when my partner keeps their mind on the game, but you take a woman like Hartsell's wife and how can they play cards when they have got to stop every couple seconds and brag about their son in Grand Rapids?

Well, the New York–New Jersey Society announced that they was goin to give a social evening too and I said to Mother, I said:

'Well, that is one evening when we will have an excuse not to play five hundred.'

'Yes,' she said, 'but we will have to ask Frank and his wife to go to the social with us as they asked us to go to the Michigan social.'

'Well,' I said, 'I had rather stay home than drag that chatter-box everywheres we go.'

So Mother said:

'You are getting too cranky. Maybe she does talk a little too much but she is good hearted. And Frank is always good company.'

So I said:

'I suppose if he is such good company you wished you had of married him.'

Mother laughed and said I sounded like I was jealous. Jealous of a cow doctor!

Anyway we had to drag them along to the social and I will say that we give them a much better entertainment than they had given us.

Judge Lane of Paterson made a fine talk on business conditions and a Mrs Newell of Westfield imitated birds, only you could really tell what they was the way she done it. Two young women from Red Bank sung a choral selection and we clapped them back

191

and they gave us Home to Our Mountains and Mother and Mrs Hartsell both had tears in their eyes. And Hartsell, too.

Well, some way or another the chairman got wind that I was there and asked me to make a talk and I wasn't even going to get up, but Mother made me, so I got up and said:

'Ladies and gentlemen,' I said. 'I didn't expect to be called on for a speech on an occasion like this or no other occasion as I do not set myself up as a speech maker, so will have to do the best I can, which I often say is the best anybody can do.'

Then I told them the story about Pat and the motorcycle, using the brogue, and it seemed to tickle them and I told them one or two other stories, but altogether I wasn't on my feet more than twenty or twenty-five minutes and you ought to of heard the clapping and hollering when I set down. Even Mrs Hartsell admitted that I am quite a speechifier and said if I ever went to Grand Rapids, Michigan, her son would make me talk to the Rotarians.

When it was over, Hartsell wanted we should go to their house and play cards, but his wife reminded him that it was after 9.30 p.m., rather a late hour to start a card game, but he had went crazy on the subject of cards, probably because he didn't have to play partners with his wife. Anyway, we got rid of them and went home to bed.

It was the next morning, when we met over to the Park, that Mrs. Hartsell made the remark that she wasn't getting no exercise so I suggested that why didn't she take part in the roque game.

She said she had not played a game of roque in twenty years, but if Mother would play she would play. Well, at first Mother wouldn't hear of it, but finally consented, more to please Mrs Hartsell than anything else.

Well, they had a game with a Mrs Ryan from Eagle, Nebraska, and a young Mrs Morse from Rutland, Vermont, who Mother had met down to the chiropodist's. Well, Mother couldn't hit a flea and they all laughed at her and I couldn't help from laughing at her myself and finally she quit and said her back was too lame to stoop over. So they got another lady and kept on playing and soon Mrs Hartsell was the one everybody was laughing at, as she had a long shot to hit the black ball, and as she made the effort her teeth fell out on to the court. I never seen a woman so flustered in my life. And I never heard so much laughing, only Mrs Hartsell

192

didn't join in and she was madder than a hornet and wouldn't play no more, so the game broke up.

Mrs Hartsell went home without speaking to nobody, but Hartsell stayed around and finally he said to me, he said:

'Well, I played you checkers the other day and you beat me bad and now what do you say if you and me play a game of horseshoes?'

I told him I hadn't pitched a shoe in sixteen years, but Mother said:

'Go ahead and play. You used to be good at it and maybe it will come back to you.'

Well, to make a long story short, I give in. I oughtn't to of never tried it, as I hadn't pitched a shoe in sixteen years, and I only done it to humor Hartsell.

Before we started, Mother patted me on the back and told me to do my best, so we started in and I seen right off that I was in for it, as I hadn't pitched a shoe in sixteen years and didn't have my distance. And besides, the plating had wore off the shoes so that they was points right where they stuck into my thumb and I hadn't throwed more than two or three times when my thumb was raw and it pretty near killed me to hang on to the shoe, let alone pitch it.

Well, Hartsell throws the awkwardest shoe I ever seen pitched and to see him pitch you wouldn't think he would ever come nowheres near, but he is also the luckiest pitcher I ever seen and he made some pitches where the shoe lit five and six feet short and then schoonered up and was a ringer. They's no use trying to beat that kind of luck.

They was a pretty fair size crowd watching us and four or five other ladies besides Mother, and it seems like, when Hartsell pitches, he has got to chew and it kept the ladies on the anxious seat as he don't seem to care which way he is facing when he leaves go.

You would think a man as old as him would of learnt more manners.

Well, to make a long story short, I was just beginning to get my distance when I had to give up on account of my thumb, which I showed it to Hartsell and he seen I couldn't go on, as it was raw and bleeding. Even if I could of stood it to go on myself, Mother wouldn't of allowed it after she seen my thumb. So anyway I quit and Hartsell said the score was nineteen to six, but I don't know what it was. Or don't care, neither.

Well, Mother and I went home and I said I hoped we was through with the Hartsells and I was sick and tired of them, but it seemed like she had promised we would go over to their house that evening for another game of their everlasting cards.

Well, my thumb was giving me considerable pain and I felt kind of out of sorts and I guess maybe I forgot myself, but anyway, when we was about through playing Hartsell made the remark that he wouldn't never lose a game of cards if he could always have Mother for a partner.

So I said:

'Well, you had a chance fifty years ago to always have her for a partner, but you wasn't man enough to keep her.'

I was sorry the minute I had said it and Hartsell didn't know what to say and for once his wife couldn't say nothing. Mother tried to smooth things over by making the remark that I must of had something stronger than tea or I wouldn't talk so silly. But Mrs Hartsell had froze up like an iceberg and hardly said good night to us and I bet her and Frank put in a pleasant hour after we was gone.

As we was leaving, Mother said to him: 'Never mind Charley's nonsense, Frank. He is just mad because you beat him all hollow pitching horseshoes and playing cards.'

She said that to make up for my slip, but at the same time she certainly riled me. I tried to keep ahold of myself, but as soon as we was out of the house she had to open up the subject and begun to scold me for the break I had made.

Well, I wasn't in no mood to be scolded. So I said:

'I guess he is such a wonderful pitcher and card player that you wished you had married him.'

'Well,' she said, 'at least he ain't a baby to give up pitching because his thumb has got a few scratches.'

'And how about you,' I said, 'making a fool of yourself on the roque court and then pretending your back is lame and you can't play no more!'

'Yes,' she said, 'but when you hurt your thumb I didn't laugh at you, and why did you laugh at me when I sprained my back?'

'Who could help from laughing!' I said.

'Well,' she said, 'Frank Hartsell didn't laugh.'

'Well,' I said, 'why didn't you marry him?'

'Well,' said Mother, 'I almost wished I had!'

'And I wished so, too!' I said.

'I'll remember that!' said Mother, and that's the last word she said to me for two days.

We seen the Hartsells the next day in the Park and I was willing to apologize, but they just nodded to us. And a couple days later we heard they had left for Orlando, where they have got relatives.

I wished they had went there in the first place.

Mother and I made it up setting on a bench.

'Listen, Charley,' she said. 'This is our Golden Honeymoon and we don't want the whole thing spoilt with a silly old quarrel.'

'Well,' I said, 'did you mean that about wishing you had married Hartsell?'

'Of course not,' she said, 'that is, if you didn't mean that you wished I had, too.'

So I said:

'I was just tired and all wrought up. I thank God you chose me instead of him as they's no other woman in the world who I could of lived with all these years.'

'How about Mrs Hartsell?' says Mother.

'Good gracious!' I said. 'Imagine being married to a woman that plays five hundred like she does and drops her teeth on the roque court!'

'Well,' said Mother, 'it wouldn't be no worse than being married to a man that expectorates towards ladies and is such a fool in a checker game.'

So I put my arm around her shoulder and she stroked my hand and I guess we got kind of spoony.

They was two days left of our stay in St Petersburg and the next to the last day Mother introduced me to a Mrs Kendall from Kingston, Rhode Island, who she had met at the chiropodist's.

Mrs Kendall made us acquainted with her husband, who is in the grocery business. They have got two sons and five grandchildren and one great-grandchild. One of their sons lives in Providence and is way up in the Elks as well as a Rotarian.

We found them very congenial people and we played cards with them the last two nights we was there. They was both experts and I only wished we had met them sooner instead of running into the Hartsells. But the Kendalls will be there again next winter and we will see more of them, that is, if we decide to make the trip again.

We left the Sunshine City on the eleventh day of February, at 11 a.m. This give us a day trip through Florida and we seen all the country we had passed through at night on the way down.

We reached Jacksonville at 7 p.m. and pulled out of there at 8.10 p.m. We reached Fayetteville, North Carolina, at nine o'clock the following morning, and reached Washington, D.C., at 6.30 p.m., laying over there half an hour.

We reached Trenton at 11.01 p.m. and had wired ahead to my daughter and son-in-law and they met us at the train and we went to their house and they put us up for the night. John would of made us stay up all night, telling about our trip, but Edie said we must be tired and made us go to bed. That's my daughter.

The next day we took our train for home and arrived safe and sound, having been gone just one month and a day.

Here comes Mother, so I guess I better shut up.

Mr and Mrs Fix-It

They're certainly a live bunch in this town. We ain't only been here three days and had calls already from people representin' four different organizations—the Chamber of Commerce, Kiwanis, and I forget who else. They wanted to know if we was comfortable and did we like the town and is they anything they can do for us and what to be sure and see.

And they all asked how we happened to come here instead of goin' somewheres else. I guess they keep a record of everybody's reasons for comin' so as they can get a line on what features tourists is most attracted by. Then they play up them features in next year's booster advertisin'.

Well, I told them we was perfectly comfortable and we like the town fine and they's nothin' nobody can do for us right now and we'll be sure and see all the things we ought to see. But when they asked me how did we happen to come here, I said it was just a kind of a accident, because the real reason makes too long a story.

My wife has been kiddin' me about my friends ever since we was married. She says that judgin' by the ones I've introduced her to, they ain't nobody in the world got a rummier bunch of friends than me. I'll admit that the most of them ain't, well, what you might call hot; they're different somehow than when I first hung around with them. They seem to be lost without a brass rail to rest their dogs on. But of course they're old friends and I can't give 'em the air.

We have 'em to the house for dinner every little wile, they and their wives, and what my missus objects to is because they don't none of them play bridge or mah jong or do cross-word puzzles or sing or dance or even talk, but just set there and wait for somebody to pour 'em a fresh drink.

As I say, my wife kids me about 'em and they ain't really nothin' I can offer in their defense. That don't mean, though, that the shoe is all on one foot. Because wile the majority of her friends may not be quite as dumb as mine, just the same they's a few she's picked out who I'd of had to be under the ether to allow anybody to introduce 'em to me in the first place.

Like the Crandalls, for instance. Mrs Crandall come from my wife's home town and they didn't hardly know each other there, but they met again in a store in Chi and it went from bad to worse till finally Ada asked the dame and her husband to the house.

Well, the husband turns out to be the fella that win the war, wile it seems that Mrs Crandall was in Atlantic City once and some movin' picture company was makin' a picture there and they took a scene of what was supposed to be society people walkin' up and down the Boardwalk and Mrs Crandall was in the picture and people that seen it when it come out, they all said that from the way she screened, why if she wanted to go into the business, she could make Gloria Swanson look like Mrs Gump.

Now it ain't only took me a few words to tell you these things, but when the Crandalls tells their story themselves, they don't hardly get started by midnight and no chance of them goin' home till they're through even when you drop 'em a hint that they're springin' it on you for the hundred and twelfth time.

That's the Crandalls, and another of the wife's friends is the Thayers. Thayer is what you might call a all-around handy man. He can mimic pretty near all the birds and beasts and fishes, he can yodel, he can play a ocarena, or he can recite Kipling or Robert W. Service, or he can do card tricks, and strike a light without no matches, and tie all the different knots.

And besides that, he can make a complete radio outfit and set it up, and take pictures as good as the best professional photographers and a whole lot better. He collects autographs. And he never had a sick day in his life.

Mrs Thayer gets a headache playin' bridge, so it's mah jong or rhum when she's around. She used to be a teacher of elocution and she still gives readin's if you coax her, or if you don't, and her hair is such a awful nuisance that she would get it cut in a minute only all her friends tells her it would be criminal to spoil that head of hair. And when she talks to her husband, she always talks baby talk, maybe because somebody has told her that she'd be single if he wasn't childish.

And then Ada has got still another pal, a dame named Peggy

Flood who is hospital mad and ain't happy unless she is just goin' under the knife or just been there. She's had everything removed that the doctors knew the name of and now they're probin' her for new giblets.

Well, I wouldn't mind if they cut her up into alphabet soup if they'd only do such a good job of it that they couldn't put her together again, but she always comes through O.K. and she spends the intermissions at our place, describin' what all they done or what they're plannin' to do next.

But the cat's nightgown is Tom Stevens and his wife. There's the team that wins the Olympics! And they're Ada's team, not mine.

Ada met Belle Stevens on the elevated. Ada was invited to a party out on the North Side and didn't know exactly where to get off and Mrs Stevens seen her talkin' to the guard and horned in and asked her what was it she wanted to know and Ada told her, and Mrs Stevens said she was goin' to get off the same station Ada wanted to get off, so they got off together.

Mrs Stevens insisted on goin' right along to the address where Ada was goin' because she said Ada was bound to get lost if she wasn't familiar with the neighborhood.

Well, Ada thought it was mighty nice of her to do so much for a stranger. Mrs Stevens said she was glad to because she didn't know what would of happened to her lots of times if strangers hadn't been nice and helped her out.

She asked Ada where she lived and Ada told her on the South Side and Mrs Stevens said she was sure we'd like it better on the North Side if we'd leave her pick out a place for us, so Ada told her we had a year's lease that we had just signed and couldn't break it, so then Mrs Stevens said her husband had studied law and he claimed they wasn't no lease that you couldn't break and some evening she would bring him out to call on us and he'd tell us how to break our lease.

Well, Ada had to say sure, come on out, though we was perfectly satisfied with our apartment and didn't no more want to break the lease than each other's jaw. Maybe not as much. Anyway, the very next night, they showed up, Belle and Tom, and when they'd gone, I give 'em the nickname—Mr and Mrs Fix-It.

After the introductions, Stevens made some remark about what a cozy little place we had and then he asked if I would mind tellin' what rent we paid. So I told him a hundred and a quarter a month.

So he said, of course, that was too much and no wonder we wanted to break the lease. Then I said we was satisfied and didn't want to break it and he said I must be kiddin' and if I would show him the lease he would see what loopholes they was in it.

Well, the lease was right there in a drawer in the table, but I told him it was in my safety deposit box at the bank. I ain't got no safety deposit box and no more use for one than Judge Landis has for the deef and dumb alphabet.

Stevens said the lease was probably just a regular lease and if it was, they wouldn't be no trouble gettin' out of it, and meanwile him and his wife would see if they couldn't find us a place in the same buildin' with them.

And he was pretty sure they could even if the owner had to give some other tenant the air, because he, the owner, would do anything in the world for Stevens.

So I said yes, but suppose we want to stay where we are. So he said I looked like a man with better judgment than that and if I would just leave everything to him he would fix it so's we could move within a month. I kind of laughed and thought that would be the end of it.

He wanted to see the whole apartment so I showed him around and when we come to the bathroom he noticed my safety razor on the shelf. He said, 'So you use one of them things,' and I said, 'Yes,' and he asked me how I liked it, and I said I liked it fine and he said that must be because I hadn't never used a regular razor.

He said a regular razor was the only thing to use if a man wanted to look good. So I asked him if he used a regular razor and he said he did, so I said, 'Well, if you look good, I don't want to.'

But that didn't stop him and he said if I would meet him downtown the next day he would take me to the place where he bought all his razors and help me pick some out for myself. I told him I was goin' to be tied up, so just to give me the name and address of the place and I would drop in there when I had time.

But, no, that wouldn't do; he'd have to go along with me and introduce me to the proprietor because the proprietor was a great pal of his and would do anything in the world for him, and if the proprietor vouched for the razors, I could be sure I was gettin' the best razors money could buy. I told him again that I was goin' to be tied up and I managed to get him on some other subject.

Meanwile Mrs Stevens wanted to know where Ada had

bought the dress she was wearin' and how much had it cost and Ada told her and Mrs Stevens said it was a crime. She would meet Ada downtown tomorrow morning and take her to the shop where she bought her clothes and help her choose some dresses that really was dresses.

So Ada told her she didn't have no money to spend on dresses right then, and besides, the shop Mrs Stevens mentioned was too high priced. But it seems the dame that run the shop was just like a sister to Mrs Stevens and give her and her friends a big reduction and not only that, but they wasn't no hurry about payin'.

Well, Ada thanked her just the same, but didn't need nothin' new just at present; maybe later on she would take advantage of Mrs Stevens's kind offer. Yes, but right now they was some models in stock that would be just beautiful on Ada and they might be gone later on. They was nothin' for it but Ada had to make a date with her; she wasn't obliged to buy nothin', but it would be silly not to go and look at the stuff that was in the joint and get acquainted with the dame that run it.

Well, Ada kept the date and bought three dresses she didn't want and they's only one of them she'd had the nerve to wear. They cost her a hundred dollars a smash and I'd hate to think what the price would of been if Mrs Stevens and the owner of the shop wasn't so much like sisters.

I was sure I hadn't made no date with Stevens, but just the same he called me up the next night to ask why I hadn't met him. And a couple of days later I got three new razors in the mail along with a bill and a note from the store sayin' that these was three specially fine razors that had been picked out for me by Thomas J. Stevens.

I don't know yet why I paid for the razors and kept 'em. I ain't used 'em and never intended to. Though I've been tempted a few times to test their edge on Stevens's neck.

That same week, Mrs Stevens called up and asked us to spend Sunday with them and when we got out there, the owner of the buildin' is there, too. And Stevens has told him that I was goin' to give up my apartment on the South Side and wanted him to show me what he had.

I thought this was a little too strong and I said Stevens must of misunderstood me, that I hadn't no fault to find with the place I was in and wasn't plannin' to move, not for a year anyway. You can bet this didn't make no hit with the guy, who was just there on

Stevens's say-so that I was a prospective tenant.

Well, it was only about two months ago that this cute little couple come into our life, but I'll bet we seen 'em twenty times at least. They was always invitin' us to their place or invitin' themselves to our place and Ada is one of these here kind of people that just can't say no. Which may be why I and her is married.

Anyway, it begin to seem like us and the Stevenses was livin' together and all one family, with them at the head of it. I never in my life seen anybody as crazy to run other people's business. Honest to heavens, it's a wonder they let us brush our own teeth!

Ada made the remark one night that she wished the ski jumper who was doin' our cookin' would get married and quit so's she wouldn't have to can her. Mrs Stevens was there and asked Ada if she should try and get her a new cook, but Ada says no, the poor gal might have trouble findin' another job and she felt sorry for her.

Just the same, the next afternoon a Jap come to the apartment and said he was ready to go to work and Mrs Stevens had sent him. Ada had to tell him the place was already filled.

Another night, Ada complained that her feet was tired. Belle said her feet used to get tired, too, till a friend of hers recommended a chiropodist and she went to him and he done her so much good that she made a regular appointment with him for once every month and paid him a flat sum and no matter how much runnin' around she done, her dogs hadn't fretted her once since this cornhusker started tendin' to 'em.

She wanted to call up the guy at his home right then and there and make a date for Ada and the only way Ada could stop her was by promisin' to go and see him the next time her feet hurt. After that, whenever the two gals met, Belle's first question was 'How is your feet?' and the answer was always 'Fine, thanks.'

Well, I'm quite a football fan and Ada likes to go, too, when it's a big game and lots of excitement. So we decided we'd see the Illinois-Chicago game and have a look at this 'Red' Grange. I warned Ada to not say nothin' about it to Tom and Belle as I felt like we was entitled to a day off.

But it happened that they was goin' to be a game up at Evanston that day and the Stevenses invited us to see that one with them. So we used the other game as a alibi. And when Tom asked me later on if I'd boughten my tickets yet, instead of sayin' yes, I told him the truth and said no.

So then he said:

'I'm glad you ain't, because I and Belle has made up our mind that the Chicago game is the one we ought to see. And we'll all go together. And don't you bother about tickets because I can get better ones than you can as Stagg and I is just like that.'

So I left it to him to get the tickets and we might as well of set on the Adams Street bridge. I said to Stevens, I said:

'If these is the seats Mr Stagg digs up for his old pals, I suppose he leads strangers twenty or thirty miles out in the country and blindfolds 'em and ties 'em to a tree.'

Now of course it was the bunk about he and Stagg bein' so close. He may of been introduced to him once, but he ain't the kind of a guy that Stagg would go around holdin' hands with. Just the same, most of the people he bragged about knowin', why it turned out that he really did know 'em; yes, and stood ace high with 'em, too.

Like, for instance, I got pinched for speedin' one night and they give me a ticket to show up in the Speeders' court and I told Stevens about it and he says, 'Just forget it! I'll call up the judge and have it wiped off the book. He's a mighty good fella and a personal friend of mine.'

Well, I didn't want to take no chances so I phoned Stevens the day before I was supposed to appear in court, and I asked him if he'd talked to the judge. He said he had and I asked him if he was sure. So he said, 'If you don't believe me, call up the judge yourself.' And he give me the judge's number. Sure enough, Stevens had fixed it and when I thanked the judge for his trouble, he said it was a pleasure to do somethin' for a friend of Tom Stevens's.

Now, I know it's silly to not appreciate favors like that and not warm up to people that's always tryin' to help you along, but still a person don't relish bein' treated like they was half-witted and couldn't button their shirt alone. Tom and Belle meant all right, but I and Ada got kind of tired of havin' fault found with everything that belonged to us and everything we done or tried to do.

Besides our apartment bein' no good and our clothes terrible, we learned that my dentist didn't know a bridge from a mustache

203

cup, and the cigarettes I smoked didn't have no taste to them, and the man that bobbed Ada's hair must of been mad at her, and neither of us would ever know what it was to live till we owned a wire-haired fox terrier.

And we found out that the liquor I'd been drinkin' and enjoyin' was a mixture of bath salts and assorted paints, and the car we'd paid seventeen hundred smackers for wasn't nowheres near as much of a car as one that Tom could of got for us for eight hundred on account of knowin' a brother-in-law of a fella that used to go to school with the president of the company's nephew, and that if Ada would take up aesthetic dancin' under a dame Belle knew about, why she'd never have no more trouble with her tonsils.

Nothin' we had or nothin' we talked about gettin' or doin' was worth a damn unless it was recommended or suggested by the Stevenses.

Well, I done a pretty good business this fall and I and Ada had always planned to spend a winter in the South, so one night we figured it out that this was the year we could spare the money and the time and if we didn't go this year we never would. So the next thing was where should we go, and we finally decided on Miami. And we said we wouldn't mention nothin' about it to Tom and Belle till the day we was goin'. We'd pretend we was doin' it out of a clear sky.

But a secret is just as safe with Ada as a police dog tethered with dental floss. It wasn't more than a day or two after we'd had our talk when Tom and Belle sprang the news that they was leavin' for California right after New Year's. And why didn't we go with them.

Well, I didn't say nothin' and Ada said it sounded grand, but it was impossible. Then Stevens said if it was a question of money, to not let that bother us as he would loan it to me and I could pay it back whenever I felt like it. That was more than Ada could stand, so she says we wasn't as poor as people seemed to think and the reason we couldn't go to California was because we was goin' to Miami.

This was such a surprise that it almost struck 'em dumb at first and all Tom could think of to say was that he'd been to Miami himself and it was too crowded and he'd lay off of it if he was us. But the next time we seen 'em they had our trip all arranged.

First, Tom asked me what road we was goin' on and I told him the Big Four. So he asked if we had our reservations and I told him yes.

'Well,' he said, 'we'll get rid of 'em and I'll fix you up on the C. & E.I. The general passenger agent is a friend of mine and they ain't nothin' he won't do for my friends. He'll see that you're treated right and that you get there in good shape.'

So I said:

'I don't want to put you to all that trouble, and besides I don't know nobody connected with the Big Four well enough for them to resent me travelin' on their lines and as for gettin' there in good shape, even if I have a secret enemy or two on the Big Four, I don't believe they'd endanger the lives of the other passengers just to see that I didn't get there in good shape.'

But Stevens insisted on takin' my tickets and sellin' 'em back to the Big Four and gettin' me fixed on the C. & E.I. The berths we'd had on the Big Four was Lower 9 and Lower 10. The berths Tom got us on the C. & E.I. was Lower 7 and Lower 8, which he said was better. I suppose he figured that the nearer you are to the middle of the car, the less chance there is of bein' woke up if your car gets in another train's way.

He wanted to know, too, if I'd made any reservations at a hotel. I showed him a wire I had from the Royal Palm in reply to a wire I'd sent 'em.

'Yes,' he says, 'but you don't want to stop at the Royal Palm. You wire and tell 'em to cancel that and I'll make arrangements for you at the Flamingo, over at the Beach. Charley Krom, the manager there, was born and raised in the same town I was. He'll take great care of you if he knows you're a friend of mine.'

So I asked him if all the guests at the Flamingo was friends of his, and he said of course not; what did I mean?

'Well,' I said, 'I was just thinkin' that if they ain't, Mr Krom probably makes life pretty miserable for 'em. What does he do, have the phone girl ring 'em up at all hours of the night, and hide their mail, and shut off their hot water, and put cracker crumbs in their beds?'

That didn't mean nothin' to Stevens and he went right ahead and switched me from one hotel to the other.

While Tom was reorganizin' my program and tellin' me what to eat in Florida, and what bait to use for barracuda and carp, and what time to go bathin' and which foot to stick in the water first, why Belle was makin' Ada return all the stuff she had boughten to wear down there and buy other stuff that Belle picked out for her at joints where Belle was so well known that they only soaked her twice as much as a stranger. She had Ada almost crazy, but I told her to never mind; in just a few more days we'd be where they couldn't get at us.

I suppose you're wonderin' why didn't we quarrel with 'em and break loose from 'em and tell 'em to leave us alone. You'd know why if you knew them. Nothin' we could do would convince 'em that we didn't want their advice and help. And nothin' we could say was a insult.

Well, the night before we was due to leave Chi, the phone rung and I answered it. It was Tom.

'I've got a surprise for you,' he says 'I and Belle has give up the California idear. We're goin' to Miami instead, and on account of me knowin' the boys down at the C. & E.I., I've landed a drawin' room on the same train you're takin'. How is that for news?'

'Great!' I said, and I went back and broke it to Ada. For a minute I thought she was goin' to faint. And all night long she moaned and groaned and had hysterics.

So that's how we happened to come to Biloxi.

How to Write Short Stories

A glimpse at the advertising columns of our leading magazines shows that whatever else this country may be shy of, there is certainly no lack of correspondence schools that learns you the art of short-story writing. The most notorious of these schools makes the boast that one of their pupils cleaned up $5000.00 and no hundreds dollars writing short stories according to the system learnt in their course, though it don't say if that amount was cleaned up in one year or fifty.

However, for some reason another when you skin through the pages of high class periodicals, you don't very often find them cluttered up with stories that was written by boys or gals who had win their phi beta skeleton keys at this or that story-writing college. In fact, the most of the successful authors of the short fiction of today never went to no kind of college, or if they did, they studied piano tuning or the barber trade. They could of got just as far in what I call the literary game if they had of stayed home those four years and helped mother carry out the empty bottles.

The answer is that you can't find no school in operation up to date, whether it be a general institution of learning or a school that specializes in story writing, which can make a great author out of a born druggist.

But a little group of our deeper drinkers has suggested that maybe boys and gals who wants to take up writing as their life work would be benefited if some person like I was to give them a few hints in regards to the technic of the short story, how to go about planning it and writing it, when and where to plant the love interest and climax, and finally how to market the finished product without leaving no bad taste in the mouth.

Well, then, it seems to me like the best method to use in giving out these hints is to try and describe my own personal procedure from the time I get inspired till the time the manuscript is loaded on to the trucks.

The first thing I generally always do is try and get hold of a catchy title, like for instance, 'Basil Hargrave's Vermifuge,' or 'Fun at the Incinerating Plant.' Then I set down to a desk or flat table of any kind and lay out 3 or 4 sheets of paper with as many different colored pencils and look at them cock-eyed a few moments before making a selection.

How to begin—or, as we professionals would say, 'how to commence'—is the next question. It must be admitted that the method of approach ('L'approchement') differs even among first class fictionists. For example, Blasco Ibañez usually starts his stories with a Spanish word, Jack Dempsey with an 'I' and Charley Peterson with a couple of simple declarative sentences about his leading character, such as 'Hazel Gooftree had just gone mah jong. She felt faint.'

Personally it has been my observation that the reading public prefers short dialogue to any other kind of writing and I always aim to open my tale with two or three lines of conversation between characters—or, as I call them, my puppets—who are to play important rôles. I have often found that something one of these characters says, words I have perhaps unconsciously put into his or her mouth, directs my plot into channels deeper than I had planned and changes, for the better, the entire sense of my story.

To illustrate this, let us pretend that I have laid out a plot as follows: Two girls, Dorothy Abbott and Edith Quaver, are spending the heated term at a famous resort. The Prince of Wales visits the resort, but leaves on the next train. A day or two later, a Mexican reaches the place and looks for accommodations, but is unable to find a room without a bath. The two girls meet him at the public filling station and ask him for a contribution to their autograph album. To their amazement, he utters a terrible oath, spits in their general direction and hurries out of town. It is not until years later that the two girls learn he is a notorious forger and realize how lucky they were after all.

Let us pretend that the above is the original plot. Then let us begin the writing with haphazard dialogue and see whither it leads:

'Where was you?' asked Edith Quaver.

'To the taxidermist's,' replied Dorothy Abbott.

The two girls were spending the heated term at a famous watering trough. They had just been bathing and were now engaged in sorting dental floss.

'I am getting sick in tired of this place,' went on Miss Quaver.

'It is mutual,' said Miss Abbott, shying a cucumber at a passing paper hanger.

There was a rap at their door and the maid's voice announced that company was awaiting them downstairs. The two girls went down and entered the music room. Garnett Whaledriver was at the piano and the girls tiptoed to the lounge.

The big Nordic, oblivious of their presence, allowed his fingers to form weird, fantastic minors before they strayed unconsciously into the first tones of Chopin's 121st Fugue for the Bass Drum.

From this beginning, a skilled writer could go most anywheres, but it would be my tendency to drop these three characters and take up the life of a mule in the Grand Canyon. The mule watches the trains come in from the east, he watches the trains come in from the west, and keeps wondering who is going to ride him. But she never finds out.

The love interest and climax would come when a man and a lady, both strangers, got to talking together on the train going back east.

'Well,' said Mrs Croot, for it was she, 'what did you think of the Canyon?'

'Some cave,' replied her escort.

'What a funny way to put it!' replied Mrs Croot. 'And now play me something.'

Without a word, Warren took his place on the piano bench and at first allowed his fingers to form weird, fantastic chords on the black keys. Suddenly and with no seeming intention, he was in the midst of the second movement of Chopin's Twelfth Sonata for Flute and Cuspidor. Mrs Croot felt faint.

That will give young writers an idea of how an apparently trivial thing such as a line of dialogue will upset an entire plot and lead an author far from the path he had pointed for himself. It will also serve as a model for beginners to follow in regards to style and technic. I will not insult my readers by going on with the story to its obvious conclusion. That simple task they can do for themselves, and it will be good practice.

So much for the planning and writing. Now for the marketing of the completed work. A good many young writers make the mistake of enclosing a stamped, self-addressed envelope, big enough for the manuscript to come back in. This is too much of a temptation to the editor.

Personally I have found it a good scheme to not even sign my name to the story, and when I have got it sealed up in its envelope and stamped and addressed, I take it to some town where I don't live and mail it from there. The editor has no idea who wrote the story, so how can he send it back? He is in a quandary.

In conclusion let me warn my pupils never to write their stories—or, as we professionals call them, 'yarns'—on used paper. And never to write them on a post-card. And never to send them by telegraph (Morse code).

Stories ('yarns') of mine which have appeared in various publications—one of them having been accepted and published by the first editor that got it—are reprinted in the following pages and will illustrate in a half-hearted way what I am trying to get at.

RING LARDNER

'THE MANGE,'
Great Neck, Long Island, 1924.

Some Notes on Baseball
DAVID LODGE

More important than the games played on the baseball diamond in stories like 'Alibi Ike' and 'Women' are the verbal games people play in the dugout or the hotel room. Alibi Ike, for instance, always has an excuse, not just for his failures, but also for his successful performances, thus implying that his true standard is above that of ordinary mortals; his exasperated teammates try to puncture this arrogant pretence by every trick of irony and forensic cross-examination. But to help British readers enjoy these stories, here are a few notes about the rules and language of baseball.

In its essentials, baseball bears a close resemblance to the British game of rounders. There are two teams, of nine players each, who take turns (innings) to bat. The pitcher of the fielding team throws the ball to the batter. The ball must pass over the batting plate, at an appropriate height, to count, unless the batter swings at it. If the batter misses or fails to hit the ball a 'strike' is called by the umpire. Three strikes and the batter is out ('struck out'). If the batter hits the ball safely he may run around the diamond-shaped circuit marked by three bases and the batting plate or home base. He may stop on one of the three bases and wait for an opportunity to continue when the next player in his team hits the ball. A run is scored when one player completes the circuit and reaches home base. A ball struck fairly over the perimeter of the field allows the batter to trot safely round the circuit for a 'home run'. A player is out if he is 'tagged' (i.e., touched with the ball) by one of the fielding team before he reaches base (in the case of first base, the baseman need only put his foot on the base while holding the ball) or if the ball is caught before it touches the ground. Three men tagged, or caught, or struck out, and the inning terminates. The ball must be hit in a prescribed segment of the field or it is a foul and the batter is not allowed to run. The first *two* foul hits count as strikes, after which they are not penalised (though the batter may be caught off one). If the pitcher throws the ball wide of the plate it is called a 'ball'; four of these and the batter is allowed to 'walk' to first base.

> In the first innin' Ike hit one clear over the right field stand but it was a few feet foul. Then he got another foul and then the count come to two and two. Then Rube slipped one acrost on him and he was called out.
> 'What do you know about that!' he says afterward on the bench. 'I lost count. I thought it was three and one, and I took a strike.' ('Alibi Ike')

'Two and two' here means that Ike had two 'balls' and two 'strikes' (his two foul hits). He is beaten by the next ball and given out. He pretends that he thought he had had three 'balls', and only one strike—otherwise he would have tried to hit the next ball instead of letting it go.

Sometimes members of the batting team who are on base will attempt to 'steal' the next base by starting their run as the pitcher throws. If a batter has teammates already on base, he may 'bunt', i.e. tap the ball without swinging at it, just far enough to allow them to move on to the next base, or score a run, and usually sacrificing himself in the process. The players have signals for such tactics.

> Along in the fifth we was one run to the bad and Ike got on with one out. On the first ball throwed to Smitty, Ike went down. The ball was outside and Meyers throwed Ike out by ten feet.

This may be interpreted as follows: in the fifth inning (out of nine), the opposing team was leading by one run when Ike got on base with one member of the team already out. On the first ball being pitched to the next batter (Smitty), Ike made a run for the next base, but the ball was wide, Smitty made no attempt to hit it, and the opposing catcher, Meyers (the catcher stands behind the batter, facing the pitcher, like a wicket-keeper in cricket) was able to throw the ball to his baseman while Ike was still ten feet short of the base. In the sequel, Ike puts up a smokescreen of different and incompatible excuses, generating a dispute about what signals he had agreed with Smitty, and whether he was expecting him to 'hit and run' (a play in which the batter hits the ball if at all possible, and runs to first base, which would compel Ike to move on to second) or intended to steal a base (a play that would require Smitty at least to swing at the ball, to distract the catcher, the 'Indian'). In 'Women', the substitutes who are not batting are sent from the 'dugout' (the place where the players wait their turn to bat) to 'coach' their teammates who are on base—i.e. to shout advice or give visual signals from the sidelines.

A player's seasonal batting average consists of the number of safe hits he makes divided by the number of times at bat. ·280 would be a good average; Ike's ·356 is outstanding.

Some other baseball jargon: 'fly ball' is a ball hit high into the air; 'fungoes' are flyballs hit to the outfield in pre-match practice. Two games played consecutively between the same teams made a 'double-header'. A 'hook' is a ball pitched so as to swerve or 'break' away from a straight trajectory as it reaches the batting plate. A base is sometimes referred to as a 'bag' or 'sack'. To 'triple' is to reach third base. To 'whiff' is to strike out. To 'pop up' is to hit a short, weak, fly ball that is caught. 'In the pinch' is a point in the game when a team desperately needs a run. A pitcher who 'boots one' makes an error that allows the batter to score a run. 'Peggin' bunts to first base' means throwing out players who have bunted. To 'shag' is to run after a ball to catch it.

I gratefully acknowledge the assistance of my colleague, Charles Whitworth, in compiling these notes.

EF.

EVERYMAN FICTION

J.G. BALLARD
The Drowned World

Ballard's classic novel, set in a tropical, flooded London of the near future, is a fast-paced narrative full of stunning images that reflect on our own society. As Robert Nye wrote about one of Ballard's latest books, 'Ballard deserves now to be taken out of the "science fiction" bracket altogether, and considered from the highest standards as what he is: a serious writer, almost a visionary, with much to tell us about the hell of the human predicament.'

'one of the brightest stars in post-war fiction'   Kingsley Amis

PHILIP NORMAN
Wild Thing

Ten fictional scenes set in the feverish world of Rock and Blues by one of the twenty Best of Young British Novelists and author of the best-selling *Shout! A Biography of The Beatles*. Seldom has a writer caught so exactly the electric waves that fizzed the blood of a generation.

'Norman has done more than most writers to take a cultural reading in a place that compelling matters.'   Malcolm Bradbury

RACHEL INGALLS
Mrs Caliban and Others

Three striking novelle in which fantasy and legend are earthed by human sympathy and humour.

'I loved Mrs Caliban. So deft and austere in its prose . . . so drolly casual in its fantasy . . . but opening up into a deep female sadness that makes us stare. An impeccable parable, beautifully written from first paragraph to last.'   John Updike

JOYCE CAROL OATES
Unholy Loves

A famous but deplorably behaved English poet visits an East Coast university in this witty and wickedly perceptive campus novel by one of America's most highly regarded writers.

'Immensely entertaining stuff . . . snide and rueful by turn' Elizabeth Berridge

'a brilliant book'   *The Times*

HUGH FLEETWOOD
The Order of Death

A compelling novel of obsession by an exceptionally talented young British author. Set in crime-ridden Manhatten, it traces the passage of Fred O'Connor—passionately dreaming of an ordered world—from a position of mad, lonely strength to one of terrible and ultimately tragic awareness.

'Hugh Fleetwood can write like a dream. He reaches down and stirs up with venomous delight the nameless, faceless things swimming far below the levels of consciousness.'   *The Scotsman*

'irresistibly readable'   *The Sunday Times*

DYLAN THOMAS
Portrait of the Artist As A Young Dog

Dylan Thomas's classic book, based on his youth in suburban Swansea—lyrical, rumbustious, brimming with life. Here is Thomas as a small boy, fighting one moment, spouting precocious verse the next; Thomas the adolescent, coping with delicious giggling girls; Thomas the aspiring reporter on a pub-crawl, his determined suavity slipping away with each pint of bitter. But there are melancholy moments, too, and a painful awareness throughout of his separate, lonely destiny as a poet.